THE BORROWED BOYFRIEND

Ginny Baird

THE BORROWED BOYFRIEND

Published by
Winter Wedding Press

Copyright © 2016
Ginny Baird
Trade Paperback
ISBN 978-1-942058-15-1

Edited by Martha Trachtenberg
Proofread by Sally Knapp
Cover by Dar Albert

About the Author

From the time she could talk, romance author Ginny Baird was making up stories, much to the delight—and consternation—of her family and friends. By grade school, she'd turned that inclination into a talent, whereby her teacher allowed her to write and produce plays rather than write boring book reports. Ginny continued writing throughout college, where she contributed articles to her literary campus weekly, then later pursued a career managing international projects with the U.S. State Department.

Ginny has held an assortment of jobs, including schoolteacher, freelance fashion model, and greeting card writer, and has published more than twenty works of fiction and optioned ten screenplays. She has also published short stories, nonfiction, and poetry, and admits to being a true romantic at heart.

Ginny is a *New York Times* and *USA Today* Bestselling Author of several books, including novellas in her Holiday Brides Series. She's a member of Romance Writers of America (RWA), the RWA Published Authors Network (PAN), and Novelists, Inc. (NINC).

When she's not writing, Ginny enjoys cooking, biking, and spending time with her family in Tidewater, Virginia. She loves hearing from her readers and welcomes visitors to her website at http://www.ginnybairdromance.com.

Books by Ginny Baird

Holiday Brides Series
The Christmas Catch
The Holiday Bride
Mistletoe in Maine
Beach Blanket Santa
Baby, Be Mine

Summer Grooms Series
Must-Have Husband
My Lucky Groom
The Wedding Wish
The Getaway Groom

Romantic Ghost Stories
The Ghost Next Door (A Love Story)
The Light at the End of the Road
The House at Homecoming Cove

Romantic Comedy
Real Romance
The Sometime Bride
Santa Fe Fortune
How to Marry a Matador
Counterfeit Cowboy
The Calendar Brides
My Best Friend's Bride
The Borrowed Boyfriend

Bundles
*Christmas Magic: The Complete Holiday Brides
Series (Books 1 – 5)*
The Holiday Brides Collection (Books 1–4)
A Summer Grooms Selection (Books 1–3)
Romantic Ghost Stories (Books 1 – 3)
*Real Romance and The Sometime Bride (Gemini
Edition)*
*Santa Fe Fortune and How to Marry a Matador
(Gemini Edition)*
Wedding Bells Bundle

Short Stories
*The Right Medicine (Short Story and Novel
Sampler)*
Special Delivery (A Valentine's Short Story)

Ginny Baird's

THE BORROWED BOYFRIEND

Chapter One

Grady flipped through the game scores on his tablet, pretending to ignore the conversation occurring across the room from him. Had he heard that right? Had his girlfriend of six months, Kate, actually offered to *loan him* to her roommate, Allison? Grady normally didn't consider himself uptight, but he wasn't sure he was into that. Besides, Allison Murphy wasn't really his type.

Grady stole a peek in their direction and spied Kate gesturing broadly to Allison. Both women stood behind the countertop bar dividing their apartment's small galley kitchen from its cozy living room area. They thought Grady couldn't hear them because he wore ear buds. Neither one knew that his playlist had ended its final track. He'd been listening to *La Traviata,* one of his favorites.

"All I'm saying is that you should think about it," Kate persisted in low tones. "Seriously consider the option."

Allison blinked in astonishment and poured herself some coffee. She wore ratty sweatpants and a plaid flannel shirt, and her long blond hair was in its typical morning disarray, but she still looked reasonably attractive. Okay, more than *reasonably...* The fact was, Allison was *hot*. But in a good girl sort of way, more like the girl next door. She was the type of woman men married, when those men were the marrying kind…

She leaned toward Kate and spoke in a hushed whisper. "Even if I did want a substitute, it wouldn't be Grady!" Allison's gaze flicked to Grady, and he saw her face flush red before he quickly returned his attention to his device. "What I mean is…" Allison lowered her voice even further, and Grady cocked an ear her way. *"Are you out of your mind?"*

"And what exactly is wrong with Grady?" Well, good, Kate was sticking up for him. "Apart from the fact that's he's all ego, and believes he can do no wrong." *Ouch. Maybe not.* "Okay, and he does tend to work long hours, and sometimes he forgets our dates. He probably would have forgotten my birthday, if I hadn't arranged for my flower delivery beforehand."

Now, that was unfair. Grady had planned to pick up a bouquet on his way to her place. But once again, Kate had jumped right in and preempted him.

"You know, you really shouldn't do that," Allison said softly. "Talk about him like he's not even there."

"Well, maybe that's because he never listens!" Kate said, her voice rising.

Grady could feel both women's eyes on him as they patiently watched for a reaction. Instead of acknowledging his eavesdropping, Grady slapped his forehead and cried, "Unbelievable! Double overtime!"

"See what I mean?" Kate asserted quietly. "Never pays attention at all."

That's where Kate was wrong. Grady O'Brien minded every detail. He simply had the good grace to let minor infractions slide. Like Kate's domineering nature, and her unfounded accusations. For Grady, the trade-off was worth it. He ruled in the boardroom and was the king of the structured buyout. In his personal life, however, Grady was content to let somebody else take charge. He hadn't been ready for a girlfriend when he'd met Kate. Then again, when she'd pestered him into it, he'd thought, *why not?* There was a certain convenience to having a woman on his arm at corporate functions. This helped rescue Grady from the slew of unwanted advances women used to hurl his way, both on and off the job.

It was a curse to be well employed and single in Marydale, Virginia, where the women outnumbered the men seven to one thanks to the small private women's college that sat at the center of town. Kate worked there as the head of the development office. That meant she was a fundraiser, which was precisely how she and Grady had met. She'd been hitting up big businesses for contributions and his wholesale operation, Total Wines, was on her list. Once she'd set her sights on him romantically, Grady had pretty much caved.

He'd only been in town a few *days* before the single women came calling. Dropping by his office with home-baked cookies, leaving potted plants outside the 1920s Craftsman house he was restoring…and offering to help wash his paintbrushes? Now to some men this might have felt wonderful, but all the unwanted attention made Grady cringe. After his disaster with Meg, he'd virtually sworn off women. Grady certainly wasn't going to take advantage of any doe-eyed coed, hopeful divorcée or single mom around here. He wasn't eager for a long-term commitment, and that was clearly what these ladies were after.

Then along came Kate Fagan. Someone equally interested in having a partner on her arm when work demanded socializing, a person who viewed Grady as a temporary asset rather than a permanent acquisition. In almost every way, their arrangement was ideal. Kate was pretty and vivacious, with short brown hair and big brown eyes. Plus, she was exceedingly organized. Kate took care of everything outside of the office, from planning their dates to booking fun vacations. Now, she appeared to be arranging one just for him. And her roommate, Allison. Weird.

A mug clanked down on the counter, and Grady surmised it was Kate's. She had a habit of setting things down before issuing statements. "You had a problem, and now—voilà! Problem solved! You get your old college friends off your back for the week, and you have a great time."

"At the beach," Allison said in stunned disbelief.

"Sure."

"In Maine."

"That's where you're going, isn't it?"

"With Grady."

"Why not?"

"You're always harping on his faults!" Allison said a little too loudly before ducking behind the refrigerator and out of Grady's view.

Kate's retort was hushed but insistent. "Those are personal things you only discover once you get to know him. A week's not nearly enough time. Your friends won't have a clue."

"Spoken like the loving girlfriend," Allison said with an astonished laugh.

Exactly! He'd come over to get Kate for their weekly Sunday morning brunch date, and she'd been taking her sweet time "getting ready," which was obviously code for bashing the guy in her life. Grady was about to yank out his ear buds and complain, when Kate surprised him with a long-suspected truth.

"Okay, listen, Allison. I know Grady's not your favorite person on earth…"

Why did Grady suddenly feel like the loser in a popularity contest? First Kate was overly critical and now this. So what if Allison didn't care for him? Plenty of people thought he was awesome, especially his employees at Total Wines. Hadn't the staff just given him the world's best surprise party on his thirty-second birthday? With a catered lunch and everything? The fact that the event had been paid for by employee donations, rather than out of the company social fund, had touched him all the more.

"But you've got to admit," Kate went on, "he presents a pretty good package on the outside." *On the outside…?* "Handsome, articulate, successful…"

"You're telling me you wouldn't mind this at all? Not even a little bit?"

That was Grady's question too. His and Kate's arrangement was casual, but they did have an agreement to be exclusive.

"Why should I? It's only just pretend!"

Ah so, there's the rub. Something like a fake engagement, but on a lesser scale. Grady had been dragged along to enough romantic comedy movies to know how those plots went. Of course, in the movies, the guy always got the girl. That's because he was secretly trying. Grady had never understood those convoluted setups. He certainly hadn't believed people did that sort of thing in real life. Women could be so diabolical. He'd have to remember to include more of them on his strategic planning team.

Kate lightly cleared her throat, then added as an apparent afterthought, "Besides, I'll be away at a conference. It will give Grady something to do."

"Grady runs a business," Allison stated reasonably from behind the refrigerator. "He probably has plenty to keep him occupied."

All Grady could see of Allison was her coffee mug and one flannel-sleeved arm. Kate peered his way and Grady quickly lowered his gaze to his screen, where the ten-day forecast scrolled across the bottom. He'd already set his weather app for Montego Bay in anticipation of all that warmth and sunshine.

"Not next week, he doesn't," Kate informed Allison. "He had his assistant clear his calendar because we were going to Jamaica. Amanda was supposed to go to this conference, but then she had her baby three weeks early." Grady could picture Kate shrugging deferentially, but he didn't dare peek again. "Kind of unavoidable. You know."

Kate had only told him about the change in plans last night, and he still hadn't decided what his next move should be. Grady was half considering going to Jamaica by himself. Except that Kate had probably booked them one of those love suites with a heart-shaped Jacuzzi overlooking a cove. It might feel a little awkward sipping champagne in it all alone. Kate was always doing things like that, going way overboard on accommodations. He suspected it was because she liked snapping couple selfies and sending them to her older sister, Marie, a stay-at-home mom with three kids and a very happy marriage. Kate was always trying to one-up Marie by proving how glamorous her life was. Perhaps he could change rooms? Or maybe even travel destinations? His meetings had already been moved to the following week, and it would be a headache for his assistant, Diane, to rearrange things again.

"And he'd say yes to this because…?" Allison asked.

A sharp silence followed. There was obviously no reason Kate could think of. Grady couldn't imagine what would make him agree to such a ludicrous idea either. Little snippets of conversation started coming back to him, things that Kate had told him in utter confidence regarding Allison's nonexistent love life. She had this annual reunion with old college friends during which everyone brought their significant other. For one reason or another, each year Allison had failed to appear with a match. Since Allison couldn't find a man for herself, her friends had started hunting them for her. Grady guessed Allison was stressed that her friends were applying so much pressure, but seriously, Katie's plan was totally wack. Not only that, it was patently dishonest.

So yeah, maybe pretending to be Allison's boyfriend would be more of a white lie than a bald-faced one. Grady could see that the intention behind it wasn't to hurt anyone. In fact, as Kate had proposed things, the reverse was true. Allison would feel less hassled while her friends could finally sit back and relax. Without them having to worry about their regular matchmaking duties—and Allison fretting over their efforts—everyone could truly unwind and enjoy each other's company. The ruse could work out splendidly for everybody but Grady, who would probably have a much better time in Jamaica.

Grady wasn't obtuse. Even before he'd overheard Kate's comment, it had been painfully obvious that Allison didn't care for him. He didn't know if it was his job or his personality she disliked, but something about him must have rubbed Allison the wrong way. She'd scarcely said two words to him since he and Kate had started dating. And that suited Grady fine. He and Allison couldn't have been more different if they tried.

Grady was grounded, analytical and in control; she was free-spirited, artistic and *a mess*. Grady had peered inside Allison's bedroom from the hall. Art supplies and clothing were piled so high you couldn't even see the floor! And she never *ever* made her bed. There was nothing on earth that could make spending a week at a chilly northeastern beach with her sound better than being in balmy Montego Bay solo, *except...*

A little lightbulb went on in Grady's head, almost like the ones in cartoon bubbles. But this lightbulb was shaped like a wine bottle with a lovely handcrafted label. The kind produced by Allison's boutique operation, Bella Fortuna Wine Designs. Of course! Why hadn't he considered that angle earlier? Grady was *this close* to cutting an international distribution deal. Purposeful product repackaging could be the key to his success.

Grady had been interviewing advertisers and industrial designers, searching for an entity that could help give his product the proper global slant. Perhaps he'd been casting his net too wide and he needed to narrow his focus? A specialty company like Allison's Bella Fortuna might be just the ticket to designing packaging with flair—something sophisticated yet fresh that would appeal to the international market. The trouble was that it was well known in the industry that

Bella Fortuna Wine Designs prided itself on staying true to its original mission. The label supplier supported local vintners by sticking to an elite client list.

Allison had thwarted more than one takeover in the past and eschewed working with large corporations. Perhaps, if she got to know Grady better and came to appreciate aspects of Total Wines' universal ambitions, she'd be willing to consider a compromise? Grady's blood pumped harder at the thought of bringing Allison's tiny venture under his larger corporate wing. It was a match made in heaven; Grady could sense it, and his business instincts were seldom wrong. Just imagine where Total Wines could go if this expansion took off... The partnership could be a boon to Allison's business too. It was a fantastic idea. Totally brilliant! Grady chided himself for not thinking of it earlier.

He'd seen Allison's work and knew it was superb. Her upscale art was sure to appeal to even the most discriminating global buyer. What better way to sell discount wines than in really lovely bottles? It wasn't like his wines were subpar. In truth, they were extraordinary. Grady got to distribute them at a fraction of their market costs due to the exclusive contracts he'd orchestrated with their vendors. But even he had to admit that their current plain labels didn't do much to convey the quality inside.

Grady wasn't one to believe in preordination, but he'd take a dose of serendipity when it landed in his lap. This beach week with Allison could be a win-win for both of them. Allison could save face with her friends and Grady could seal his deal. But Grady understood that he would need to finesse this. He couldn't agree to Kate's plan straightaway, as that might look suspicious. Allison probably wouldn't want him tagging along if she knew about his ulterior motives up front—even if they *were* to her ultimate benefit.

Grady lowered his tablet to find Kate and Allison goggling at him. He removed his ear buds one at a time and shot them each a charming smile.

"Hey, ladies! What's up?"

Chapter Two

Allison stared at Grady shell-shocked, hoping he hadn't absorbed any of her and Kate's conversation. It was mortifying that they'd discussed the whole thing right in front of him. Then again, as Kate always said, Grady rarely listened. Allison sure hoped he hadn't been listening this time. Kate's idea was ridiculous. What could make Kate even *think* she and Grady would go for it?

"We were just talking about you," Kate said. "And our canceled trip to Jamaica."

"Who says it's canceled?" Grady asked smoothly. "I still might go."

"Why would you do that?" Kate asked.

Grady set his tablet down beside him on the sofa. "Because it's booked."

Kate walked toward him and pulled a frowny face. "But baby, can't you see? You'd be bored."

"I'll ask Diane to plan things," he said. "Chart out a full itinerary."

"I have a better idea!" Kate took his hand, her face brightening as if she'd just thought of it. "Let's save Jamaica for later! For when the two of us can go together. We purchased the travel insurance. We can rebook."

Grady's hair was nearly black and his eyes were slate blue. At the moment, they were dancing with mischief. Perhaps he *had* overheard her and Kate's conversation, and now he was toying with them. That devastating dimple in his left cheek deepened as he repressed a smile. "Then what will I do next week?"

"Go to Maine!" Kate proclaimed, as if it were decided.

Grady wrapped his arms around himself and gave a fake shiver. "Not a great choice for springtime. The Caribbean sounds better."

As Allison listened to them, she gave Grady a long look. He wore jeans and a charcoal-gray sweatshirt that stretched across his broad chest and offset his morning stubble. She begrudgingly admitted that Kate was right. Grady did present a pretty nice package—on the outside. Not that she was considering Kate's ludicrous idea. Not even for a second. Despite his stellar appearance, Grady's priorities and hers were worlds apart. He ran an empire that crushed smaller businesses into submission…and just look at the overpriced car he drove. Allison couldn't even pronounce its name.

Kate leaned over Grady with a coarse whisper. "You're not helping!"

"Helping with what?" he gruffly whispered back.

Kate motioned him toward her and he angled forward, resting his elbows on his knees while she murmured in his ear.

"Hmm. Um-hum… I see… That's too bad… *Never?*" Grady clasped his hands together with a worried frown. "That *is* distressing."

Now Kate was going too far. Allison strode toward the couple, raising her hands. "Guys, wait!"

Kate and Grady drew apart and viewed her expectantly.

"Kate, look. I appreciate that you're trying to help… Really, I do. *I think.* But honestly, you don't have to go there. I'm perfectly capable of defending myself during seven days—"

"And seven nights!" Kate reminded her.

Allison sputtered her reply. "What do the nights have to do with it?"

"You told me yourself, they put the last guy in your room!" Kate rejoined quickly.

"That's because the house was small! We were tight on space!" Allison set a hand on her hip, thinking it was really none of their business, but she was going to tell them regardless. "Anyway, he slept on the floor."

"Sounds like a charming vacation," Grady said wryly. "For the guy."

Kate shot him a look.

"What?" he told her. "I'm not sleeping on the floor!"

"You're not sleeping in her bed either," Kate warned sternly. "That's not part of the bargain."

Allison wheeled on Kate, her head spinning. "Whose bargain?"

"Your bargain." Kate gestured between them. "Both of yours!" She licked her lips, then spoke more calmly. "The plan is for you to *pretend* that you're an item… not really, ha-ha, *you know.*" Kate rolled her eyes heavenward. "As if that would ever happen between the two of you."

Allison had probably shared too much with Kate about her dislike of corporate America. Allison's parents' bookstore had been run out of business by the big chains, and now the major wine warehouses were threatening to do the same to small and midsize vineyards. Places like Cost Club sold memberships to millions who purchased items in bulk. Total Wines had an exclusive deal with the retailer to supply all of its generic wines at bottom-of-the-barrel prices. It was no wonder the wines were cheap, given their really ugly labels. They were totally bland, with just a big, brick-red "CC" in Verdana font set against a pale yellow background. Seriously? No one could get any more creative than that?

Grady slowly shook his head, assessing Allison. "Good point, Kate," he said blandly. "No worries there."

Hey! Allison didn't consider herself that bad a catch, even a fake one. What did Grady think he was? Irresistible? She issued her reply, her cheeks steaming. "Not a snowball's chance in…in the…hot sun!"

"Great!" Kate loudly clapped her hands together like that settled it. "There's no risk of anything going wrong because you two obviously can't stand each other. The boundaries are clear! *So* then, what's the problem?"

There were two major issues that Allison saw. One, she was against the idea. And two, Grady wasn't interested either. Well, fine. What did she expect? That he would leap at the opportunity to help her? Grady wasn't any sort of knight in shining armor, and Allison wasn't a damsel in distress.

She definitely wasn't into it any more than he was. Why, then, did Allison feel the slightest sting of rejection? She was overwrought, that's what she was. The tension of this impending beach trip was getting to her, just as it did every year. Heat prickled her eyes and she quickly turned away as her cell phone buzzed. She lifted it off the countertop and stared down at the text. It was a photo of a guy sent by her college friend Carla. He looked to be in his forties and was plump and balding on top. *Oh, yikes. Is that hair growing out of his ears?*

Great personality.
Dentist.

Allison pushed "ignore" and the phone buzzed again.

This man was very thin and closer to her age. He wasn't *bad looking,* but he wasn't necessarily attractive either. Not that Allison was so shallow as to focus only on looks. Other things mattered too. She read the description beneath the new photo.

Podiatrist.

What was this? Medical week?

Loves your red pumps.

Ew! Carla had shared a picture? Allison wondered if she'd been wearing the pumps in the photo, or if it had been of the shoes alone. That second thought made her feel a little queasy.

The phone buzzed again and Allison looked down, spotting an attractive guy in his late thirties. He had a manly jaw and kind brown eyes. So what if he was graying a bit around the temples? There was nothing wrong with maturity. Within limits. Given that she'd just turned twenty-nine, Allison had decided her limit was thirty-seven. All right, maybe thirty-eight...thirty-nine…forty? So much of everything depended. She couldn't wait to see what this guy did.

Pediatrician.

It was definitely medical week. Well, she supposed Carla had connections… The pediatrician sounded promising until she read the next line.

Six kids.

Six? Allison loved children, honestly she did. But she'd hoped to get started on them individually, not by the half dozen! A single dad wasn't necessarily out, but Allison didn't think she had the wherewithal to play Sister Maria to a ready-made brood. She couldn't even sing!

Before she could respond, Carla rapidly typed:

Come on, you loved The Sound of Music.

Allison switched off her phone and laid it facedown on the counter.

"And so it begins…" Allison looked up to see Kate had settled herself in beside Grady on the sofa. "The litany of inappropriate matches for Allison," Kate continued, "and her poor lovelorn soul."

"Carla's just trying to be helpful," Allison answered dejectedly.

"That was Carla?" Kate gasped. "Isn't she always the last one to offer choices?"

Allison's heart sank because it was true. "We're getting down to the wire, here."

"That means...there've been—"

"Twenty-two of them so far."

Grady sat up a little straighter. "Wow. Impressive. All these guys want to date you?"

Allison shook her head. "You haven't seen the guys."

"What's wrong with them?" Grady asked.

"Nothing's really wrong. In fact, I'm betting they're all great guys…"

"Just not the guys for you?"

Grady had nailed it.

Allison gestured to her phone and frowned. "Everyone thinks I'm lonely…lost. And all my college friends are—"

Grady quirked a smile. "Found?"

Allison laughed in spite of herself. But it was a sad little laugh, not a joyful one.

"If you want to look at it that way. They all claim to be in love. Madly and deeply enamored." Allison gave a resigned sigh. "They can't imagine what's wrong with me because I'm not."

"Hey, there's nothing wrong with that," Grady said kindly. "Lots of people are not."

Kate scrutinized him.

"I mean, *not* in the perfect relationship, or in any relationship at all."

"I know it's true," Allison answered. "But thank you for saying so." She'd always thought of Grady as brash and insensitive. Perhaps because that's the way Kate painted him. Now, Allison wondered if Kate's sweeping portrayal of Grady as a self-focused macho male was entirely accurate.

"So, how does it work, anyway?" Grady asked her. "Do you audition these men by text?"

"Audition? No!" Allison spouted, horrified. "It's nothing like that!" She didn't know why Grady's opinion of her mattered, but Allison didn't want *anyone* thinking of her as being that uncaring. Even if there were dating apps that did approximately the same thing, she'd never used them. Allison had never even been on any Internet dating sites. True love couldn't be reduced to algorithms or simple technology. Matters of the heart were much more complicated than that. At least in Allison's view they were. She was a believer in fate. When the timing was right, the perfect guy would find her. Or maybe they'd simultaneously find each other.

While Allison used her head in business, when it came to relationships, she was a *feeler,* not a *thinker.* Love couldn't be planned for or analyzed in advance. It just sort of rolled over you like a truck, and when that mother lode hit you, you simply *knew it.*

That's what Allison thought it would be like, anyway. She'd never experienced the emotion personally. Sure, she'd dated, and Allison had liked some guys a lot. Contrary to what her college friends thought, Allison had even had a real-life boyfriend or two. But none of them had bowled her over.

"Her friends text Allison the guys' pictures," Kate explained to Grady, "and one or two things about them."

"And then you choose?" Grady turned his eyes on Allison and her heart caught in her throat. Grady made it sound like she was shopping for a new appliance. Allison couldn't help but feel humiliated. This entire situation made her look inept—incapable of coming up with a passable date for one short week out of the year. Even though it was just Kate and Grady here with her, Allison felt exposed. As if the whole world had seen her in her underwear. Next week was creeping up on her and Allison didn't have a plan. It was probably too late to take up the guitar and become a singing nun. And in that case, the pediatrician was out. So was the hairy-eared dentist. Allison didn't even want to *think* about the guy who liked shoes. She was a wreck.

"Truth is, she's never even chosen one!" Kate revealed a bit gleefully. "Can you imagine anyone being that picky?"

Picky was not the word Allison would have used. *Selective* sounded better. Besides, she didn't want to *select* from a text photo! Where was the destiny in that? This was all wrong, and every year things had only gotten worse, with her friends' efforts becoming more desperate.

"Sometimes being picky is good," Grady answered. "Too many people settle for the wrong one."

"Or settle too quickly," Allison replied.

Grady locked on her gaze. "I've heard of that happening too."

Seconds ticked by, but neither one looked away. Allison had never fully appreciated the smoky hue of Grady's eyes. They were a deep blue infused with touches of gray, and unlike any she'd seen. Allison found herself falling into them. Heat swept across her face and her pulse pounded harder. She tried to think of something to say, but Grady's stare rendered her mute. In fact, it took her breath away.

"Yes, well!" Kate said a little too loudly. "Everyone makes mistakes."

Grady and Allison turned to her.

"Present company excepted!" Kate blurted out. "I mean, in our case," she said eying Grady oddly, "everything is cool, right?"

Grady rolled back his shoulders, seeming to shake something off. "Yeah…right." He glanced uncertainly at Allison before answering Kate. "It's all good."

Chapter Three

Allison appeared chagrined that Kate had started this unwieldy ball rolling. Probably the last person on earth she'd intended to dump her personal troubles on was her roommate's boyfriend. Grady and Allison had barely had any interaction at all, and now he'd been privy to her embarrassing plight. Allison shot Kate an agitated look, then glanced apologetically at Grady. "I'm sorry Kate tried to get you involved in this."

Grady pursed his lips, sensing her discomfort. He didn't know why Kate seemed to be having such a good time exploiting Allison's misfortune. The situation was clearly painful for her. "I'm sorry too, Allison. Sorry your friends are putting you through this."

"They mean well," she answered quietly. "Really, they do."

Allison's sad baby-blue eyes were on him and, all at once, something *ping*ed inside. It wasn't a big *ping,* but still, it was there. Like the sound of a pin dropping in a really quiet room. Only that room was Grady's heart, and the *ping* was a tug at his heartstrings. Maybe he'd been working too hard, or maybe his supposedly ideal arrangement with Kate was finally getting to him. A more likely scenario: the pub chili he'd eaten for dinner last night was giving him heartburn. But if heartburn was to blame, what about that weird connection he'd felt when he'd stared at Allison earlier and she'd failed to look away?

Just watching Allison grow weepy-eyed was enough to break a grown man's heart. The very thought of another beach week fix-up clearly tormented her. While Grady felt certain Allison had the strength to confront her friends eventually, at present she didn't seem up to it. So why not go in with both barrels blazing and stage a counterattack? Grady could help Allison out of this tight spot, and then maybe she'd be amenable to helping him. Wasn't that how life worked? *You scratch my back and I scratch yours.*

Even if Allison didn't agree to his business deal at the outset, she at least might be willing to listen to Total Wines' proposal. Grady was fairly confident in his powers of persuasion once he turned on the charm. All he needed was an opportunity, one that a week at the beach might provide.

Grady had intended to play this out a little longer, but he couldn't let Allison suffer for one more minute. Not when it was within his power to alleviate her worries.

"Allison," he began carefully. "I've been thinking it over, and I've decided that maybe Kate is right. Maybe I *should* go with you to Maine."

Allison looked like she'd been thrown a curveball. "What?"

"I don't mind doing you the favor, helping you through this rough patch."

"Ye-es," Allison queried skeptically, "and why is that? What's in it for you?"

Grady decided if he told her the whole truth now, she might instantly reject his coming along. Better to wait and ease her into any work discussions after she'd gotten to know—and appreciate—him as the good-natured guy that he was. Allison had never really spent any time with Grady. Perhaps once she had, she'd see he wasn't the ogre she imagined him to be. Grady wasn't sure what he'd done to offend Allison, but somewhere along the line, it must have been something. Grady could ask her about it at the beach and smooth things over between them. *Shortly afterward,* Grady thought confidently, *I'll seal our deal.*

"Like Kate said, I've already taken the time off. It will keep me from getting bored."

"You said Maine was cold this time of year."

"I'll pack sweaters." He hesitated a moment, then couldn't resist. "There's just one small thing."

Allison arched an eyebrow.

"I'm not sleeping on the floor."

"Agreed," Allison said firmly. "Because you're not going."

"Okay," Kate said defiantly. "Then turn your phone back on."

"What?"

Grady nodded in agreement. If what Kate had whispered in his ear was true, Allison would find another barrage of text messages waiting. Her bosom-buddy friends would harass and hound her right up until a few days before her trip. And if she didn't choose someone herself, which according to Kate she never did, then her friends would pick a love interest for her. Maybe one day they'd get it right. But honestly, what were the odds?

Allison reached for her phone, her fingers twitching in resistance, like it emitted some rare biological disease and she might catch it.

"Go on," Kate urged. "What are you waiting for?"

Allison snatched up her cell and switched it on. Seconds later her face fell as she scanned through the messages. "Thirteen new alerts."

"Could be your lucky day," Kate ventured. She smiled at Allison encouragingly. "I mean, if you agree to take Grady along. I think it's a great plan—just for the week."

"Just for the week," Allison echoed, her resolve crumbling. Though she didn't like the idea of pretense, she hated the thought of another blind date disaster even more. One of these days she was going to stand up to her friends and show them what she was made of. That she was capable, strong and sure, and didn't need a man to validate her. But *one of these days* wasn't right now, Allison realized with a touch of shame. She was chicken, and—all right, she'd admit it—the slightest bit embarrassed that eight years had passed, and she'd not managed to produce a legitimate boyfriend for one short vacation. In part, that was due to bad luck. A few of those years, she'd actually *had* steadies, just not at the precise time of the annual beach trip. When she'd tried to explain that to the others, nobody had totally believed her.

Allison shut her eyes and imagined the perfect getaway. Lazy walks along the beach, glorious sunshine and absolutely no stress. If bringing Grady along as a faux beau could help her achieve that nirvana, then maybe the ruse would be worth it. So yeah, she'd be sort of deceiving her friends. But honestly, didn't they deserve it? They were the ones who wouldn't accept her without another couple-half.

If anyone was to blame for some potential dishonesty, it certainly wasn't her—or Grady, who was curiously offering his assistance. She didn't know why he was, other than the fact that he probably felt sorry for her. Which represented a whole other load of emotional baggage. Then again, Allison had no real relationship with Grady, so why should any emotions come into play at all?

Grady was a grown man, capable of making his own decisions. Dreadful decisions that often meant the demise of smaller companies... Allison was starting to recall one of the very big things she disliked about him. But, really. Couldn't she set that aside? For just seven days—and seven nights? It wasn't like she was planning to marry the guy! Allison didn't have to agree with Grady's corporate values—or lack thereof. All she had to do was acknowledge how impressive he might look to other people. Other nosy, interfering, presumptuous people who thought they knew what was best for her. And *that* was being in love!

Allison's phone buzzed again and her eyes popped open. She was down to two choices. She could either go to the beach with Grady, or take a chance on being saddled with another virtual stranger. At least, with Grady, Allison understood what she was getting into. Plus, they could work out the sleeping arrangements ahead of time.

"Okay, Grady," she said, meeting his eyes. "You're on."

Kate couldn't contain her excitement. "Really?" she asked with a happy squeak, but Grady didn't utter a word. Instead, he was staring at her like...like Allison didn't know what. Like he was genuinely pleased.

"We'll have things to discuss."

Grady's mouth tipped up in a smile. "Naturally."

"Ground rules to establish."

"Of course."

"And I'll take the floor."

"I wouldn't expect anything less."

Allison couldn't decide whether she wanted to thank—

or throttle—him. "You're sure about this?"

"Extra sure."

"Hmm."

"What's *hmm* supposed to mean?" Grady asked her.

"I guess that makes one of us."

Chapter Four

The minute Allison buckled her seatbelt in Grady's tiny sports car, she regretted her decision to let him drive. "Do we have to have the top down?" she asked loudly as wind whipped across her face, carrying long strands of blond hair with it.

Grady smiled at her congenially and shouted back, "What's wrong? It's a beautiful day!"

Allison glanced up at the clear blue sky and the smattering of clouds offsetting the brilliant sun. The morning was certainly gorgeous, but it was still windy—and cold, as far as Allison was concerned. She zipped up her jacket with a grumble, then fished in her purse for a hair tie.

"What are you doing?" Grady queried before cranking the ignition. He wore slim sunglasses and a brown leather jacket. If Allison didn't know better, she'd swear he was an Italian film star. But Grady's heritage was Irish, according to what Kate had told her.

"Fixing my hair." Allison pulled a coated rubber band from her pocketbook and fashioned a makeshift ponytail, combing through her wildly flying tresses with her fingers until she secured them in place.

"Your hair looks great." He gave her a cockeyed grin and Allison brought her hand to her head, realizing she'd missed several long strands on her left side.

"Right," she said, flipping down the passenger-side mirror and making the needed adjustments. The wind kicked up again and a stone-cold sensation settled in the pit of Allison's stomach. She was having serious second thoughts about this whole *meet Grady, my boyfriend* thing. Allison stared at her reflection in the tiny mirror, spying terror in her own eyes. "Grady," she said, avoiding his gaze. "Maybe this wasn't such a hot idea. Maybe we should—"

"It's going to be all right." Grady laid a hand on her shoulder and gave it a reassuring squeeze. "It's only for a week and we've rehearsed what we're going to say."

Allison turned to him in a panic. "About the sleeping arrangements—"

"The bedroll's in the trunk, along with a sleeping bag."

"And how are we going to explain that?"

"I've got a bad back," Grady replied easily. "Sometimes, during the night, I need to sleep on a hard surface."

"Like they're going to believe that."

"It probably won't even come up. You can squeal and catch up with your friends while I unload the car. Nobody will see what I carry in. And if too many folks are hanging around the driveway when we arrive, I'll just sneak out to the car and grab those things later."

Allison started to feel better until her mind focused on the *squeal* part. "What do you mean, 'squeal' with my friends?"

Grady shrugged. "You know how women do." He affected a high falsetto. "'Eeeeek! I'm so happy to see you!' Kiss-kiss, hug-hug and then more shrieking."

"That's not fair. Men shriek too."

"No, they don't."

"Some do."

"Not any that I know."

"Fine." Allison testily tugged on her oversize sunglasses and sat back against the seat, her arms crossed in front of her.

"Ready to hit the road?" Grady asked from beside her.

This was it: Allison's final chance to turn and walk away. More like, leap from the car and race back up the stairs and into her apartment. But it was too late. She'd already told her friends she was coming and bringing her new boyfriend. Allison hadn't had the nerve to do this over the phone, so she'd sent a group text.

Grady O'Brien wasn't Allison's first choice for a substitute boyfriend. He probably wasn't even her second or third. He might be good looking and successful. But much of his success came out of causing other people misery. Allison wondered if Grady even *knew* how many businesses he'd closed down, or how many people he'd put out of work. They were probably just numbers to him. "As ready as I'll ever be," she answered.

"Mind if I turn on some music?"

"It's your car." Allison said, still miffed by his earlier comment about women squealing. Even if what Grady had said was true, she hadn't particularly cared for it. Allison was starting to put her finger on another thing she disliked about Grady. He was a self-assured know-it-all.

Grady reached toward the dashboard and punched in a button. To Allison's surprise, loud opera music poured from the speakers of the car's surround-sound system.

"Now, *that's* shrieking," she said, covering her ears.

"That's not shrieking, that's Puccini's *La Bohème*."

"Ah, thanks for clarifying the difference."

"You don't like opera?"

"It gives me a headache."

Grady studied her with amusement. "I'll bet you've never even been to one."

She stared at him agape. "Whether I have—or haven't—is totally beside the point."

He gazed thoughtfully in the distance. "Hmm. Bella Fortuna Wine Designs. Say, isn't that Italian?"

"So?"

"So's this opera," he said with a smirk.

Allison ignored the comment, refusing to take any more of his bait. She'd given her company an Italian name because Italy was where she first fell in love with the wine process, and beautiful packaging. She'd studied in scenic Cortona and had taken day trips to places like Florence, Siena and Montepulciano. In between studies and sightseeing, she and her college friends had toured many wineries. One of those friends, Carla, was meeting her at the beach today.

"So, what kind of music *do* you like?" Grady pressed after a pause.

The aria came to a frenzied crescendo and Allison cringed, the pain at her temples spiking. She wrinkled her forehead and sent him a petitioning look. "Silence?"

Grady looked at her in surprise.

"I'm sorry, but I actually am getting a headache." That was understating things. Allison was bound to have a raging migraine by the time this day was through. Could she and Grady really get away with this in front of Allison's closest friends?

Grady viewed her sympathetically, then punched off the music. "Silence it is. And hey, I'm sorry about the headache. I can put the roof up. It's no big—"

"That's all right, really."

"Do you need me to stop by a drugstore?"

"I keep some ibuprofen in my purse." She popped it open and tugged a bottle out of its brand new packaging before slipping two tablets in her mouth. She downed them quickly with a swig from her water bottle.

"Are you sure about this?" he asked with concern. "It's not too late to—"

"I couldn't do that to my friends. They're expecting us."

Grady put his car in gear. "Then let's not let them down."

Allison and Grady drove a full three hours with neither one speaking. They headed north toward Washington, DC, and picked up Interstate 95, which would take them all the way to Portland. Allison's friends had rented a bungalow on a small private beach about twenty miles north of there. Way back in college, when all the other kids were headed south to sunny Florida or the islands, Allison and her friends decided to be different. None of them had been to New England and they'd heard the Maine coast was incredible. Plus, they'd found a really cheap rental at that time of year. They'd had so much fun that first spring that, afterward, a Maine vacation had become an annual group tradition. She and her friends took turns picking out a place each year, always in a new section of the coast they'd not yet explored.

She glanced over at Grady, fearing she'd been rude in criticizing his kind of music. Allison might have guessed he listened to jazz or rock. Maybe even soul. Never, in a million years, Puccini. She'd have to think up a way to apologize later. Perhaps she could explain it by saying her headache had made her cranky.

Grady motioned to a road sign ahead that indicated a coffee shop and a gas station were at the next exit. "Feel like coffee? We can grab some and I can top off the tank while we're there."

"Coffee sounds great!" Allison called above the wind. To her relief, her headache had abated. In fact, she barely felt it at all. Though she'd protested riding with the top down initially, the day had warmed up considerably and the fresh air actually seemed to have done her good. It really was a gorgeous springtime day. It would be even nicer at the ocean. It was a shame that it would already be dark by the time they reached their destination.

Grady exited the highway and pulled into a service plaza. "Why don't we gas up first? Then we can get our coffee at the drive-through," he said, motioning to the coffee shop across the way. "That is, unless you'd like to step inside there?"

"That's fine," Allison answered. "I'll just dash into the restroom here, and…powder my nose!" She wasn't sure how soon they'd be stopping again, and Allison wanted a chance to check her appearance in a proper mirror. She probably looked a wreck after riding in the wind, and the last thing Allison wanted to do was appear unpolished during this trip. Her girlfriends were all accomplished professionals, engaged in fulfilling romantic relationships. Allison, by contrast, had work worries and couldn't even get a man. By the way he was looking at her, Grady was probably thinking the same thing. That she was an utter disaster.

He lowered his sunglasses to study her. "If you're worried about your hair again, it looks terrific. In fact, all of you looks terrific."

Allison's cheeks warmed. "Thanks, Grady, but you don't have to—"

"I know I don't," he cut in. "But there's nothing wrong with me telling the truth."

"Are you this slick in business?" she queried.

"Slicker."

"I'll just bet," Allison said with a giggle. Then she climbed from the car and made her hasty retreat, catching runaway strands of hair as she went.

Grady watched her scurry into the convenience complex that housed the restroom, thinking everything was right on target. Allison was already warming up to him, he could tell. So what if she didn't like opera? He supposed he could live with that for a week. It wasn't like they'd have tons of time for music appreciation at the shore anyway.

Grady stepped from the car and filled his tank, whistling the tune to "Light My Candle" from the film *Rent.* Perhaps Allison didn't know the movie was based on *La Bohème,* and he could get away with playing the soundtrack?

Allison returned in record time, appearing just as stunning as she'd looked when she'd left. Grady conceded to himself once again what an attractive woman she was, which made him curious as to why

Allison had not yet nailed down a man. Surely, with a face like hers, she'd had plenty of opportunity. Plus, she was brainy and talented. The way she filled out the pair of stretch jeans tucked into her calf-high leather boots wasn't bad either. Grady mentally slapped himself for even thinking that. He had a girlfriend! Sort of. "That was fast!" he said as Allison climbed back in the car.

"Long line," she explained with a grimace. "Maybe I'll try the coffee place?"

"Sure thing." Grady replaced the gas cap and opened the driver's door. "Allison?" he said suddenly. "I forgot to ask. How do you take your coffee?"

"Coffee?"

"Seems like something we should know about each other. Don't you think?"

She teased him with a smirk as he slid into the driver's seat. "You should know. You've seen me drink it often enough."

Grady tightened his fingers around the steering wheel and thought hard. After a moment, a mental picture appeared. "Milk, no sugar."

"Yes!"

Grady didn't know why she seemed surprised. "How do I take mine?" he asked.

Allison looked blank. "I...uh..."

"You don't know, do you?" Grady wondered why he felt a dig. It wasn't Allison's job to pay attention to how he took his coffee. Just like it wasn't Grady's fault that he always minded details, as well as remembered them.

"Black?" she finally guessed.

Grady nodded. "With sugar."

Allison smiled tightly. "I was about to say that," she lied.

Grady gave her a serious look. "I thought we'd covered everything. Little details like that could trip us up."

"I'll remember now!" she blurted out. Her face reddened.

Grady rumbled a laugh. "I'm sure you will. I just hope there's nothing else."

"It's not like anyone's going to quiz us," she told him.

"Maybe we should go over everything one more time, just in case."

"Grady, you're being paranoid."

"I like to think of it as being prepared."

Allison sighed with resignation. "All right. Once we've made our pit stop and picked up our coffees— *one black with sugar,*" she added pointedly, "we'll review our story."

Grady plastered on a grin. "It's a sweet one."

"Let's keep it *short* and sweet," Allison returned, deadpan. "That will leave less opportunity for messing up."

Chapter Five

When they were a little more than halfway through their journey, Grady felt his stomach rumble. He guessed Allison was hungry too. Neither one had grabbed anything to eat with their late morning coffees, so she couldn't have eaten since breakfast. Neither had he. "Hungry?" he asked, getting her attention.

"Starved!" She still seemed to be battling the wind, but somehow appeared less troubled by it. Perhaps Allison was actually starting to unwind and enjoy this trip. That would make things go more smoothly for the two of them.

"There are a couple of choices in the next town!" Grady called back. The road sign ahead showed a burger joint, a hoagie shop and a pancake restaurant. "What do you feel like?"

Allison shot him a megawatt grin from behind her glam girl sunglasses. "Breakfast!"

Grady didn't mind her choice, particularly since the place was a chain known for serving big, greasy burgers too. While he generally tried to eat healthy, road food was in a category unto itself. No one could fault a guy for getting his grease on during a ten-hour drive. That, plus a few more cups of strong coffee, would keep him stoked for the rest of the trip. They'd planned to arrive at the beach house right around dinnertime, and another one of the couples, Patrick and Deb, had offered to cook. That's apparently how things were done. Allison had explained that each of the four couples took turns cooking one night; that they ordered something simple, like pizza, on another; and that they all went out to eat one night as well. On some random evening in between, at everybody's choosing, the entire group cooked one mega meal together, to which each of them contributed.

Grady supposed it must have been awkward for Allison when she'd been paired with some guy she didn't know for chef duties. Then again, that couldn't have felt any weirder than sharing a bedroom with a stranger. Grady didn't know *what* her friends had been thinking. It wasn't like Allison was some endangered species that could be put in a pen to mate. That might work in the animal kingdom, but it was hard to imagine such a scenario playing well for someone like Allison. Didn't artists need to feel inspired, in one way or another?

Grady steered them off the interstate and onto the rural road that housed the restaurant, thinking things were looking up. Though Allison had begun this excursion in a sour mood, her spirits had seemed to brighten throughout the trip. Who knew? A meat-stuffed omelet might push her right over the edge and clear into euphoria!

"Thanks, Grady," she said, when he pulled into one of the empty spots in front of the building.

"Not a problem. I like this place too. Besides..." He studied her slyly. "I hear they make great omelets."

She gaped at him. "How did you know what I was in the mood for?"

"I've seen you make that thing with eggs, sausage and bacon..." He raised an authoritative finger. "And ham! Can't forget the ham!"

Her cheeks went pink. "You remember all that?"

Grady winked and her color deepened. "I pay attention."

Allison entered the restaurant ahead of Grady, feeling her face flame. She was wrong to think Grady had been flirting with her. He'd just made a simple statement. It wasn't such a big deal that he knew how she liked her eggs—and took her coffee. Lots of people who'd hung around her might make similar observations. But, the truth of the matter was, none of them had. She'd dated Colin a full eight months and he'd still thought she was a tea fanatic. Turned out he hadn't been able to get his former girlfriend, a yoga instructor who owned a juice bar, out of his mind. She'd let that be a lesson to her. Any man who repeatedly failed to note her beverage choices spelled trouble.

Allison didn't know what to make of a guy who paid such great *attention*. If this were a normal dating situation and Allison was interested in Grady—which she absolutely, positively wasn't—she might even be flattered that he'd taken care to note her preferences. As things stood, she'd do well to recall this entire arrangement was a farce and nothing like a real date. To top it off, Grady was dating Kate! Allison found herself puzzling over that. For a man who noticed so much, Grady seemed patently unaware of how shabbily Kate treated him.

Perhaps that was just from Allison's perspective, as she had keener insight into her roommate's behavior.

Allison was sure Grady didn't know how blatantly Kate flirted with other guys during their "girls' nights" out, and Allison understood it wasn't her place to tell him.

A pleasant waitress greeted them and led them to a snug booth near a front window. "Would you like to hear our specials today?" she asked, handing each one a plastic-coated menu.

"I think we know what we want," Grady said confidently.

Allison raised an eyebrow. Wasn't he even going to give her a chance to order?

"But I'll defer to my lady friend," he continued. "Just in case she surprises me."

The slight, middle-aged waitress with springy dark curls positioned her pen above her order pad and waited.

Allison fixed her gaze on the menu, tempted to select something different just to show Grady he didn't know everything. Though that ham and cheese omelet did look awfully good. If only they could throw in—

"Say," Grady asked, interrupting her thoughts. He pointed to an item on the menu and the waitress craned her neck to see. "Would it be possible to add bacon and sausage to that?"

The woman appraised him wryly. "I guess you're not worried about your cholesterol." She winked conspiratorially at Allison. "These young guys never are."

"Oh, it's not for me," he said, beaming. "It's for my girlfriend."

"What?" Allison practically croaked before she realized what he was doing. Of course, a dress rehearsal…and why not? It might help them to practice.

"What's the matter, dear?" the waitress asked her. "Not watching your figure, I hope. You seem very fit to me."

"Boy, is she ever," Grady said suggestively.

Allison swatted him—hard—with her menu, then smiled sweetly at the waitress. "I'll take the omelet, please."

"With ham and cheese, *and* bacon and sausage…?" she asked, as she wrote.

"Yes, please. And a glass of water and a cup of coffee."

"And I'll take the BLT burger with a side of fries," Grady said when the waitress looked up. "Also with water and coffee."

"All good choices for a windy day."

Grady and Allison stared out the window, seeing a nearby stand of pines move as fierce winds rustled through them.

"That's what we get for driving north," Grady said when their server departed. "I told you Jamaica would have been better."

"My friends aren't vacationing in Jamaica"

"Oh, right," he said, pretending. "I forgot."

Allison shook her head and peered back outdoors. "Those look like rain clouds moving in. I guess it's a good thing you put up the top."

Their waitress returned a few minutes later carting two cups of coffee and two iced waters on a tray. Grady scanned the table, then queried politely, "Do you think we could have some cream for the coffee?"

Since he didn't use it himself, Allison knew he was asking on her behalf. She couldn't help but find the gentlemanly gesture endearing. Why did Grady have to be such a lout in his professional life? She'd read about his recent "successes" in the papers, and each one of them had involved closing a smaller business down.

That wasn't progress to Allison; it was imperialism. It was like Grady's megacorporation thought it was some huge king that could annex anybody's land that it wanted. Lately, Grady's firm, Total Wines, had been doing exactly that—eating up more and more of the fertile ground surrounding Marydale by buying out the independent vineyards.

The waitress tugged some individual creamers from her apron pocket and placed them on the table. "Sugar's over there," she said, motioning to the metal bracket stand beside the napkin holder. "Help yourselves." She laid down their flatware, and they thanked her as rain began to streak the window.

Grady fixed his coffee while Allison added creamer to hers. "Looks like we're in for a storm." Just as he said it, thunder boomed and lightning tore up the sky.

"I hope it won't make for bad driving," she said, unable to mask her concern.

"No worries. I grew up in Seattle. We get rain there too." He seemed so confident sitting there, as if he hadn't a care in the world. Wasn't Grady the least bit concerned about the week ahead?

Allison toyed with her cup before asking, "So, you think we can be convincing?"

"As a couple? Sure. Just look at the waitress." He furtively glanced sideways. "She already thinks we're an item."

Allison leaned toward him and whispered, "How do you know?"

Grady's eyes twinkled. "Because I told her so," he whispered back.

Allison's shoulders drooped. "Are you used to *everyone* believing what you tell them?"

Grady stroked his chin in thought. "Pretty much, yeah."

"Some would call that arrogant," she said, annoyed. Nobody got everything they wanted. Not even the stupendous Grady O'Brien.

"Others might use *confident...convincing...captivating...*"

Allison narrowed her eyes at him, then said coolly, "These are the charms you use during your take-overs, I suspect?"

Grady's mouth dropped open. For ten seconds he said nothing. He just assessed her. "You don't think much of my career, do you?"

"I never said that."

"Didn't have to."

"What do you mean?"

"I observe things."

"What things?"

Grady scrutinized her for a beat. "Like how you're pretty dismissive of me whenever I come over to visit Kate. And the little digs about 'big business' you tend to drop into casual conversation. Oh yeah..." He scratched his head as if remembering. "And then there was that front-page newspaper article covering my buyout of Voltaire Vineyards..."

Allison slunk down in her seat. "What about it?"

Grady leveled her a look and wriggled two fingers behind his head, miming devil horns.

Allison was consumed by a lava wave of heat.

Oh no, he couldn't have. She'd tossed the paper in the recycle bin! Right after scratching "*sacre bleu*" across the newsprint in big angry letters with permanent marker…and drawing pointy horns and a beard on Grady's picture. It may have been childish, but it had felt pretty good at the time. Voltaire's owner was one of Allison's good friends and someone who'd pledged never to sell out. Then, Total Wines had come along like a huge bulldozer and crushed them right into the earth.

"Your assessment held a certain—*je ne sais quoi*—degree of poignancy? A certain bite—almost like a very sharp cheese? Blue cheese in particular."

Allison peered up at him, her heart pounding in her throat. "How do you know it was me?" she asked with a squawk.

Grady took a very slow sip of coffee, then raised his eyes to meet hers. "Kate doesn't speak French."

Allison felt like a heel. Grady had seen that and still he'd been willing to do her a favor? She pushed herself upright and gathered her nerve. "Grady…" she began sheepishly. "I'm sorry about the newspaper. I never intended for you to see it."

He carefully set down his coffee. "I'm not the Big Bad Wolf, you know. It's not like Total Wines gobbles other businesses up. We're helping them."

"*Helping?*" Allison asked, flummoxed. She couldn't possibly see how.

"Sure. Most of the businesses we go after stand to benefit through their alliance with Total Wines. We never shut anyone down. Our mission is to maintain operations and to keep any current workers in place. With Total Wines' distribution reach, we can do that, plus offer greater security as an employer."

"Greater security? How?"

"By providing a complete benefits package. Expanded health insurance coverage, retirement plan options, things that a smaller business can't possibly provide on significantly lower revenues."

Allison felt like she was being sweet-talked into believing Grady was really the good guy, but she had a gut feeling he was sugarcoating things by omitting any negative aspects. "You said *most* of the businesses stand to benefit," she countered. "What about the others?"

"When I said 'most,' I was talking about the healthy enterprises, those with sound financial standing. For them, expansion is a snap. Total Wines can easily assist with further growth."

Allison leaned forward on her elbows. "And the others?" she asked caustically. "They're not so lucky, are they?"

To her astonishment Grady frowned. "You're absolutely right, they're not." He shot her a sad look. "Those are the companies that are the hardest to help, the ones that are going under. But we still try."

"Going…?" Allison bit her lip, thankful Grady didn't have long-distance, X-ray vision and the ability to see into her ledger book. While she'd told virtually no one, Bella Fortuna Wine Designs was in financial straits. Though business had boomed initially, the recent hits to the economy had taken their toll on Allison's product line. When she'd started out, her handcrafted labels, based on prints from her original art, had been extremely popular and brought top dollar. Then suddenly, the market tanked and even some of her most loyal clients began to cut back by sacrificing quality for quantity. They'd started buying prefab labels that supposedly looked just as good to the untrained eye, and could be commissioned for less than half the cost, since they were produced in bulk.

Grady gazed at her with interest. "I'm sorry. You were saying?"

Allison was at a loss for any sort of intelligent reply. Her mind was muddled from Grady's gibberish about Total Wines being some industry savior. Plus, she found herself swimming in his deep blue eyes. Dog-paddling, really. Allison had never exactly mastered freestyle, or the butterfly, or the sidestroke, now that she thought of it.

"So, how's business for you?" he asked with a penetrating stare.

"I'd rather not talk about work on this trip," Allison said, backpedaling quickly. That maneuver she remembered quite well.

"I'm not the one who brought work up."

"Sorry!" She took a quick gulp of water and an ice cube slugged down her throat. Allison coughed into her napkin, getting over the shock.

"Are you all right?"

"Yes, fine. Thanks!" She drew a rushed breath. "And Grady…I'm sorry about Puccini!" she added before losing her nerve.

"Puccini?"

"I'm afraid I've not just insulted your job today, I've dissed your music too."

Grady laughed warmly as their waitress appeared. "All's forgiven," he whispered to Allison. "I'm a fan of silence too."

The waitress set their plates on the table with a loud clatter as they banged against the flatware.

"Oops!" She abruptly squared their place settings before nodding toward the window. "Wow. It's really pouring out there!" Rain was coming down in buckets, sweeping across the parking lot in drenching gray sheets.

Allison surveyed their food, which had arrived piping hot and smelled delicious. The scent of spicy sausage, ham and bacon wafted toward her. "I guess we'd better eat up and get going soon. Could be a long drive."

Grady lifted his burger and prepared to dig in. *"Bon appetit."*

Chapter Six

By the time they finished their lunch, the rain had stopped. Grady motioned to the waitress for their check, then spoke to Allison. "Looks like a lull. Maybe we should make a break for it."

"Agreed." She reached for her purse beside her on the bench, determined to pick up the bill. Although her bank account was ailing, Allison had her pride. It was the least she could do to make up for her earlier rudeness.

The waitress arrived speedily with their check and laid it on the table before hustling away to refill another customer's coffee.

Grady was quick on the draw with his wallet.

"Here," Allison protested. "Let me!" But when she snapped open her purse it tipped sideways on the table, then somersaulted onto the floor. Allison stared aghast at the mound of personal belongings that had landed on the carpet by her open bag, which gaped wide like a landed fish. There in a heap were her wallet, a pack of tissues, lipstick, sunglasses, a chewing gum container, assorted wrappers, the ibuprofen bottle and… "Eeek!" She dove onto the grimy carpet and got down on hands and knees, scraping it all together.

Grady's head dipped below the table. "Can I help you down there?"

Allison stared in mortification at the box of condoms clutched in her hands, then tried to cover the label with her fingers. "Er, no thanks."

Grady's forehead rose. "Looks like you came prepared."

"These aren't mine!" she blubbered. "Actually, they're yours!" Her face steamed. "For you!" That hadn't come out right at all. What she meant was that Kate had asked her to buy them for him, or for Kate and him! Oh, she didn't know!

Grady grinned and her heart hammered.

"Sorry, Allison. I'm taken."

Allison gulped. She'd totally forgotten they were in her purse! Not being the regular condom-buying type, she'd quickly shoved them in there without requesting a bag when she'd bought her ibuprofen. Was it her fault that her biggest client from Meritage Estates, Lou Ellen Smith, had walked up to the counter at the precise moment she'd been paying? That would teach her to buy birth control for her roommate. Let Kate pick up her own darn condoms!

Grady cupped a hand to one side of his mouth and whispered. "Though I must say I'm flattered."

Allison shot up so fast her head knocked the table. "Ow!"

Grady's hand reached out and rested on her crown. "Bad joke. Sorry." His face creased with concern. "Are you okay?"

Allison nodded numbly, then scooped the items off the floor and into her open bag with a few fast sweeps of her hands. Grady wasn't totally convinced the

condoms were for him, but he was a little surprised that
Allison was packing. Somehow, she didn't seem the
casual-sex type. That just showed how much Grady
knew about her. On the outside, she was quietly
conservative. But underneath, Allison was clearly a
party girl. Grady would need to tread cautiously during
this beach trip. When he'd figured Allison for the
hands-off type, he didn't envision sharing a room with
her would be a problem. Now that he knew Allison was
ready to throw down under the covers, he'd have to be
careful not to encourage her. He had his understanding
with Kate to honor, after all.

Grady had started to question that "understanding,"
especially after overhearing the various nasty things
Kate had to say about him. But now wasn't the time for
a big showdown. He needed to get through this week
with Allison first. On a purely platonic basis, he
reminded himself. That should prove easy, given that
his attention would be less focused on the woman and
more keenly on his work during their getaway in
Maine.

Allison backed out of her perch on all fours, her
nice, toned backside wiggling...

Grady braced himself against the tabletop and tried
to look away. But he didn't...quite...get there. Okay:
mission. He'd do well to focus on his goals and not
become distracted by something as base as physical
attraction. Grady'd thought he might have an
opportunity to talk business when Allison had inquired
about his work earlier, but then she'd squashed the
topic of conversation quickly.

She stood awkwardly, dusting off the front of her
jeans and tucking her purse under her arm. Her face

was bright pink. No, make that scarlet. "They really weren't..." she began feebly.

"I know," he cut in.

"I mean it."

"Of course."

"This isn't for real, Grady. You know that?"

"I remember our deal."

"And the condoms are Kate's," she said hurriedly.

That was a likely story. "I'm sure they are."

"Good." She was clutching her purse so tightly, her knuckles were turning white. "I'm glad you believe me." Allison's eyes darted toward the door as thunder boomed again. "We should get going."

"Sounds like a plan."

Grady stood and Allison fumbled with her purse, still flustered. "Let me pay the tab first."

"Already taken care of," he said.

"What? When did you do that?"

Grady couldn't resist a smile. "When you were under there."

Allison stared at the grimy carpet in horror. One lone condom package had somehow escaped from the box. *Glow-in-the-Dark, XL-Long.* "Oh, terrific," she breathed into her hand. Then she darted back under the table and snatched it up.

Chapter Seven

Okay, Allison mused later, *let me think of ten sure ways to humiliate myself.*

1. Reveal my embarrassingly bereft love life to my roommate's boyfriend.

2. Agree to have him pose as my boyfriend, even though he knows I can't stand him.

3. Lie to my friends by text message.

4. Prepare to lie to my friends in person. (I mean, create a really elaborate plan, with sexy girlfriend outfits and everything.)

5. Affront the man who's offered to help me by insulting his taste in music.

6. Offend the man who's offered to help me by bad-mouthing his job.

7. Discover that Grady knows I think he's the devil.

8. Lie to Grady by telling him my business is going fine. (Not that it's really any of his business that it isn't.)

9. Blush like a hormonal teenager whenever Grady looks my way. (I mean, come on, Allison. Get a grip!)

10. Make Grady think I want to jump his bones! (Who knew there was a glow-in-the-dark variety? They come in sizes? Seriously?)

"You're being awfully quiet over there," Grady said, his voice pitched below the pounding rain. They'd been driving for nearly an hour and Allison hadn't said a word. Not one little peep. She was frankly too stunned to speak. Even she hadn't known she was capable of messing things up this badly. Had that all really occurred over the last week? She felt like she ought to win a medal or something. Her cumulative feats were Olympic.

"I'm, um…just enjoying the silence," she said as the rain thrummed harder. To her mind, silence wasn't simply golden; it was safer than opening her mouth again. Events had transpired so quickly, Allison had scarcely had a chance to process them. Perhaps she'd rushed into this charade with Grady, but the clock had been ticking with her annual beach holiday just seven days away. In any case, it was too late to turn any clocks back now. They were already approaching Boston.

"Why don't you tell me about your friends?" Grady said chattily.

Allison turned to him with a blank expression on her face. She'd been seriously out of it ever since the restaurant. Grady guessed the pocketbook episode had embarrassed her, but it wasn't like either of them had to mention it again. Grady certainly didn't intend to—not unless it somehow came up in another context. For instance, like if Allison was putting the moves on him. Grady gave her a quick perusal from her head down to her boot tips, then back up past her snug-fitting jeans and windbreaker. She wore a powder-blue sweater underneath that picked up the color of her eyes. At the moment those eyes looked distant, as if Grady had spoken in a foreign language. Mandarin, maybe.

"I was asking about your friends?" he said, fixing his gaze back on the road. Night had fallen and the highway ahead revealed patterns cast by brilliant headlights traveling the other way. Grady squinted against the glare and added, "I'd like to know something about them before we get there. I mean, six new people will be something to adjust to. Especially since they'll all think I've been hearing about them since…"

"January," Allison filled in. She took a swig from her water bottle, appearing to collect herself. "You and I met in January. That's what we decided."

That was a good call too. If anything appeared awkward about his and Allison's relationship, or if they made any minor missteps in regards to their interactions as a couple, the others would simply believe it was because he and Allison hadn't been dating that long.

Allison took another drink and set the bottle back in the cup holder. "What do you want to know?" she asked, still in a trancelike state. Grady peered her way to spy her staring between the swishing wiper blades.

"Well," he began tentatively, "you could tell me their names. That might be a start?"

Allison folded her face in her hands and wailed, "This is nuts! What are we doing?" Uh-oh, oh no. Next she was crying. Make that *sobbing,* shoulders hunched forward as she wept. "None of them will ever believe this! I'm such a sorry mess!"

He attempted to comfort her while dividing his attention between Allison and the road. "No, you're not," he said gently. "You're just stressed."

She wheeled on him, mascara streaming down her cheeks. Grady couldn't help but think she looked like a frazzled raccoon. A cute one, but still... He'd never say that in a million years. "Why wouldn't I be stressed?"

"You're right, you should be. Absolutely."

"It's a very stressful situation!"

"I can see that."

"Year after year!"

Grady reached into a box on the console and handed her a tissue. "Allison, listen to me. This year doesn't have to be that way. We've worked things out. Everything's going to be okay."

"Okay?" She loudly blew her nose and it honked. "How can things be *okay*? My whole life is a disaster!"

"No... It's just taken a turn you didn't expect."

"A turn? You call this *a turn*? I'm lying to everyone, Grady! Even myself!"

"Yourself?" Wait. What? This comment threw him. "I don't see how—"

"By telling myself this is a one-off! That I'm not a total loser!"

"Allison..." he said steadily. "I think you'd better calm down."

"They weren't my condoms, I swear!" She broke down sobbing again. "I can't even get that lucky!"

A horn blared and Grady looked around for the source apprehensively. A car had cut in front of him, nearly clipping his bumper and almost rear-ending the vehicle it slipped behind. They were going to stop for coffee. He wasn't even going to ask. Executive call.

"We need to get off the road," he told her. "Take a breather."

"I don't want to take a breather!" she yelped like an indignant child.

"Yeah, well, I do," he said. "And I'm the one driving." *Thank goodness,* Grady thought to himself.

Allison wiped her cheeks again, blinking in astonishment at the huge dark smudges soiling the tissue. They'd been sitting in the parking lot of a doughnut shop for at least ten minutes while she recovered from her meltdown. She didn't dare look at Grady. He had to think she was a raving lunatic. *Great, now I have a number eleven: fall apart like a crazy person in the car.* Allison didn't know whether to laugh or cry at this point. Everything was too surreal.

The defroster was running and so was the heat. Allison saw from the thermometer on the dashboard that the temperature had dipped down quite a bit. She stared through the rain-speckled windshield at the shop's glowing neon lights, thinking that Grady had been right to get them off the road. Her outburst had put them both in danger. "I'm sorry, Grady," she said softly. "My behavior was inexcusable. I apologize."

Grady exhaled beside her. "It's okay, really. Trust me, I have my moments too."

She turned to him in the shadows. "I'll bet not like that one."

There was agreement in his eyes. "Probably not." He studied her a long while in silence, then finally said, "Why don't you let me get you some coffee?" He paused, then added kindly, "I know how you like it."

Her lips trembled into a smile. "Coffee sounds great." She dabbed her nose with a new tissue and sniffed. "Maybe I'll go and clean up while you order."

"Can I get you something to eat? Something for your blood sugar?"

"Blood sugar?"

"My Grandma O'Brien swears low blood sugar is the cause of all ills."

"Does she now?" Allison asked, heartened. "Even meltdowns in the car?"

"How long has it been since lunch?"

Allison checked her watch against the car clock. "About four hours."

"There you go! It was a natural dip."

"Felt kind of supernatural to me."

"You mean, like an out-of-body experience?"

"I was certainly experiencing some kind of mental disconnect."

Grady laughed warmly. "I know just the thing to fix that right up."

A short while later, they were settled back in the car, with Allison actually feeling human again. She'd brushed her hair and washed her face, and had applied fresh makeup.

Grady handed her a cup of coffee with a smile. "Feeling better?"

She smiled gratefully in return. "Much."

"Good," he said, opening the bag in his hands and handing her a chocolate-topped doughnut. "Have one for the road."

Allison giggled and took a bite, eagerly digging into the yummy confection with its delicious custard-filled center. "Boston cream!" she exclaimed with happy surprise. "How did you—?" She stopped herself suddenly, her cheeks warming. "You pay attention."

Grady grinned broadly. "Yeah, I do."

Allison set her doughnut on a napkin on her knee. "You're not the only one."

Grady watched in amazement as she pulled a small bag from her purse. She handed it to him, extremely pleased with herself. By the time she'd exited the restroom, Grady had already purchased their coffees and returned to the car. That had left the coast clear for her to pick up a little surprise. While the shop sold mostly doughnuts, it had a small bakery section in the back offering other sweets. She handed him the paper sack and he peered down inside.

"What are they?" he asked, obviously pleased.

"Irish soda bread cookies. I didn't know if you liked them, but after you mentioned your grandmother…"

"Thank you, Allison." Grady's Adam's apple rose and fell. "I think that's the nicest thing anyone has ever done for me."

"It can't have been the *nicest,*" she teased.

"All right," he conceded. "Close second."

Allison grinned from ear to ear. "It was the least I could do after all you've done…*are doing*…for me. It was so sweet of you to agree to come along for this week, especially with you not wanting anything in return."

Grady suddenly choked on his cookie.

"Are you okay?" Allison asked with alarm.

Grady pounded his chest a few times, then took a sip of coffee. "Fine. Really great. Just went down the wrong pipe."

She studied him worriedly, then noted that her water bottle had been drained. "Maybe I should go get you some water? It will just take a minute."

She gripped the door handle, but Grady stopped her. "No, seriously! I'm great." He polished off his cookie, making appreciative sounds. "Mmm, really terrific. What a treat."

"My…pleasure," she said cautiously, concerned that he still looked a little peaked. Allison hoped he wasn't secretly allergic to soda bread or something like that and wasn't merely trying to be polite.

Grady checked the GPS. "Looks like we've got just a little over an hour left." They buckled in and he cranked the engine. "Maybe you'd better tell me about those friends soon."

Allison felt better about this trip than she had since they'd started. Maybe her blood sugar had been low after all. "Right!" she said sunnily, finishing up the last bit of her doughnut.

Chapter Eight

"I'm not sure where to start," Allison said as they pulled onto the highway.

"How about with Carla?" Grady asked. "She's the one who was texting you last Saturday, wasn't she?"

"Yeah, and the last one to join our group."

"What do you mean?"

"Carla and I met in Italy, but I already knew the other two. Deb and Queenie were my roommates in a triple room freshman year."

A grin tugged at the corners of Grady's mouth. "Queenie?"

"Long story." Allison sighed happily at the recollection. "I'll explain it when we get to her."

"All right."

Thankfully the rain had stopped, but it had left the air hazy, with big puffs of steam rising off the asphalt. "So, Carla Sanchez—Carla Allen, now, since she married Bruce…" Allison said, "is half Cuban, but she barely speaks a word of Spanish. Only enough to trip her up with her Italian when she was in Cortona."

Grady laughed at this. "I can see how that might have been confusing."

"Some people have a gift with languages." Allison shrugged. "Carla's not one of them. But I shouldn't really talk…"

"Your Italian's no good?" Grady asked with surprise.

"It's about like my French," she admitted with a blush. "Passable. Just not the world's best. Some kids in the program picked it right up and were speaking like natives in no time."

"And you?"

"The dried fruit man at the market used to tease me about my poor command of it all the time. But it was lighthearted teasing."

"Maybe he was flirting with you."

"He had to be in his sixties!"

"Even so. I've heard about those Italians…"

Allison shook her head and laughed. "Anyway! Carla and I met there; we were roommates during the program and got along famously from the start. She thought she wanted to be an oil painter at the time, but later changed her mind and majored in kinesiology."

"That's a pretty big leap."

"Not really. Carla was always into athletes. So, training to be a physical therapist fit right in with her interests. She married a baseball player."

"Really?" Grady asked with interest. "The majors or minor league?"

"Neither. Bruce played ball in college. Now he's doing his residency in sports medicine in Philadelphia."

"Sounds like an ideal match," Grady commented.

"Yeah, they're a pair! They've been together five years and married four."

"No kids?"

"They're waiting until Bruce is completely finished."

"Gotcha."

"One important thing about Carla," Allison said suddenly. "It's best not to mention her hair unless she does first."

"What's wrong with her hair?" Grady asked, taken aback.

"She tries a different color every year. This year she went for blonde, but according to Queenie it came out sort of neon orange."

"Yikes. What color is it naturally?"

"We've all lost track."

"And in college?"

"She even colored it then. When I met her in Italy it was a dramatic pitch black with purple highlights. In any case, she's expressive!"

"Carla sounds terrific," Grady answered. "Now tell me about Queenie."

Allison rolled her eyes and grinned. "Queenie is larger than life. When she walks into a room, everyone notices. She's a fashion buyer for an upscale women's clothier in SoHo and always dresses to the nines. She used to swap out men as breezily as she traded outfits. Then she met Brevard Little. They've been together nearly a year and he's supposedly been writing a book all that time."

"Supposedly?"

"You never know for sure about things like that, do you? He could just be saying it, but I hope not. Brevard has a PhD in English and is apparently very good at getting fellowships. He's on his third one to date."

"Wow."

"Queenie keeps saying that her mother wishes Brevard would get a real job. But that could just be what Queenie is secretly thinking."

"You said you'd tell me about the name?"

"Oh, that!" Allison laughed at the memory. "Queenie's real name is Laticia Morris, but in college nobody could get her first name straight. She's an imposing-looking woman—five foot ten with a broad smile and gorgeous caramel-colored skin. Whenever she introduced herself as Laticia, the inevitable reply was, 'Oh, like Queen Latifah…?' After a while, Deb and I started razzing her by calling her 'Queenie.' She got a kick out of the nickname and began introducing herself that way. Of course, that was a long time ago."

Grady bellowed a laugh.

"Sounds like she's got a great sense of humor. I can't wait to meet her, and Brevard."

Grady didn't know where the time had gone. Allison's stories about her friends had not just been entertaining, they'd helped the time fly. They were already approaching Portland and nearing the exit to 295. While Grady hadn't been particularly nervous about playing Allison's boyfriend, he hadn't liked the thought of going into the situation unprepared. Getting a handle on Allison's friends in advance made him feel far more ready for the week. Plus, they sounded like fun people. Grady found himself thinking that he might actually enjoy this vacation.

"Deb and Patrick are the ones with dinner duty tonight," Allison continued. "Deb is a pro bono lawyer specializing in women's rights. She's got really short brown hair and runs marathons just for fun. Sometimes her partner Patrick runs with her."

"What does Patrick do?" Grady asked as he took their exit. They turned onto a side road and headed east to hook up with Highway One.

"He's the golf pro at the club near where Deb lives in the DC suburbs. They met when she was representing a woman in a divorce case whose husband had been openly carrying on with a very rich widow on the course. And when I say 'openly,' I mean in broad daylight. Poor Patrick caught the two of them in action right by the fourteenth hole, and then had to give a deposition."

Grady shook his head in wonder. "Wow."

"I know, right?" Allison said in tones of disbelief.

"What happened with the case?"

"Deb's client took her ex to the cleaners."

"It seems things worked out for everyone, then. Except for the cheating husband. How long have Deb and Patrick been together?"

"Three and a half years. Deb had just started practicing when they met. That was one of her first cases."

The GPS signaled for them to make a few consecutive turns and he and Allison stayed quiet as they drove through the darkness, anticipation filling the air. He couldn't help but feel excited. Grady loved the beach, and Allison had told him the rental property sat right on the oceanfront. According to his navigational map, they were almost there.

Grady centered his hands on the steering wheel, setting everything in its proper bracket in his mind. "Thanks, Allison. That was a very good wrap-up. I think I've got it straight now."

"Just in time!" she said, gleefully grinning and waving to someone in the driveway framed by their headlights. A quaint beach bungalow came into view. It was two stories tall with white clapboard siding and a red tin roof. The tail end of a wraparound porch led to the back door, which was just few steps up from the sandy gravel drive studded with seashells. High northern bayberry bushes hugged the house's perimeter, giving it a fortressed effect. Grady also thought he spied the telltale signs of sweet fern, meadowsweet and staghorn sumac illuminated by the cheery glow emitting from the cottage's windows. The early burst of unseasonable warmth the East Coast had experienced over the past few weeks must have tricked them into blooming early.

Grady returned his attention to the statuesque beauty flailing her arms about wildly and shouting excitedly. She wore a colorful flowing coat and had a turban wrapped around her head. Big gold bangles knocked into each other on her wrists as she bounced up and down. "Let me guess," Grady said, grinning. "Queenie."

Chapter Nine

The second Grady put the car in park, Allison leapt from it. "Yay! I can't believe it! Queenie!"

She raced to Queenie, who folded her in her arms amid the colorful fabric of her coat. Queenie's splendid natural curls cascaded to her shoulders from the turban on her head as she hugged five foot seven Allison to her. They briefly pulled apart to stare at each other in wonder before yelping "Eeeek!" in unison, hands waving toward the sky.

"Oh my gosh!" Allison cried.

"Girlfriend!" Queenie shrieked back.

"Ahhhh!" they both screeched together.

At that precise moment, a tall, slim, man appeared from around the side of the house, carting firewood. He had chocolate-brown skin, cropped salt-and-pepper hair and heavy, black-rimmed eyeglasses. He acknowledged Grady with a nod, then raised his brows at Queenie and Allison. "Don't you love it how women squeal?" he put in amid their high-pitched revelry.

Grady had a feeling he was going to like this guy. "You must be Brevard," he said, holding out his hand.

Brevard shifted his load and gripped Grady's hand firmly. "Pleasure. I take it you're Grady?"

"Guilty. Can I give you a hand?" he asked, indicating the pile of logs.

"Thanks, I've got it."

Grady scanned the drive, noting two other cars in place besides his: a Lexus SUV and a vintage Volvo. Just beyond them, he spied the outline of a stone chimney, and gray smoke curling from it into the night. There was a nip in the air, but neither Queenie nor Allison seemed to feel it.

"Let me add a few of these to the fire," Brevard said, "and I'll help you get your bags."

Grady thought of the bedroll and sleeping bag in his trunk. "No, that's all right. We really don't have a lot, but thank you anyway. I appreciate the offer."

Brevard shrugged and began to move away. "Cold beer's in the fridge," he said as the women pulled apart, then collapsed together again with more gleeful shouts. "You might need it."

Grady laughed and turned back toward Allison, who'd stopped her hugging and now was dragging Queenie in his direction. "Queenie," she said brightly. "I'd like you to meet—"

"The *boyfriend*." Queenie sharply arched an eyebrow, her dark eyes boring into his.

Grady held his breath. He wasn't often at a loss, but Queenie was formidable—and more than a little scary up close. If she knew why he was really here, she'd probably thrash him.

"I hope you have honorable intentions."

"Of course," Grady answered, finding his throat a bit scratchy.

A nanosecond later, Queenies lips parted in a grin. "Look at you!" She whacked him across the shoulder with approval. "What a big strong man! And, handsome!" She nudged Allison. "You've done *good,* girlfriend." She lowered her voice a notch. "What's he looking so pale for? Did I say something?" Her innocent gaze was on Grady. "I hope you didn't…? No, no, *no,* sugar! I was just playing, that's all." It was Grady's turn to be embraced in a bear hug. "Come here and get some Queenie love!"

Allison pulled them apart with a laugh. "That's enough, Miss Madame."

"Oh, shucks. I was hoping you'd share." Queenie's mouth puckered in a play frown, then she said brightly and in a much more sophisticated tone. "Laticia Morris, nice to meet you."

Grady took her manicured hand and shook it, glancing briefly at Allison, who appeared ready to burst into giggles. "Grady O'Brien. It's really great to meet you, Latic—"

"Please," she said with a genuine smile. "Call me Queenie." She chuckled warmly. "Otherwise, my girlfriend here won't have a clue who you're talking about!" Then she wrapped her arm around Allison and started chattering again as she escorted her toward the house.

"You look awesome, Queenie." Allison pulled back to survey her as they walked. "And svelte! Where did the rest of you go?"

"On a five-mile walk four times a week," Queenie said, glowing.

"Seriously?"

Queenie batted her eyelashes and asked coyly, "Does it show?"

Allison laughed and gave her a squeeze before they headed up the beach house steps arm in arm.

"Don't mind me!" Grady shouted after them. "I'll just get the luggage!"

Allison turned suddenly. "Oh, sorry, Grady! Do you need help?"

"No, you go on ahead. We don't have that much anyway."

Across the length of the driveway he saw Allison's eyes widen. "And what we don't need right away, we can grab later!"

"Good thinking," he said, giving her and Queenie a thumbs-up.

Grady popped open the trunk of his car, his residual tensions easing. If the interaction between Allison and Queenie was any indication, playacting as Allison's boyfriend this week would be a breeze. The women would spend all their time focused on each other, and the men would scarcely get noticed. Maybe that's what Brevard meant about the beer. Grady chuckled to himself, thinking he was going to like Brevard, and Queenie was an absolute riot. Underneath that brazen bravado was a very warm woman. Grady could see why Allison loved her, and the feeling was obviously mutual. Grady slung his backpack and Allison's canvas tote over one shoulder, then hefted their two carry-on bags from the trunk. Grady appreciated that Allison didn't overpack like some women he knew, meaning Kate, who had to pay excess baggage fees wherever she went.

It was nearly seven, so he guessed Kate had already landed in San Francisco. He'd text her later tonight to see how her flight was, and let her know he and Allison had arrived at the beach without incident. *Well, nearly without incident,* Grady thought, recalling

Allison's highway hysterics. He didn't entirely blame her for falling apart under the circumstances. Now that they were here and she was reuniting with her friends, she hopefully felt better. Grady's perspective on the situation had certainly improved. He'd met Queenie and Brevard, and had apparently passed muster. That was two down and four more introductions to go, with Allison's other girlfriends and their significant others.

Grady had counted cars and surmised one of the couples had yet to arrive, which was perfect. He wouldn't be pressured to get to know everyone at once. He guessed that Deb and Patrick were in the house. Since they'd volunteered to fix the first night's dinner, they must have arrived early. As Grady approached the wooden steps leading up to the house, the rhythmic pounding of waves seemed to swell and the scent of salt heightened in the air. The smell of burning birch and the image of a blazing hearth inside made the retreat all the more inviting. Grady couldn't wait to meet Patrick and Deb, and see what was for dinner. He'd also like to take Brevard up on one of those beers.

Chapter Ten

Allison threw her arms wide and greeted Deb with a hug. Deb drew her in tightly with her forearms, keeping her flour-dusted hands in the air. "Welcome! Welcome! Just preparing a fish fry." Allison saw whitefish on the counter, a bowl of beaten eggs, another bowl of flour, and a smattering of herbs and spices standing in bottles nearby. "We picked some up at the market on the way here."

"Sounds delicious," Allison said, greeting Patrick next.

"Hi, lovely." He leaned over to give her a peck on the cheek. "Where's the boyfriend?"

"Just bringing up the rear!" Queenie proclaimed loudly. "And he's got one too. A nice one."

"Queenie!" Allison exclaimed while Brevard cleared his throat by the fire, where he repositioned a few logs with a poker.

"What?" Queenie asked, forcing a blank expression.

Deb grinned at Queenie. "That good, huh?"

"Why don't you judge for yourself?"

Grady stepped through the entrance wielding their luggage and Brevard went over to help hold the door. "Evening, everyone!" Grady entered and Brevard shut the door behind him as he set his things on the floor. Hardwood gleamed beneath area throw rugs, catching the glow of the firelight.

Grady's gaze took in the low-hung ceiling with exposed beams and the cozy great-room area with expansive framed windows facing the sea. A rustic farm table was positioned in front of two of them. It had a bench on either side and the table was set for eight. Glowing candles, protected by hurricane globes, adorned end tables flanking the plush plaid sofa and were also positioned elsewhere around the room. A fat one was set on a bookshelf, beside two high-end stereo speakers from which mellow jazz played.

Artwork and knickknacks with a nautical theme were tastefully distributed throughout. A replica of a nineteenth-century schooner stood on the mantel, and matching decorative seashell pillows were carefully arranged on each hefty canvas-covered chair facing the enormous stone hearth.

"Great place!" Grady said, accepting Patrick's outstretched hand.

"Patrick Howard, nice to meet you."

Grady smiled at the tall, tanned man with sandy-colored hair and light green eyes. "Thanks for including me."

"Any friend of Allison's is a friend of ours."

"Especially a boyfriend," Queenie added devilishly.

"Okay, Queenie," Allison warned lightly. "Knock it off."

Deb smiled at Grady. "I'm Deb Thompson. We're so glad that you could join us." She nodded to a door at the far side of the stairs and to the right of the kitchen. "Your room's over there, if you guys want to settle in."

Allison viewed her with surprise. "You gave us the master?" The rule was that the first couple to arrive got first dibs on a room. Since Allison always arrived alone, she'd never felt right taking the biggest room for herself, even when she knew she'd be forced to share it. In these houses, the master was often the only bedroom on the first floor and the one made for romance, with its own en suite bath. The other rooms upstairs generally shared a hall bath.

Deb and Patrick nodded in understanding. "We thought it was time."

"Enjoy," Patrick said, his face sunny. "Say, would either of you like a beer?"

"I'd love one," Grady said.

"Allison?" Patrick asked.

"That's a definite yes!"

Patrick pulled two bottles from the refrigerator and uncapped them as Deb returned to her work. "Why don't you carry these back to your room for you and Grady while you unpack?"

"Don't you need any help around here?"

"Yeah," Grady inserted, "I'd be glad—"

"Uh-uh," Deb said firmly. "Tonight's on us. Tomorrow, you may not be so lucky."

"Tomorrow's our night!" Brevard protested. "Beer-braised short ribs on the grill!"

"With homemade au gratin potatoes," Queenie added temptingly.

"Very gourmet!" Grady said, hefting the luggage off the floor. "Allison and I will have a hard time keeping up."

"That's okay," Queenie said smoothly. "We're willing to cut you new lovebirds some slack."

"Just no fast food," Brevard requested.

"Or anything processed," Deb agreed. She glanced apologetically at Grady. "It's kind of our rule."

"Sounds like you all run a tight ship." Grady called. "But a very healthy one."

Allison led the way down the hall and paused between two identical-looking doors.

"The one on the left!" Deb shouted. "The other is the laundry and the half bath."

Allison nodded and repositioned the beer bottles in her grasp so she could open the door.

"Have fun in there!" Queenie called.

To everyone's surprise, Brevard added. "And check out the claw-foot tub!"

Allison shut the door at her back and burst into giggles. "Oh...my...goodness!"

"Your friends are really sweet," Grady said, placing their luggage beside the queen-size sleigh bed with an oversized down comforter and a stack of big plush pillows. "They welcomed me without question." Grady appeared a little in awe of this.

Allison angled toward him and whispered, "That's because they have no reason to doubt you."

"Queenie gave me a scare."

"In the beginning, you mean? She's just a big tease. You'll understand her better once you get to know her."

Allison set their beers on two coasters on a bedside table and glanced around the well-appointed room. It had its own wood-burning fireplace, centered between two windows to the right that afforded partial ocean views. A sturdy reading chair and a brass lamp were positioned beside it. A fire had been laid in the hearth, and was ready to go at the strike of a match. At the back of the house, abutting the cove, a solid oak dresser with a swivel mirror stood opposite the bed between two ocean-facing windows.

Grady followed Allison's gaze around the room. "Whoa. Nice."

This wing took up the width of the house, with the laundry room and half bath situated behind the master and facing the drive. The en suite bathroom and large walk-in closet backed up to the kitchen, forming a buffer between the bedroom and the great room, and making this area as private as you could get in a house of this kind. If that wasn't enough, there was also an exterior door leading directly onto the wraparound porch, which was likewise accessible through the kitchen.

Beyond the darkened windows, the ocean rolled in waves as skittering gray clouds partially cloaked the moon. Allison couldn't resist a peek outside and Grady was two steps ahead of her. He pushed open the porch door and they both went outdoors. The slap of brisk air against Allison's face was refreshing. She inhaled deeply, absorbing the salty breeze, and tugged the door shut behind her.

A charming set of rockers lined the broad covered porch separated from the soapstone patio below it by a low railing. Center steps led down to an outdoor seating area, complete with a fire pit in the center. To the patio's left, Allison spied a gas grill housed in a brick surround that included a separate gas cooktop large enough to accommodate a hefty lobster pot. To the right, a raised boardwalk led over the low-lying dunes and out toward the sea. Sea grass danced in the wind, prettily offsetting the patio's ocean panorama. Allison caught her breath. "It's—"

"Amazing," Grady said, taking her hand.

Suddenly, Grady realized what he'd done, and he froze, staring aghast at Allison's hand in his. He didn't know why, but he'd been overcome. Unexpectedly swept up in the moment. The view was so spectacular, and the timbre of the waves had been particularly romantic. There'd been music in his soul and a pounding in his heart and he'd instinctively reached out. Grady generally thought with his head, but in that instant, emotion had overwhelmed him. After her meltdown on the road, Allison had seemed to change. She'd been so thoughtful in buying him the sort of cookies his grandmother used to make, and the gesture had warmed his heart. Perhaps a little too much.

"There you two are!" came a bright voice from the other end of the porch.

Grady squinted through the shadows, willing himself to release Allison's hand. But somehow he couldn't. It was like his fingers were stuck, clamped tightly around hers.

"Carla?" Was it Grady's imagination, or had blood flooded Allison's face? "Is that you?"

Footfalls echoed across the planks as a woman with wavy orange hair dressed in a puffy jacket approached. A buff-looking guy in a field coat trailed her, his face lighting up in a grin. "It *is* them!"

"Bruce! Carla!" Allison cried, tightening her fingers around Grady's in surprise.

Bruce and Carla both looked down to find Allison and Grady's grips sweetly entwined. "I guess this must be Grady!" Carla said with an approving smile.

Chapter Eleven

After the necessary introductions, Allison asked. "So, when did you all get here?" She also developed the presence of mind to reclaim her hand. She slipped it out of Grady's grasp and into her windbreaker pocket, before it could cause her any more trouble. She didn't know what had gone on just then, but Grady's move had surprised her. It was like he'd lost track of where he was, or—even worse—who he was with. She and he had established firm ground rules. One of the most important ones, and something Kate had naturally insisted on, was that their interactions would remain platonic. Plenty of couples weren't big on PDA. It wouldn't make her and Grady's relationship appear any less legitimate if they each employed a degree of reserve.

"We just pulled in," Carla explained, "and were getting the lay of the land."

"We decided to check out the porch, and that's how we found you two." Bruce motioned to the pair of them with his beer bottle and Allison recalled that she and Grady had left theirs on the bedside table.

"We forgot our beers," she said to Grady. "Maybe we should grab them and join the others in the great room?"

"I'll get the beers," Grady offered quickly. "You go ahead with Carla and Bruce and start catching up."

Allison nodded and Carla pulled her into a one-armed hug as Bruce walked ahead of them. "He seems really cute," Carla whispered. "I can't wait to get to know him." With her free hand she pinched up a handful of tresses. "What do you think of the color?"

"Oh! Um… It's hard to say in the dark."

Carla frowned with disappointment.

"But it looks really good!" Allison rapidly amended. "I mean, from what I can see of it! Love the new shoulder-length cut!"

"It's a little on the orange side, isn't it?" Carla asked worriedly as Bruce held open the kitchen door in front of her. Light streamed from the kitchen, casting a halo-like glow around Carla's hair. Allison had to admit it appeared tangerine.

"Orange?" Allison nearly choked on the word. "Not at all! What would make you think that?"

"Queenie," Carla whispered in annoyance. "When it's obviously strawberry blonde!"

Grady ducked into the bedroom as the threesome disappeared into the kitchen. Good thing he had the excuse about getting the beers. Grady needed a chance to gather his wits. He also needed to send Kate a text. Posthaste. It wasn't just guilt prodding him along. He'd planned on doing it earlier. Grady slid his cell from his pocket and sent Kate a quick note, saying he hoped her flight had gone well and that he missed her. The telling truth was that Grady didn't miss her. Not in any sort of overwhelming way. He'd barely considered Kate at all until he'd gotten his and Allison's luggage out of the car, and then it had been to make an unfavorable comparison.

Grady sighed to himself, wondering if his deal with Kate was all that it was cracked up to be. It occurred to him that playing the fake boyfriend wasn't exactly a new role. It was in fact becoming routine for him. He and Kate weren't in love; they were together for the sake of convenience. Yet when others saw them together, they naturally assumed them to be an amorous pair. That was clearly the picture Kate was trying to paint for her sister, Marie. Hence all the extravagant vacations with lavish accommodations. Grady didn't mind funding these excursions, because he could afford them and he and Kate generally had a good time. They got along and were compatible enough. And having Kate organize his downtime left Grady free to focus his energies on his job. He was doing well at it too, and making loads of money. But sometimes, when Grady was being very honest with himself, like after fending off another round of questions from his grandmother, he felt that something about his ultrasuccessful life rang hollow.

Grandma O'Brien's voice came back to him.

When are you going to find a nice girl for yourself?

I have a nice girl, Grandma, he'd answered. *I'm dating Kate.*

I've met this Katie Fagan, his grandma had said in her deep Irish brogue. *She's not the one for my Grady.*

When he'd asked what made her think that, his grandma claimed to have seen it in Kate's eyes. *You can always read a woman by looking in her eyes,* his grandma had said. *Particularly when she's observing her man.*

Grady had caught Kate staring at him once, when she hadn't expected him to. He'd been working at his desk in the office while his assistant had been away on her lunch hour. Kate had apparently walked right in and then had stopped to study him a moment without interrupting. When Grady looked up and met her eyes there was a weird gleam there, almost like Kate had been scheming. Or maybe she'd been summing him up. In either case, her gaze hadn't felt warm and complimentary. In a really weird way it had given him shivers.

Grady shook off the memory and picked up the beers, thinking it wasn't the time or place to question his arrangement with Kate. It wasn't her fault that she'd been called away to a conference, and Kate certainly had her strengths. Didn't the fact that she'd wanted to help out a friend, by urging Grady to spend this week with Allison, attest to the better side of Kate's character? Nobody was perfect. Least of all Grady. If there was any fault in his arrangement with Kate, he was equally to blame. But there'd be time for relationship evaluation later. At the moment, Grady needed to set thoughts of any problems with Kate aside and focus on the task at hand: getting to know Allison better and impressing the daylights out of her friends.

Chapter Twelve

When Grady returned to the great room, Allison was settled comfortably by the fire with her friends. Deb and Patrick had apparently finished any early dinner preparations and had decided to join them.

"Just let us know when you get hungry," Deb said as Grady approached, "and we'll start the fish."

Patrick glanced pleasantly around the room. "We don't mean to starve anyone. The slaw, cornbread and fruit salad are ready."

Deb nodded and added, "The fish won't take more than ten minutes." She and Patrick sat companionably together, with her in an armchair and him perched on an ottoman beside her. Queenie was in the other armchair and Brevard had pulled up a ladder-back chair from the corner of the kitchen to join her. Carla, Bruce and Allison sat on the large three-cushioned sofa. Carla nudged Bruce and he instantly scooted toward her to make more room. "There's plenty of space here on the sofa," Carla said sweetly. "I'm sure Allison won't mind the close quarters."

Allison glanced at Grady, her cheeks rosy pink. "Of course not." She politely patted a sofa cushion. "Please, sit."

Grady handed her one of the beers and then, almost as an afterthought, passed her the second one too. "Would you mind hanging on to this for just a sec?"

Allison's brow rose with a question.

"I've just remembered our housewarming gifts!"

"Housewarm…" Allison's words fell off, then she added a little, "Oh. Yes! That!" clearly having no clue what Grady meant.

"That's too sweet!" Carla said.

"Aren't housewarming presents generally for home-owners?" Deb questioned.

"Yes, but we're all warming this house," Grady said with a wink. "Just look at that roaring fire, and this great company! I…I mean, *we*…brought you all some small presents. It was the least we could do for you all agreeing to let me tag along. Right, Allison?"

The color in her cheeks intensified. "Ye…es."

Then he retreated to the bedroom, leaving the others goggling at Allison.

"That's some man you've got there," he heard Queenie remark as he strode away.

A few minutes later, Grady returned with three decorative wine bottle bags. He handed one to Queenie, one to Deb and one to Carla. "I'll let you ladies do the honors. Though the wine is for both of you."

"Oooh," Queenie said, extracting a bottle from her bag and scanning its label. "Grady…" she said in low tones. "How did you know pinot noir is our favorite?"

"It's from both of us," Grady quickly corrected. "Me and Allison too."

Brevard took the bottle and examined it, appearing pleased. "A very good year too. Thank you both."

Carla opened hers next. "Merlot!" she said, excitedly handing the bottle to Bruce. "We love merlot, don't we, baby?"

"Absolutely! It's the best. Thanks, Allison and Grady. Nice touch."

Deb lovingly hugged her bottle. "A Bordeaux! How fantastic."

Patrick's eyes shone with pleasure. "We can open it tonight. Serve it with the fish."

"No, please," Grady protested. "Allison and I intended these as couples' gifts. They're for your private time. You know…" he uttered confidentially. "For when you're alone in your rooms."

"Or—you can take them home!" Allison burst in, her cheeks blazing.

"This was so kind," Deb said. "Only, we've never really done this."

Queenie's lips puckered in a frown. "I'm afraid we didn't bring anything for you."

"We didn't either," Carla said with dismay.

"Don't worry!" Allison said, shooting Grady a sideways glance like she wished he'd discussed this with her earlier. "It's all good. Grady gets his wines at a discount."

"Sure, right. Yeah." Grady sat uncomfortably beside her, not wanting anyone to believe he'd brought poor-quality wine. "But these are all special bottles, great years. Sometimes my suppliers send samples. I keep a stock of the very best in my cellar."

"You have a wine cellar?" Brevard asked, evidently impressed.

"It's pretty basic at the moment," Grady said. "It's in the basement of the house I'm currently restoring."

Patrick viewed him with admiration. "On your own?"

"I'm doing most of the work," Grady said. "For some things, like the wiring, I've had to hire contractors. The house is pretty old."

"How old?" Bruce questioned.

"It was built in 1922. It's a Craftsman-style bungalow."

"I've seen those!" Queenie said enthusiastically. "They can be gorgeous when restored."

"Utterly charming," Deb agreed.

Carla eagerly turned to Allison. "I bet you just love it. What color is it outside?"

"White!" Allison said quickly at the same time Grady said, "Gray!"

The others exchanged startled glances.

"She means it's gray, but we're painting it white," Grady explained.

"Sounds great," Bruce said. "Do you have a picture?"

Allison stared at Grady and he stared back. After a second he said, "Sure, yeah. Right here on my phone." He tugged it from his pocket and Carla leaned toward him as he switched it on. To Grady's dismay, a photo of him and Kate immediately popped up on the screen. It had been taken in Barbados and she'd been wearing a very tiny string bikini. "Who's that?" Carla asked at once.

Grady lowered his phone, sensing all eyes on him. "Oh, that!" he said coolly. "That's…um…Kate!"

One of Queenie's eyebrows shot up. "Kate?" she asked darkly.

"His sister!" Allison yelped.

"Sister?" Deb asked with a dazed expression. She stood and walked toward the phone, which Grady wanted to shove under a sofa cushion. Instead, he held up the phone like he had nothing to hide and pointed it toward Deb, then showed it around the room.

"You've got a very hot sister," Bruce said and Carla whacked his knee.

"We were…" Grady thought fast. "On a family vacation. Scuba diving. Mom and Dad really loved it. It's not often the four of us can get together."

"Wait a minute…" Deb stroked her chin and inclined her head toward Grady's cell. "That looks a lot like Kate Fagan." She turned her gaze on Allison. "Say, isn't she your roommate?"

Grady could see little dabs of perspiration forming at Allison's hairline. "Yes, she is…ha-ha. Small world. Well, you see, the truth is—"

"That's how we met!" Grady said suddenly. "Through Kate!"

Carla cocked her orange head at Grady. "Your sister?"

Allison nodded furiously her head bobbing up and down. "And my roommate. Exactly! Kate introduced us!"

Well, Grady thought to himself, *at least that part's true.* "That's right," he offered. "It was really very sweet of Kate. She set us up."

"That she did!" Allison chirped shrilly. "That's the truth!"

"If she's your sister," Queenie asked cagily, "then why is her last name Fagan?"

"Married!" Allison quipped. Grady shot her a cockeyed look.

"And divorced!" he added. "That's why she lives with Allison. Still getting over the shock."

Deb returned to her seat and a stunned silence gripped the room, except for the low, quiet crackling of logs in the fireplace.

"So," Grady asked, looking around. "Anyone still want to see a picture of the house?"

Everyone noisily burst in with their answers, saying yes, of course, and how nice about Kate, and it wasn't it fun he liked to travel with his sister. They must be such a close family. Fortunately, after a few perfunctory glimpses of photos of his house, everyone decided it was time for dinner.

Thirteen

A little over an hour later, the group lingered around the dinner table, chatting amicably and sipping coffee. Candles burned low and the firelight waned as soft music hummed from the stereo, underscoring the lively conversation. Allison was grateful they were discussing generic topics. Favorite places people had traveled and films people had seen.

Since she and Grady had supposedly just been dating two months, it was easy to explain that this was their first joint getaway. Allison noticed Grady purposely left Kate out of the previous trips he mentioned. While Allison was aware Kate had gone with him to France and Greece, Grady had obviously decided there were only so many trips he could describe taking with his *sister* without the whole thing sounding weird.

The topic of popular movies was just as lighthearted. Many in the group had seen the same films and had similar favorites. Bruce verbally replayed a funny scene from a recent action-comedy, and everybody laughed.

"Speaking of entertainment," Carla said, turning to Brevard, "tell us about that book you're writing."

"Yes, do tell," Deb petitioned. "I'm a huge reader. I'd love to know what you have in store."

Brevard shared a look with Queenie, then leaned forward. "To tell you the truth," he said in a rough whisper, "I'm writing a novel."

"How exciting!" Allison exclaimed. "What's it about?" She asked just as much for Queenie as for herself. Queenie had confided that she hadn't been able to pry the subject of the novel out of Brevard, which made her question whether he was actually writing one. *I mean, I want to believe in my man,* she'd confessed to Allison earlier while Brevard was stoking the fire. *But you never know, do you?*

Allison saw her point. If they were as serious about each other as Queenie thought, why wouldn't he share? Carla and Deb also thought it was odd, she could tell. So tonight, without even needing to plan it, they'd circled their sisterhood wagons. They'd been friends for so long, it was easy to pick up on cues and follow each other's lead.

"Well, I…" Brevard cleared his throat and Queenie surreptitiously shot Allison a wink behind the back of her hand. "Don't normally discuss it."

"Why not?" Grady asked congenially. "We're among friends, here. I mean, I suppose I'm the new friend in the crowd."

Carla surveyed him warmly. "Don't worry, Grady. You're already one of us."

"Absolutely," Deb and Patrick said together.

"We're glad you could join us," Bruce agreed.

"Boy, are we *ever,*" Queenie saucily added.

Brevard took a casual sip of coffee, appearing relieved that the subject had changed. But no one was letting him off the hook that easily. Allison dabbed her mouth with a napkin and smiled at him sweetly. "Grady's right, you know. We're all friends."

"And we're interested because we *care*," Carla put in.

Deb folded her hands together and rested her chin on them, waiting.

Brevard appeared as if he'd been caught in a trap. "Well, if you must know…"

Queenie's dark eyes lit up. "Yes?"

"It's about a group of friends that gets together each year. Old school friends from college…"

Deb dropped her hands to the table, palms down. "Wait a minute."

"Three of them met freshman year, but two of them met in Italy."

Carla's face flushed with alarm.

Brevard glanced around the table at their stunned expressions and his mouth twitched. "That is so seriously *not* my story," he admitted after a beat.

The group sighed a collective breath, then began to heckle and toss napkins at him.

"And that was *so* not nice!" Queenie told him, but in spite of herself she was laughing. For a heart-stopping second, he'd fooled them all.

"All right," Brevard relented, his shoulders sagging. "Since this seems so important to all of you, I'll tell you. Although the four-friends-at-the-beach tale is probably much more commercial…"

The crowd leaned toward him with bated breath.

"It's a psycho-thriller—"

"I knew it!" Queenie's manicured finger shot up. "I mean, I suspected it was something dark."

"It's not so much dark as intriguing," Brevard answered. "It's a mystery, really. A murder mystery."

"That sounds dark to me," Carla answered. Heads swiveled in her direction. "But in a good way!"

The others quickly agreed.

"What's it called?" asked Allison.

Brevard hesitated a moment, then enunciated carefully. *"The Dean's Wife."*

"An academic thriller?" Grady said. "Brevard, that's fantastic. You've spawned a new genre."

"I hope so." Brevard shrugged modestly. "In the story, the dean's wife is accused of having an affair with an esteemed member of the faculty. Later, that faculty member winds up dead and the wife is accused. But there are other suspects too—"

"Like the dean," Grady guessed correctly.

"She did it, didn't she?" Carla's face lit with imagination. "I bet she did it!"

"Innocent until proven guilty," asserted Deb.

Queenie patted the hand Brevard had resting on the table. "Sounds fantastic, sugar. A sure *New York Times* best seller."

"I'll keep my fingers crossed on that one," Brevard said, and everybody laughed.

Deb was the first to call it a night. "Wow, will you look at the time," she said, checking her watch. A silent signal passed between her and Patrick. "I think we'll clean up and head on to bed."

"What? No fun and games tonight?" Queenie asked, referring to the charades or cards the friends sometimes played.

"I didn't say that," Deb returned, deadpan.

The others stared at her with admiration and Bruce tilted his chin at Patrick. "You guys have done enough already. Go knock yourselves out." Patrick's neck turned slightly crimson. "Carla and I can clean up."

"Yeah—right!" Carla shot to her feet. "Great idea, Bruce." Her panicked eyes swept the kitchen. "There *is* a dishwasher here?"

"A very efficient one," Deb said.

"Super," Allison offered. "Grady and I can help too."

"Of course." Grady stood and grabbed a few empty plates.

"No, you don't," Queenie said, swatting his hand. "You and Allison drove the farthest, which means you must be the most *tired.*" She shot Grady a very pointed wink, and Allison's temperature rose. She didn't know why she should feel embarrassed. No matter how much innuendo her friends tossed around, between her and Grady the boundaries were clear. At least, she thought they were. She'd need to bring up that hand-holding episode on the porch and help him get things in perspective straightaway.

"Laticia's right," Brevard said, standing. "She and I can help Carla and Bruce. You two run along and enjoy your own private fireplace."

Allison swallowed hard. She found it endearing that Brevard was the only one among them who called Queenie by her proper name. Perhaps that was because that's how she'd introduced herself. Queenie was only "Queenie" to this group here. After college, she'd dropped the nickname in favor of a more professional-sounding moniker.

Allison glanced across the room and saw Deb leading Patrick up the stairs hand in hand. To her delight, Patrick carried their new bottle of Bordeaux and a couple of wineglasses. Grady had really made a good move with that. "Good night, you two, and thanks again for the dinner!"

They waved and said their good nights, then scurried up the stairs, Deb giggling ahead of Patrick as he trailed her. Grady also watched them disappear, then turned to Allison with a suggestive grin. "Ready for bedtime, darling?"

Allison's cheeks blazed. "Yeah, I'm beat."

"Let's hope you're not *too* tired," Queenie called from the kitchen.

Carla hooted. "Have fun, you two!"

"See you in the morning," Bruce said.

Brevard nodded politely. "Good night."

Grady impulsively reached for Allison and she stared aghast at his outstretched hand. This absolutely had to stop.

The foursome in the kitchen eyed her with curiosity when she hesitated.

Well, fine.

She slapped her palm into Grady's so hard the sound *popped.*

He tightened his grip on her fingers and pulled her toward the bedroom, giving the others a cheery wave. "See you in the morning!"

Chapter Fourteen

Allison shut the door behind her and huffed loudly. "Okay, Grady, let's make one thing clear." To his astonishment, she appeared perturbed. Hey, he was the one with the stinging hand. All right, so maybe hers was smarting too. She'd really walloped him. "This is a hands-off arrangement, remember?"

He glanced at his palm, which burned bright red. "Come on, it was for show and you know it."

"And on the porch?" She set her hands on her hips and challenged him with piercing blue eyes. "I don't think Kate would have appreciated it. Either time. Do you?"

Grady felt awash with shame. She was correct, of course. There was no way around it. He resisted the urge to check his cell to see if he'd heard back from Kate, deciding to take a peek later. "No, I don't suppose she would have approved, but Allison…"

"Yes, Grady?" She took a step toward him and his pulse pounded. Her cheeks were flushed and little wisps of hair had escaped from her ponytail band, framing her face. It was an angelic face, prettier than he'd ever noticed. Then again, he'd never stood this close.

Grady swallowed past the lump in his throat. He'd been about to say that sometimes things happen. That those had been impulsive moves made on the spur of the moment, and he hadn't thought things through. But what would that say about him? That he couldn't keep himself under control? Talk about mixed signals! Those certainly weren't the ones he wanted to send. Grady normally wasn't prone to such unstoppable surges of emotion. So what about Allison had sent his heart racing and his judgment askew? He shook his head, determined to do better. "I'm sorry. I'll make sure it doesn't happen again."

"Good."

He attempted to soften the moment by highlighting one of his successes. "I think the wine gifts went well."

The little tension lines around her eyes eased. "Yeah, they were excellent. How did you know? I mean, which wine to give to whom? And furthermore," she said, adding a thought, "where did you keep them? I didn't see any wine bottles in the car."

"They were in my backpack, along with the other one."

"Which other one?"

"The one I brought for you...us...but you mostly. You don't have to share if you don't want to."

She blinked at him, obviously touched. This was clearly a turn she hadn't expected. "You brought me a gift?"

Grady could still pull a rabbit or two out of his hat, even if he had ticked her off with the hand-holding. He strode to his backpack and lifted it off the bed, unzipping it. "I really just guessed with the other wines, but this one I picked out specially. I hope I got it right." He reached into the backpack and took out a top-quality wine from the region in Italy where Allison had studied. He'd asked Kate about it, and she'd said Tuscany. He handed the bottle to Allison. "I thought you might like the label."

She gripped the bottle with two hands and gave a happy gasp. "I can't believe it! This is from the first vineyard I ever visited."

Grady grinned. "Then I guess I made a good call."

Allison stared at the bottle agog, spinning it around slowly to study every inch of its packaging. The label was elegant and artistic, and just the sort Allison might have designed herself. Grapevines heavy with fruit climbed a trellis framing the rustic wooden door of a villa, while blue and purple mountains rolled gently in the distance, meeting a grenadine sky. The font was Century Gothic and exquisite, perfectly picking up the hue of the red roof tiles and lending the name of the vineyard a stylish pop of color.

She gave a breathy sigh. "It's almost too pretty to open."

"We can open it later if you want. Or you can save it and take it home."

She locked on his gaze and her eyes glistened. "This is a really wonderful surprise. Thank you." Allison bit into her lip, considering. "You know what? I think we should open it now. Of course, we'd have to get a corkscrew from the kitchen."

"No need." He extracted a Swiss Army knife from the front pocket of his backpack and flipped out the corkscrew portion. "Wine steward, at your service," he said with a flourish.

Allison laughed lightly. "In that case, I think we should each have a glass tonight—to celebrate your getting through all those introductions unscathed."

"That bit with Kate nearly tripped us up." He grimaced in apology. "Sorry."

"Your sister!" Allison giggled. "That was fast thinking."

"Yeah, thank *you* for thinking of it."

"No one can accuse me of not thinking on my feet."

"That was some pretty fancy sidestepping you did."

"You too. I noticed how you left Kate out of your travel discussions at dinner."

"Was she on those trips with me?" Grady questioned playfully. "Really?"

Allison laughed again, but this time it was a deep belly laugh. Grady loved seeing Allison like this, all lit up and happy. "I have to admit the evening was kind of fun," she said. "It was certainly a relief not having to make small talk with a total stranger."

Having met Allison's friends, it was hard to imagine how they'd ever put Allison through that. They must have somehow convinced themselves they were doing the right thing. "I'm sure that was hard, Allison. You're a trouper for surviving those occasions and living to talk about them."

"I'd rather not," she said with a blush. "Talk about them, I mean. They were all such horrible disasters. Especially the last one."

"The guy who got to sleep in your room?"

"Uggh! Please, don't remind me!"

"That bad, huh?"

Allison shook her head at the memory. "He slept on the floor, but kept trying to move into the bed—all night long."

"Oh, no."

"Oh, yes," she replied, "and for seven nights running. I didn't sleep a wink all week."

"This trip will be different," Grady assured her. "You're guaranteed to get plenty of shut-eye."

"Especially after a nice glass of wine," she agreed, handing the bottle back to him. "Why don't you open it? I'll get a couple of glasses from the bathroom."

"Good idea. I'll set it out to breathe while I grab the sleeping bag from the car. The coast should be clear now."

"Yeah, particularly since we've got our own private door," Allison said. Then she added, "Maybe you should go around the other side of the house, rather than walking past the kitchen windows, just in case they're still in there?"

A few minutes later, Grady made his way around the side of the house, grateful he'd scored with the wine gifts. Not just with Allison's friends, but also with Allison herself. She'd seemed genuinely pleased by the Montepulciano, and Grady was glad he'd chosen well. That beautiful little bottle would prove a lovely entrée into Grady's discussion with Allison about the wine label industry. He could get her to open up a bit more about her business and he could hint at Total Wines' international expansion. He'd need to ease into his interest in Allison's company, so he certainly wouldn't mention it tonight. Still, there were things he could do to pave the way for smoother sailing during the negotiations that were bound to occur in time.

Grady reached his car, noting several of the lights in the cottage's windows had been extinguished, indicating the other couples had gone to bed. He'd genuinely enjoyed meeting Allison's friends and didn't envision having any problem getting along with them during this trip. However, his primary mission was

winning over Allison. As his *fake girlfriend,* Grady
reminded himself sternly. Not an actual one. It was
Allison's friendship that he was really after. He wanted
her to trust him so she'd be more open to talking
business. Meanwhile, he had a legitimate girlfriend in
San Francisco. He tugged his cell from his pocket and
checked it, seeing Kate hadn't replied. Perhaps her
flight had been delayed and she was running behind in
getting to her hotel and checking in.

Grady pressed his key remote and popped open his
trunk, lifting the sleeping bag and bedroll out of it. He
felt a tad guilty about Allison sleeping on the floor,
even though she had agreed to it. Her last beach trip had
apparently been a disaster, and he'd promised she'd get
more rest this time. It wouldn't kill him to take the
sleeping bag. It was the gentlemanly thing to do, and
the gesture also might win more points with Allison.
Grady never got involved in any games he couldn't
win, and he was determined to come out ahead in this
endeavor. Naturally, a deal would benefit Bella Fortuna
Wine Designs as well. Grady just had to find the right
method for helping Allison see that.

Grady was nearly back to the house when a dark
figure emerged from around the corner, nearly running
smack into him. "Whoa!"

"Oh! Sorry!" It was Bruce, holding an armload of
firewood.

"Bruce!" Grady said with surprise. "I…we…
Allison and I thought everyone had gone to bed."

"Queenie and Brevard turned in," Bruce explained.
"Carla and I decided to stay up awhile and have some
of that merlot you brought by the fire." His gaze
roamed over the bedroll and sleeping bag in Grady's
grasp. "Planning a campout?"

Grady blanched. This obviously didn't look good. What could he say?

Bruce shocked him by leaning forward with a husky whisper. "No worries, man. Your secret's safe with me."

"Ah, well. Thanks." Grady mentally kicked himself. How could he break the news to Allison that their jig was already up? It was only their first night here!

Next, Bruce stunned him with another revelation. "Carla and I used to do that too," he confided, keeping his voice down. "Sneak down to the beach late at night." He appeared pensive a moment. "It was pretty romantic actually. We haven't done that in a long time. That's what happens when you're an old married couple, I suppose." He slapped Grady firmly on the shoulder. "Anyway! Have fun!"

"Right. Uh-huh. Will do!" Grady said, his face steaming.

Chapter Fifteen

Allison found a set of glasses on the double vanity in the very fancy bathroom, with its super plush towels folded elegantly over brushed steel towel racks. The fixtures were top-drawer, and the classic claw-foot tub was fantastic. She was a bit road weary and achy from the long drive. A nice hot soak would feel terrific. Still, the idea of Grady being right outside the door while she was covered in suds, but otherwise naked from head to toe, made her flush all over. It was absurd to think that way and Allison knew it. She hadn't worried over this silliness with any of her previous blind date fix-ups. Then again, this was the first time Allison had been appointed the master suite, with its very own, private bathroom. When she and her date had shared a hall bath with other couples, the situation had not felt nearly as intimate.

Allison conceded to herself that today had gone better than expected. Though she'd been a nervous wreck on the road, once she and Grady had arrived at the beach house, she'd been more comfortable. Never mind that Allison was pulling a big fat one over on her friends. Since none were aware of the ruse, it had no real impact on any of them. What mattered was that Grady had been accepted by her friends with open arms, as she'd suspected he would be. All she and Grady had to do now was continue their couple act for six more days—and nights.

Allison was glad the awkwardness about her former blind date sleeping on the floor had come up. That had given her and Grady a chance to discuss it, and get any miscommunications out of the way. Allison didn't anticipate any trouble with Grady. While he was clearly assertive in business, she didn't judge him to be the physically aggressive sort. He was also a lot more thoughtful than she'd imagined. His bringing wine to her friends had been such a nice touch, and the bottle he'd selected just for her had really moved her. Kate was fond of saying Grady didn't pay attention to things, but she was so wrong. From Allison's perspective, Grady was a very keen observer of many details, including particular ones pertaining to her.

Allison recalled their pit stops on the road, musing over the way Grady had seemed to know very specific things about her: how she took her coffee and liked her eggs. Those certainly weren't big deals, but they'd made Allison sit up and take notice...shortly before she'd dumped her purse contents all over the floor, she remembered with a rapid blush. Perhaps one day she'd look back at that incident and laugh about it. She wasn't there yet. Allison heard the outside door pop open and stepped into the bedroom, seeing that Grady had just entered carrying the bedroll and sleeping bag.

"Everything go okay?" she asked him.

Grady heaved a breath before volunteering, "You're never going to believe this."

An hour later, the two of them laughed companionably while finishing up their glasses of

Grady's delicious wine. The wine tasted just as good as Allison remembered, and she hadn't had it in years. She sat on the bed, her back bolstered by pillows, and had kicked off her boots onto the floor. She'd been too tired to hang up her belongings so had left most of them in the suitcase, while laying her coat, gloves and scarf across the dresser. Her purse was around here somewhere. *Oh yeah, there! On the floor, and thankfully closed this time.* Grady relaxed in the armchair by the hearth, his face catching the glow from the fire. They'd decided to light it after Grady had returned with the sleeping gear and he'd filled Allison in on his hilarious encounter with Bruce.

They'd been reliving the highlights of the evening and presenting various imagined plot twists to Brevard's book, each of their proposed scenarios designed to outlandishly outdo the other's.

"Maybe the dean's wife isn't his wife at all," Allison suggested. "Perhaps she's an impostor put in place to impersonate the real wife, who's being held hostage somewhere! Maybe by the…tenure committee!"

Grady laughed heartily and raised his glass. "I still say the butler did it. In the conservatory. With the candlestick."

Allison roared, then pulled a throw pillow over her mouth to stifle her hilarity. "We're going to wake the others up!"

"No, we're not," Grady said. "Bruce and Carla are having a romantic moment by the fire, and the others are either…um…occupied or fast asleep. Speaking of slumber parties…" Grady's eyes sparkled in the firelight and Allison's cheeks warmed. "You tired yet?"

Allison fought back a yawn. "A little."

"Maybe we should hit the hay." Grady stood and reached for the bedding beside his chair. "If you want to wash up first, I can set things up here."

"All right." Allison scooted off the bed and nabbed her toiletries and pajamas from her suitcase, while discarding the items that were in the way on the floor. Who knew she'd packed so much stuff! Three more pairs of shoes, including the cute cowgirl boots with swirly stitching, and six new scarves with matching gloves and hats! What did Allison think? That she was preparing for a fashion show?

"Are you sure you're color coordinated enough?" Grady teased her.

Her hand landed on a mound of silky undergarments and she shoved them down below the pile of stuff still in her bag. Grady certainly didn't need to know that all her bras and panties matched as well, even though she was fairly proud of her fashion choices.

Allison flushed and set a fourth pair of stretch jeans aside before laughing lightly. "Just enough!" Then she clutched her nighttime supplies to her chest and scurried toward the bathroom, nearly tripping over a pile of designer sweaters as she went.

As soon as Grady heard the door lock turn, he set down the bedroll and took out his phone. That was odd. There was still no reply from Kate. Perhaps she'd arrived in San Francisco exhausted, had grabbed a quick bite and had gone to bed early. She'd shared that her conference registration wasn't until Sunday morning, with most of the activities beginning on Monday.

Grady shrugged, then got to work setting up the bedroll and sleeping bag, carefully stepping around Allison's belongings. It wasn't as if she'd unpacked, it was more like her suitcase had exploded. Grady had no idea how she'd been able to cram so many things into such a small bag. Perhaps she'd had years of practice. Allison certainly was skilled at making a mess of things quickly, he thought, glancing around. Ah, well, he could deal with that tomorrow. For now, he was feeling beat from the drive and the long night of conversation.

He stretched the bedroll and sleeping bag out before the fire, adding a pillow and a throw blanket from the bed. At least he'd be warm on the floor, and his sleeping gear was comfortable enough. He'd broken it in during several trips to the mountains outside of Marydale. Camping was one thing Kate absolutely wouldn't do, so he'd taken those trips solo. That had actually suited him fine. Grady enjoyed being outdoors, and there were several hiking trails and waterfalls within less than an hour's drive of downtown.

One reason he'd pursued acquiring a new company in that part of Virginia had been due to the area's natural beauty. It was also obviously very good wine country, and the operation in question was booming. Though Total Wines had been performing well prior to his arrival, once Grady took charge, their profits soared. Grady had been there less than ten months, and already their revenues were predicted to double by the end of the year. Largely, this was due to the company's rapid expansion, which had led to increased distribution. This international deal would be the final feather in his cap for the fiscal year, if he could pull it off as intended.

Allison exited the bathroom, looking fresh faced and wearing pajama pants and a T-shirt. "It's all yours!" She headed for the sleeping bag and stumbled over a mound of balled up socks. Grady reached out his hands and caught her. The woman was a menace to herself!

Her eyes rounded and her cheeks tinged pink.

"Allison," he said sincerely. "I've thought it over. I'll take the floor, so you don't have to."

"But I... We made a—"

"I know, but you're probably not as used to sleeping bags as I am."

She lifted an eyebrow and responded, "First Class Girl Scout."

"Were you really?"

Her smile was captivating. "I can hold my own in the wilderness."

Grady surreptitiously scanned the room, thinking, *Even the bears would be scared of her. She'd bury them alive in outfits.* "Huh. Who knew?"

"There are likely many things you don't know about me, Grady O'Brien," she said lightly, and Grady had the keen sensation she was flirting with him.

"That so? Name one."

Allison appeared to be considering it, then changed her mind. "I'm afraid you'll just have to discover them on your own."

Grady chuckled, then said warmly, "Challenge accepted."

Allison plopped down on the floor and snuggled down in his sleeping bag, zipping it up around her. She yawned and brought a hand to her mouth. "Do me a favor, and turn out the light when you're done?"

Grady nodded and carried some things from his suitcase toward the bathroom. When he reached for the doorknob she called his name. He turned to find her looking sleepy-eyed and cozy by the fire. "You don't have to keep thanking me," he said, anticipating her words.

"I know." She smiled sweetly, and Grady felt that *ping* again. That little heartstring *ping* that he suspected spelled trouble. "But thank you, anyway."

Grady got ready for bed in the bathroom, preparing to insist he take the floor. Even if Allison had been in Girl Scouts, that was bound to have been years ago. Besides, Grady was buff and trained up for harsh sleeping environments. His rugged mountain excursions had conditioned him. He was ready to say so, and offer to swap sleeping locales with Allison again. But when he returned to the room, she'd already drifted off to sleep, her long blond tresses catching the firelight's glow.

Chapter Sixteen

Allison awoke feeling chipper until she heard rumbling thunder. She sat up with a jolt to find a sleeping bag pooling around her waist, and a man's arm draped over the edge of a mattress beside her. The sound boomed again, and her mind whipped into focus. That wasn't a rainstorm, it was snoring... *Grady!* Allison gasped, seeing the sheets were folded back, exposing Grady's torso. He lay on his stomach, his head turned away from her, his bare back streaked with morning sunlight. Just at the point where the rumpled comforter met his tailbone, Allison spied the elastic band of a plaid pair of boxers. Grady stirred, and Allison quickly collapsed back on the floor, shimmying down in her sleeping bag.

Grady lazily lifted his head, then thunked it down on the pillow, opening one dazed eye to face her. "Morning," he said groggily. "Is it coffee yet?"

Coffee sounded like a great idea. Allison had nearly forgotten where she was or what they were doing here. She stared out the window, catching a glimpse of a bright blue sky dotted by puffy white clouds. Seagulls sailed below them and darted into the waves. That's right; they were at the beach in Maine. And Grady was pretending to be her boyfriend. He pushed himself up on his elbows and shook his head, apparently trying to clear it. "Where's Kate?" he asked, obviously still foggy-brained.

Allison tried to avert her gaze from his broad chest and the smattering of dark hair that covered his pecs, then trailed down his taut six-pack in a tantalizing V. Allison had never seen Grady shirtless before and he afforded quite a view. She swallowed hard, then spoke with a squeak. "San Fran-*cis*-co." Hopefully, Grady just thought that was her morning voice.

"Oh, yeah." He sank back into his pillow facedown and mumbled something unintelligible.

"What?"

He turned his face to hers again, apparently with great effort. *"Coffee?"*

Allison sat up and clutched the front of the sleeping bag against her. "Are you asking me to bring you coffee?"

Grady groaned plaintively. "Please?"

"I take it you're not a morning person."

His arm flopped back over the bed, dangling off the mattress. "You're a goddess. You know that."

Allison laughed in amusement. "Well, I don't know about the goddess part, but I *do* know how you like your coffee."

She wiggled out of the sleeping bag, retrieved a bathrobe from the bottom of her suitcase and slipped into it. "Maybe you could think about putting some clothes on while I'm gone?" she suggested, her back to him.

Grady didn't utter a word until she was halfway to the door. It was hard to make out since he seemed to be talking into his pillow again, but Allison distinctly thought she heard the words *party pooper.*

"So?" Queenie asked with a gleam in her eye. "How did everybody *sleep* last night?"

Allison glanced around the great room and saw no one else there, except Brevard, who was sitting by the fireplace and busily typing on his laptop. Considering that she and Queenie were the only occupants of the kitchen, Allison understood the query was specifically addressed to her. "Brevard appears rested," she answered brightly, avoiding the question.

Queenie noisily cleared her throat. "Ah-hum, and so—love bug—do you!" She stared into Allison's eyes, waiting. What did Queenie imagine? That Allison would provide blow-by-blow details?

"That's because I did sleep well. Like a rock, really. Thanks so much for asking!"

Queenie scrutinized her oddly as Allison poured two coffees and added sugar to one of them. "Where's your man?"

"Grady's having a little trouble getting started this morning."

Queenie became suddenly animated and nudged her. "You go, girl! That must have been some night, huh?"

"I don't know what you're talking about," she said, purposely naïve. She turned to grab some milk from the fridge. Deb and Patrick had laid in the initial supplies, and they'd all take turns picking up more groceries later.

Allison's hand had just settled on the milk carton when Queenie jokingly purred behind her, "Don't play cute with me, Miss Sex-on-the-Beach Kitten."

Allison spun to face her, nearly dropping the milk. "What?"

Queenie sported an informed look. "We all heard about the sleeping bag, sister."

Allison's jaw dropped open. "Sleeping bag?" she asked lamely. Oh no, it couldn't have possibly gotten around. Not when Bruce promised Grady...

Queenie clapped her hands together and roared, "Doing it in the dunes!" She threw her hands up with glee, and Brevard stopped what he was doing to stare at her. "What, sugar?" she told him. "We can do it too."

Brevard's natural skin tone deepened.

"But look at you!" she said, squeezing Allison's shoulders with approval. "You thought of it first! No, wait..." Queenie brought a hand to her chin. "I guess that was Carla."

"Carla?" Allison asked, flummoxed. She suddenly felt chilled and realized she was standing in front of the open refrigerator door. She reached behind her and slammed it shut, setting the milk on the counter. "What's Carla got to do with anything?"

"It doesn't matter," Queenie said authoritatively. "That was a long time ago. That's what comes of being married, I guess."

Allison tried to keep up the pretense of ignorance. "Carla and Bruce seem very happy to me."

"Oh, they are! That's one reason they're so excited for you! Bruce couldn't wait to tell Carla, who naturally had to tell me. She thought I'd gone to bed, but then she spotted me in the hall... Of course, after that, we simply couldn't leave Deb out! So Carla and I shoved a note under her door! She and Patrick *obviously* were still awake, because she sent one back. Very efficient. Just *WTG Allison*. But, you know." Queenie shrugged. "That's Deb. I suppose she has to be concise in court."

Allison's cheeks grew warm. Wait until she told Grady! They'd been here less than twenty-four hours, and already, as a couple, they were legendary. "Yes, well." Allison licked her lips and spoke primly. "I guess I'll just finish fixing our coffees then. No doubt Grady needs his."

By the time Allison returned with their coffees, Grady was dressed in a sweater and jeans and seated in the chair by the hearth. He'd rolled up the sleeping bag and bedroll and stashed them in the closet, while he was at it. He'd also made the bed, and hung more female outfits than he could count in the closet. While Grady hadn't been invasive enough to touch anything still in Allison's suitcase, he'd felt fully justified in nabbing stuff off the floor. The room had been a minefield, with little traps lying around everywhere. It was a miracle Allison could safely navigate her own space back home and hadn't yet landed in the hospital. Grady congratulated himself for getting so much accomplished caffeine-free. He normally didn't function well without his java.

"Well..." Allison face brightened as she looked around the room. "I see you picked up in here."

"And got dressed."

"Hmm, yes." Grady didn't know why, but he detected a hint of disapproval.

"Don't tell me," he said, only half teasing. "My sweater's a fashion fail?"

She kicked the door shut with her foot, juggling the two mugs of coffee. "That's not it at all."

Grady rose and reached for the mug she extended in his direction, preparing to offer his thanks, but

Allison unexpectedly pulled it back. "I was thinking maybe you should apologize."

Grady couldn't believe she was stuck on that hand-holding thing. He thought they had that settled. He knew he'd done wrong, two times. But he'd already admitted his mistake. What did Allison want him to do? Grovel? Grady really wasn't the groveling kind, but in the interest of fake couple harmony, he supposed he could make an exception. They'd be sharing this room together for six more nights. "Allison, I apologize. I'm generally quick on the uptake, but in this case, I hope you'll forgive me for being a slow learner."

"Slow learner? What are you talking about?"

"Well...I...uh... What are *you* talking about?" he asked cautiously.

"Your comment, of course!"

"Comment?" Grady asked, stupefied. He reached desperately for the coffee, but Allison held it away from him.

"I want you to apologize for calling me a party pooper."

"I didn't call you that." Grady repressed a grin. "To your face."

"No, you said it to your pillow."

"So, maybe my pillow's a good listener."

Allison smirked and waved his coffee temptingly in front of him. He tried to snatch it, but she pulled it back. "Ah!" He grabbed for it again, but she lifted it higher. "Ah-uh!"

Grady ran a hand through his hair. "Allison, you're killing me."

"Then say you're sorry."

"Okay," he said like a petulant child. "I'm sorry for calling you a party pooper."

"Good."

Finally, she handed him his coffee. Grady took a grateful swallow, then murmured, "Even though you are one…"

Allison's eyebrows shot up. "I most certainly am not."

"I thought we were having a pajama party," Grady said brazenly. "You made me take my pajamas off."

Allison blew out a breath. "You weren't *wearing* pajamas, Grady."

His lips twitched. "Minor detail."

"I can see why you drive Kate nuts," Allison said. "You're really irritating in the morning."

Grady took a giant step backward, defending his mug with his other hand. "That's better than being a…."

Allison looked like she wanted to tackle him. Grady questioned whether he'd really mind that. If he were unattached that might not pose a problem. In fact, he'd probably enjoy it. Then the picture of him and Kate on his phone popped into his head. Grady couldn't even remember why he'd saved it as his wallpaper. That's right! Kate had done it for him during their layover in the airport between their connecting flights. She'd saved the same photo as the wallpaper on her phone as well. He was pretty sure she'd also texted a copy to Marie.

Allison was still standing there, glaring at him, issuing a silent dare. It was too much. He couldn't resist. He stepped past her and shot for the bathroom, shouting, "…party pooper!" Then he slammed the door shut and locked it.

"Grady!" She pounded it hard from the other side. "Unlock this door!"

"No!"

"Why? What are you doing?"

He casually lifted his electric razor off the sink and switched it on. He held it out to the side in one hand while slowly sipping his coffee. "Shaving!" he lied, savoring the moment.

Allison sat down on the bed in a huff and folded her arms. She was *not* a party pooper. She absolutely wasn't. Just ask her friends! Everyone knew Allison was a lot of fun! And she was going to prove it. Just as soon as she got done strangling Grady. He was such a pain. Allison massaged the side of her neck, realizing it felt sore. She must have gotten a crick from sleeping on the floor.

Tonight she'd let Grady take a turn and see how he liked it. Maybe then he wouldn't wake up in such an aggravating mood.

Allison lifted her gaze to the windows facing the sea, absorbing the fabulous view. Beyond the patio and rolling dunes, waves crashed against the shore of the tiny inlet. The small private beach was ringed by craggy boulders and steep drop-offs overlooking the churning ocean. And slightly to the north, a sandy footpath led through mossy hills dotted with occasional wildflowers. Allison stood and walked to the window, peering out as far as her eyes could see. There, on a faraway spit of land, she found the treasure she sought: the spindly tower of a lighthouse.

While she and her friends came to Maine each March, they'd made a pact to investigate a different section of the coast each year. So this landscape was breathtakingly new to her. She couldn't wait to get out and explore it. With—or without—Grady, she thought with a surly pout.

The sound of Grady's razor clicked off, then Allison heard water running. Great, now he was taking his shower. Allison flopped back on the bed, thinking this was going to take a while. This was the thanks Allison got for bringing Grady his coffee. Tomorrow, she was not only waking up refreshed after having slept in the bed—*alone*— she was also getting first dibs on the bathroom.

Chapter Seventeen

By the time Allison finished her shower and got dressed, Grady was holding a captive audience around the dining table. She found him there, his coffee mug at his elbow, eagerly answering questions from the others. Allison's stomach clenched with worry. She hoped he wasn't revealing things about their "relationship" that would trip her up later.

"Morning!" Carla called brightly from beside Bruce at the table. The couple shared a knowing look, then Carla grinned at Allison. "Sleep well?"

Deb and Patrick were also at the table, as were Queenie and Brevard. All of them exchanged glances, while Queenie giggled behind her hand. Allison noticed Deb's lips firmly pressed together, as if she was going to burst into giggles any moment herself.

Grady, on the other hand, appeared dead serious—and very proud of himself. He sat up straighter, flexing the muscles of his chest as he inhaled deeply. "Nothing like exposure to the night air to help one sleep more soundly." Was it her imagination, or had Grady not really shaved? Dark stubble covered his chin when he stroked it. He shot her a playful look and his deep-blue eyes twinkled. "Right, darling?"

Allison grinned tightly and went to pour herself more coffee before joining them at the table. "I'm not sure how I'd know."

"She's just embarrassed," Queenie whispered to the others.

"I don't see why," Carla returned.

"We all only want what's best for her," added Deb.

Allison spun on her heel toward them and the chatter stopped. Grady glanced at her friends and shrugged. He lowered his voice and spoke confidentially. "Allison's always been the modest type. Doesn't like to brag."

"Hmm, that's true," the group seemed to agree in unison.

Allison approached the table, feeling her cheeks burn. There was only one seat left and, thankfully, it wasn't next to Grady. He was still being obnoxious enough for her to want to pinch him. Okay, so yeah, she wanted her friends to think they were an item, but did Grady have to carry things so far? She settled herself in at the free spot across from him instead. He was facing the great room with his back to an oceanside window, and the bright blue sky brought out the hue of his eyes.

"What does everyone have planned for today?" she asked, changing the subject. She noticed bagels and cream cheese laid out on the table along with a plate of pastries. She picked out a cheese Danish and set it on a napkin by her mug.

"Brevard and I are going shopping," Queenie said. "We're cooking tonight."

Brevard nodded. "Beer-braised short ribs slow-cooked on the grill." He stopped and surveyed their faces with a worried frown. "Everyone's okay with that? No vegetarians among us?"

"Just make sure the beef is free-range," Deb said between bites of her whole wheat bagel.

Queenie, who was to Allison's right, leaned toward Brevard beside her and quietly whispered, "It's all right. She'll never know the difference."

Brevard cleared his throat, and Bruce piped up. "Carla and I were going to take a drive into Portland. Tool around the town. Anyone want to join us?"

Though Allison had been there before and found it lovely, what she really wanted to do during this trip was spend time in nature. "I was thinking I'd take a long walk on the beach, maybe head up to the lighthouse."

Grady smiled at Allison. "I love how we think alike." He reached his arm toward her, almost like he was ready to take her hand. She stealthily slid hers back from where it rested on the table.

"Can you please pass the sugar, Patrick?" Grady asked innocently, like that was what he'd been after all along. "I can't quite reach it."

Allison fumed, realizing he'd been razzing her on purpose. She narrowed her eyes at Grady, but he just smiled pleasantly in return.

Patrick complied with Grady's request, then said, "Deb and I discussed going biking later. We can get some rentals in town."

"We've heard colder weather's moving in tomorrow," Deb offered. "So we thought it might be good to go today. Anyone else interested?"

"I'm taking a vacation from exercise this break!" Queenie declared.

Everyone laughed and Carla said, "Me too. Sightseeing at a slow pace is about my speed."

"As long as we can stop for beer," Bruce put in.

"He just wants to stop into a sports bar to check on March Madness," Carla said in a mock whisper.

Grady scanned the great room, his eyes landing on a large flat-screen TV. "We don't get ESPN here?"

"We don't turn on the television," Allison explained. "It's something we all agreed to in the beginning. No one monopolizes the TV and everyone gets to enjoy the sound of the waves."

"We do watch movies as a group sometimes," Carla said.

Deb nodded. "But only by popular vote."

"So!" Queenie took a sip of coffee. "It sounds like we're all going our separate ways today. What time should we meet back here for dinner?"

Everyone agreed on seven, before Allison asked casually, "What were you all talking about earlier?"

"Earlier?" Grady asked innocently.

"When I walked in?"

"Oh, that!" Patrick's green eyes lit up. "Grady was just telling us about Total Wines."

"And its plans for world domination," Bruce said with a laugh.

Allison couldn't mask the disapproval in her voice. "Oh really?"

"You remember, darling," Grady said. "I told you about it on the drive here."

No... No, he didn't. What's more, Allison wished he'd stop calling her *darling*. It was getting on her nerves.

"Grady's company is expanding," Carla explained gently, as if reminding her. "I think it's fantastic he's exploring an international angle. Just think, Allison! Italy! I'd love to go back someday, wouldn't you? Maybe you could go there with Grady."

"Or maybe we could all go together!" Bruce suggested. "Next year, when I'm done with my residency, I'll be ready to celebrate. I mean, assuming I nail down a job."

"Of course you will, honey." Carla reassuringly patted his hand. "A really brilliant one too."

Deb cocked her head to the side. "I like that idea, actually." She glanced at the others. "All of us going to Italy. We could rent a villa."

"Sounds good," Patrick said.

Brevard lifted a shoulder. "Well, maybe if my book sells…"

"I think we should *save the date*!" Queenie declared.

Wait a minute. How did they go from a discussion about Grady's job to all eight of them going to Italy? This deal was for *one week.* One week only! Allison and Grady weren't supposed to making plans beyond that. Especially not as a couple.

Allison folded her face in her hands.

Queenie tenderly laid a hand on her shoulder. "What's wrong, sugar?"

"She's just overwhelmed," Grady said warmly. "By everyone's love and support. To imagine you'd all want to come with us to Tuscany! I think that's awesome! What a great plan!"

Chapter Eighteen

Allison tugged a ski vest over her sweater and headed for their private outside door. "You don't have to come with me, Grady. Really you don't." Her head was still spinning from the conversation at breakfast. She should have thought the details through a little better. Getting off the hook by letting her friends think she had a boyfriend for one week was one thing. Arranging future vacations with them and Grady was something else entirely. Well, fine. Allison could fix this. She'd already decided to tell her friends later that her relationship with Grady hadn't worked out. She just didn't realize how instantly they'd bond with him. *I mean, really! He's been here less than twenty-four hours, and already he's included in future vacation planning?* Didn't anyone think to ask her?

Grady quickly typed something into his cell, then left it charging on the dresser. "Wait up!" he said, grabbing his jacket and chasing after her. "I want to see the lighthouse too."

Allison paused midstride and wheeled on him in utter disbelief. "You want to see the lighthouse?" she asked as if she were speaking to a child. Allison placed a hand on her hip, then added more coldly, "Well, bully for you."

Grady scanned her with alarm. "Where's all this anger coming from?"

"From you!" she said thumping his chest with her finger. "You, you, *you!*"

Grady reached down and grabbed her finger, pinning it to his chest. "Is that really the way to speak to the guy who's taking you to Italy?"

"Argh!" Allison wanted to yell, then she considered his words. What had Grady just said? "Taking me?" she asked, confounded. "You must be joking."

"Maybe the three of us could work it out. You, me and Kate. She could let you borrow me again?" His expression was totally impassive, but Allison understood he was teasing. She was starting to get the hang of Grady and his weird sense of humor. Unfortunately.

"Let go of my finger," she snapped, her nostrils flaring.

"Why?"

What an insolent question! "Because I want it back, that's why. It's mine."

"Not if you're going to use it as a lethal weapon."

"It's not lethal, Grady. I don't even have long fingernails, see?" She flashed him her other hand as evidence. "I'm an artist. I keep them short."

"Well, it still hurt. All that poking."

Allison sighed in disbelief. A big strong guy like him probably didn't feel it. Hello! He tightened his grip until it pinched. "Ow!"

"Let's make a deal."

They already had one, and Allison was starting to regret it. "What kind?" she asked suspiciously.

"I'll give you back your finger if you tell me what's wrong."

Why, oh why, did she have to spell it out for him? "Fine!" She set her chin. "Where do you want me to start?"

"From the top, I guess."

"Hmm, well…" Allison thought fast. Her finger was going numb. "One," she said, surveying his stubble, "I don't appreciate that you lied to me about shaving."

Grady's brow shot up.

"Two, tonight I think that *you* should take the floor."

She gulped in a breath as he stood there waiting. Grady apparently realized this was going to be a long list.

"Three, I don't appreciate you talking to my friends and telling them things behind my back. Things like we're all going to Italy!"

"But I didn't say—"

"Please," she said, assuming an air of dignity, "let me finish… Four, I don't want you to come with me on my walk. I want to go solo."

"And five?" he asked mildly.

Allison gritted her teeth and tried to pry free her finger, but Grady clamped down tight. "I want my hand back! I've told you time and time again, no—"

He stunned her by letting go so quickly, she nearly toppled backward into the door. "It's all good, Allison. You go on…" He gestured grandly. "Take your little walk on the beach. Have a great time."

"And what's all this about Total Wines going global!" she shrieked, having just thought of it. "That's six! You can't stop taking, Grady, can you? Take, take, take. First it's Voltaire Vineyards. Next, the world!"

To her astonishment, Grady's lips pulled into a grin. "Now that you put it that way, it sounds kind of good, doesn't it? Going global. I like that."

Allison drew a deep breath and released it. "I'm going for a walk," she said, laying her hand on the doorknob. "Please, stay here."

Grady leaned into the doorframe as she stormed away. "I'm surprised you could only think of six!"

Allison threw her hands up in the air and turned to glare at him. "That's because I only started counting with today!" she hollered back.

Queenie and Brevard stared out the window from where they sat at the dining room table making up their shopping list. The other two couples, Deb and Patrick and Carla and Bruce, had already departed on their excursions.

"What do you suppose is going on?" Brevard asked quietly.

Queenie thumped her pen against its matching notepad. After a minute she spoke, her face falling. "Lovers' quarrel. Has to be."

"I hope they work it out."

"Of course they will, sugar. Didn't you hear? They're already making plans for next year. That spells *long-term.*"

Brevard unexpectedly took her hand. "Laticia, about the future…?"

Her big dark eyes went round. "Yes, Brevard?"

He slightly adjusted his glasses. "I was thinking we should talk about it."

"Of course, we'll talk about it." She sweetly squeezed his hand. "But not just yet, all right?" She shot him a confident wink. "You finish that book first."

"I really am writing one. I know you suspect that maybe I'm not."

"Phooey! What would make you think that?"

He grabbed his laptop from the far end of the table and turned the screen toward her, opening a collapsed window. "Were you Googling my agent and checking his client list?"

Queenie blinked like a kid who'd been caught with her hand in the cookie jar. "What?" she asked, her voice rising. "Now, don't be silly, baby." She rolled her eyes toward the ocean, obviously thinking fast, then turned to him with an exaggerated grin. "I was only checking my e-mail."

Chapter Nineteen

Allison walked briskly along the beach, a sharp breeze whistling off the ocean and whipping through her hair. It was nippy out, but still pleasant enough with a big, bright sun shining in the sky. It was hard to imagine a cold front was coming in tomorrow, possibly even bringing snow. Allison was glad she'd gotten away from Grady to take this walk alone. She needed time to clear her head.

It was true she'd snapped at him when she shouldn't have. At the end of the day, Grady was doing her a favor, no matter how aggravating he tried to be. She didn't know why, but she felt like he was doing it on purpose. It was like he was learning where all her buttons were and having fun pushing them. The one thing Grady didn't know about was her parents. Their bookstore closing down had been a big blow. While very few people were aware of this, Allison had been forced to return from her semester abroad early. With her parents' income suddenly reduced to almost nothing, they hadn't been able to cover the extra bills and student visa restrictions had prevented Allison from finding a job in Cortona to help pay her own way.

Three months later, her mom's cancer had returned. It came on with such a vengeance that, by the time it was discovered, there was nothing the doctors could do. Allison had always secretly believed that the stress of the bookstore's closing had contributed to the illness's resurgence and her mother's subsequent demise. Her mom had been only fifty-six when she'd died, leaving her husband of thirty years behind, as well as Allison and her younger brother. Josh hadn't even finished high school before her death. If Allison found the situation hard to deal with as a college junior, it had been even tougher on him. Their mom had died two weeks before Josh's high school graduation. Allison liked to believe that her mom had been there in spirit. Though in person would have been much better.

Allison dragged a hand across her cheek, wiping back a tear. Now was not the time to be sentimental. But she couldn't help it. This random talk of returning to Italy opened up those old wounds. Grady O'Brien wanted to take over the world. Ha! How many families would Total Wines destroy in the process? Did he really have any idea what he was doing? While he claimed his buyouts helped people, it was difficult to see how. Sure, Grady was full of glib stories about improved employee benefits and stability. But was that really the way things played out? It was impossible to believe his success rate was as high as he claimed, and much more reasonable to assume that when the people at Total Wines saw something they wanted, they took it, regardless of the collateral damage.

The path followed a steep incline among the dunes, then carried her higher to the grassy hills that she'd seen from the window. She could spy the lighthouse gleaming in the distance, with the lighthouse keeper's cottage and another outbuilding beside it. Allison climbed toward them, and the sole of her boot slipped against the rocky slope.

Allison stared down in horror as bits of gravel mixed with crushed shells catapulted toward the churning sea below. This path cut precariously close to the ocean at certain points, and the higher she climbed, the more daunting the cliffs with sheer drop-offs became. Things were still slick from the heavy rains yesterday. She'd have to watch her step.

Grady plunked down on the bed and dropped his head in his hands, not knowing what to think. If the idea had been to have Allison get to know—and like—him, the plan obviously wasn't succeeding. Just because he was a bear before his coffee didn't mean he needed to add that bit about Allison being a party pooper. He never expected for her to get so bent out of shape about it, which had only inspired him to tease her more. That had been wrong of him, as had the hand-holding fake-out attempt at the breakfast table. What on earth was his problem?

Grady was a polished professional at the top of his game, yet his interactions with Allison left him feeling like a clumsy oaf having trouble putting one foot in front of the other. Everywhere Grady turned, he made a misstep. And *this* was supposed to win favor with the woman?

At least his tactics seemed to be working with Allison's friends, but they weren't Grady's main target. He'd meant to slowly introduce the topic of Total Wines' global expansion to Allison. But when her friends had pressed him for details about his business, his chest had swelled with pride and he'd been all too interested in discussing his exciting endeavors. Perhaps he'd been trying to impress them, by making them think he was good enough for Allison. In return, he'd apparently turned the object of his pretend affections off by making her super angry.

But why *was* Allison so angry? Although she'd given him six reasons, they somehow didn't seem enough. Her distaste for Grady appeared to run deeper than that. He didn't know how things had changed so suddenly, because last night when they'd been talking over wine, everything had been going beautifully. Even this morning she'd seemed all right, until they got into that exchange over the coffee.

Grady ran both hands through his hair and stared out the window, considering his options. He could see Allison in the distance, making her way through the hills overlooking the sea. She'd definitely been eager to get away and put some space between them. Grady hoped the walk would do her good, and that she'd return refreshed, maybe ready to discuss things like a rational person.

That would mean Grady would have to be a grown-up too, and quit all this nonsense about trying to get Allison's goat. He'd been a real ass, when he could have played the perfect gentleman. Grady questioned his own motives in this regard, and wondered if he'd perhaps been acting that way because, way down deep, he'd sensed Allison's genuine dislike of him. It was like his inner child was urging him to make trouble in retaliation. Grady heaved a sigh, thinking maybe he should have taken another social psychology course in school. Perhaps he would have learned more about himself, and developed a better clue as to how to handle this situation.

Not that book learning could ever prepare anyone for a setup like this. His first instinct about the idea had been the right one. This was ludicrous!

Just then, Grady's cell phone buzzed. He got up to check it, seeing Kate had finally answered. She'd gotten there fine and asked how things were going in Maine. At this precise moment, Grady decided he'd better not tell her.

Grady walked to the kitchen for some water, weighing his next move. Allison was bound to have calmed down by the time she returned, and perhaps she'd be in better spirits. Grady glanced around the great room, where sunlight streaked across the floor, pouring in from the oceanside windows. There was an empty notepad sitting on the table along with a closed laptop computer. "Hello?" he called out, but he got no reply. It was evident the others had gone. He fixed himself some iced water, thinking maybe that was what he and Allison needed too. A little excursion to bring them closer together. Perhaps he could offer to take her to lunch.

Grady surveyed the contents of the refrigerator, finding deli meats, cheeses, bread and condiments. If push came to shove, they could make lunch here, but it might be fun to go out. They didn't need to go into Portland; he and Allison could explore the quaint seaside village nearby. Grady had researched it ahead of time and found it had a fish market, a small supermarket, a coffee shop and two restaurants, as well as a few knickknack stores selling beach supplies and offering bike and equipment rentals. There weren't a whole lot of choices, but he and Allison should be able to rustle up a midday meal.

Grady set his water glass on the counter by the kitchen sink, observing the small cove ringed by rocky shores and the tall white-capped waves that swept toward the house. Even with the cottage windows shut, he could hear them crashing melodically against the shore. It was gusty out today, with wind whipping through the sea grass, bowing it sideways. He cast his gaze toward the lighthouse, looking for Allison. He spotted the small speck of her scaling an enormous boulder. Then, suddenly, she was gone. Grady tightly shut his eyes, then opened them again, wanting to be sure of what he'd seen. He leaned toward the window and peered north with all his might, willing an image of Allison to appear.

Grady's heart pounded in his throat.

She'd fallen over the edge.

Without thinking of his jacket, Grady banged open the kitchen door and raced for the beach. In seconds, he was tearing along the rocky terrain that led toward the lighthouse and calling her name. Yet nothing came back to him but the fierce pounding of the surf.

Chapter Twenty

Allison was falling, falling…plummeting toward the sea in a frightful rush, icy winds swallowing her up as she kicked and flailed her arms, desperately trying to reach something…*anything! There!* Her left palm slammed into an outcropping as her right hand made purchase with a gnarly branch. No! It was the narrow trunk of a tree forcing its way out between two boulders, its spindly bare limbs fracturing the sun. Allison's heart thudded as she clung for dear life, teetering forty feet above the ocean, where a deadly embankment of rocks threatened to tear her apart. She'd never survive the fall.

Allison's palms grew slick as her feet dangled below her. She had to hold on—and find a way to pull herself up. Her overextended arms were burning from supporting her weight and felt as though they might snap apart at any minute, and her left hand was sliding…losing its grip on the moss-covered ledge. She couldn't support her weight with one arm alone. She'd need to move her left hand over and use both to grip the tree. Allison squinted against the sunlight and questioned whether the sapling could hold her. But what choice did she have?

She heard her name in the distance. Was it her imagination, or…

"Allison!"

Grady! She attempted to shout, but fear strangled her cries. Just like in the most horrific nightmare, Allison worked her mouth and couldn't scream. She summoned her courage and willed her voice to work. A short syllable scraped from her throat, gravelly and unintelligible. "Gray..." He'd never hear her. Not above the wind.

Hot tears blistered her eyes as she heard her name again. *No, not this.* Her left hand slid suddenly on the ledge and she clawed at the earth, digging in with her fingers. She had to grab the tree…get both hands around it. But she was too weak to hold on with just her right hand while she made the effort. Trying could mean certain death.

Sobs racked her body, threatening her hold and causing her arms to strain harder. *I'm not going to make it.* Fear seized her heart. *This is it.*

Allison unexpectedly thought of her mother and instantly felt cradled in her arms. It was like her mom was telling her to hang on, that this wasn't her time. Strength surged through her and Allison tightened her right-handed grasp on the tree. In a flash, she jerked her left hand off the outcropping and slammed it toward the tree. *Wham!* Bark burned against her palm as she clamped the fingers of her left hand around the trunk, just above her right hand, frantically holding on.

Next, she found her voice. "Grady!" The words wrenched from her throat. "Down here!"

Allison heard rapid footfalls approach, then skid to a halt. A torrent of pebbles cascaded toward her, and she quickly turned her head as they bounced off the rocky ledge. Then Grady was staring down at her, hands perched on his knees, his eyes rapidly assessing the situation as he caught his breath. "Allison," he said, keeping his voice steady. "Hold on."

Allison released a ragged cry. Her elbows ached and her fingertips felt prickly, like they were losing sensation. "I don't think I can. Much longer."

"Don't let go. I'm coming down to get you."

"Grady, no!" Her voice echoed off the side of the cliff. "The shelf! It will give way!"

He glanced to the left and then the right, before setting his gaze back on her. "It's the only chance we have. There isn't any time."

"Then we'll both die."

"Not if I get you to safety first."

Chapter Twenty-One

Grady set his lips in a hard line and assessed the situation. The outcropping was five feet below the main path, so if he got to Allison he could hoist her up. It would be tougher for him to make it without anyone giving him a boost, but he was tall enough to reach the upper rim of the cliff—if he could only find something to hold onto. He spied the spiky edge of a large boulder that appeared embedded in the earth. A piece of it had broken off, leaving a rocky sheath he could use as a handle. Grady tested his grip against it, trying with all his might to dislodge the cut stone, but it held steady. It wasn't ideal, but it was something. He also thought he'd be able to reach it from the outcropping.

But first, it was going to have to help support him on the way down, or else he risked falling himself and tumbling straight into the ocean. Or worse, he could land too hard on the outcropping and the sudden shock could send the entire thing plummeting. Even if he took it easy, Allison was right…their combined weight could cause the outcropping to collapse. But there wasn't another soul in sight and Grady was out of options. He had to use what he had.

Grady's earlier plans and the real reason he'd come here seemed inconsequential. Being successful in business meant nothing compared to this. All that mattered was protecting Allison from serious harm.

Her grasp seemed to slip on the tree and she shrieked as it bowed toward her. Her holding on wasn't the only problem. The tree trunk itself could snap in two.

The second he'd thought it, he heard a bone-chilling *crack.*

The narrow tree trunk collapsed against the outcropping and Allison's grasp slid further toward the top of the tree, which now darted past the crown of her head and extended over the ocean. "Ahh!"

Allison's lips trembled as she locked on his gaze. "Grady…"

Grady had to go *now.*

"Don't move!" he commanded. He gripped the rocky sheath with his right hand and stabilized his descent with his left, gingerly setting his shoes down one at a time on the portion of the outcropping that most closely abutted the cliff. There; he was steady. His full weight was on the outcropping and it hadn't given way, but he still had to reach Allison and he had nothing to hold on to. If he shifted the bulk of his weight in her direction, the outer edge of the outcropping might break off, sending them both to an untimely death.

Allison sucked in a breath, then spoke, her voice warbling. "My hands…are…burning. I can't…feel my…fingers."

Grady got an idea. He'd lie down on the outcropping to more evenly distribute his weight. Anything was worth a shot. "I'm coming to get you."

"No! It's too late." She looked like she was giving up.

Not on his watch, she wasn't.

Grady deftly got down on his knees and lowered himself onto his belly, extending an arm in her direction. The tree trunk teetered beyond him, three or four inches away. If he could grab the section where it had bent forward and gently swing it toward him, he might just reach her. "Allison, I need you to listen to me. I'm going to have to move the tree trunk."

"Move it? No!"

"It's going to happen really quickly, so I need you to stay with me."

"Grady! You can't! I'll fall!"

"I'm going to grab you."

Her eyes widened in panic. "What if you miss?"

Slowly, he inched toward her. "I won't."

Her chin trembled. "I don't think—"

"Allison!" he barked fiercely. "Do you trust me?"

"No!"

"Not in business. With your life."

She blanched, then said softly, "You're not giving me a choice."

"You got that part right." He shifted his left shoulder and grabbed the tree trunk just above where it had bent. "We're just going to take it easy."

Allison appeared as if she might faint.

"I need you to stay with me. Hold on tight and tell me number seven."

"What?"

"All those terrible things you think about me. You only gave me six."

Almost imperceptibly, the tree trunk began to move in his hand, swinging toward him. "Come on," he forced a grin. "I know you can do better than that."

"You're a lunatic!" she screamed, but she appeared to tighten her hold.

"Good. That's seven. Now, what's number eight?"

Just half an inch more and he had her.

"I hate you!"

"No, you don't." Grady's right hand clamped onto her wrist, and his heart stuttered. "Allison," he told her, "When I say *go,* we're going to rock and roll."

"What's that mean?"

"You're going to let go of that tree and grab on to me."

"How do you know I won't pull you over the edge?"

"Because I'm stronger than you and outweigh you by seventy pounds. Plus, the second I've got you, we're heading that way." He motioned with his chin. "I'm pulling you up and on top of me then we're rolling toward the cliff where the earth is steadier. Are you ready?"

"No!"

The outer edge of the outcropping started to crumble.

"It's now or never, Allison."

"Okay!"

"Go!"

Grady whipped his other hand around and firmly gripped her wrist, so he held both her wrists in his grasp. Allison shrieked and jerked her left hand off the tree, clawing into Grady's wrist. But her other hand still had a death grip on the sapling.

"Allison!" He gritted his teeth against the strain as rocks plummeted around them. "Let go of the tree!"

Horror flashed across her face. "Don't let me go."

"Never."

The fingers of her right hand left the tree and found his forearm. Allison wailed in terror as her grasp slid. Adrenaline pumped through him and Allison's body quaked. "Ready?" he asked with a labored breath.

She gulped in air and nodded.

Grady clenched his abs and hauled her toward him, flipping onto his back and pinning her against his chest. In a flash, he rolled them over, holding Allison fast in his arms, and slammed them toward the cliff wall. The edge of the outcropping gave way, and the tree that had been Allison's lifeline plummeted into the waves.

The back of Allison's head smacked the dirt as she came down hard, Grady ramming into her. "You okay?" His voice was husky and his strong forearms nestled beneath her.

Allison's pulse pounded in her ears and her mouth went dry. "Yes. Yes, I think so."

"Good," he said, "because it's not over yet."

Allison stared at the edge of the outcropping, which was breaking apart and free-falling toward the ocean in rock-laden chunks, and her panic spiked.

"We're going to take this nice and slow," Grady said, carefully easing off of her and standing. He checked something near the top of the cliff, then held out his hand. "Don't make any sudden moves, but see if you can try standing."

Allison nodded, still in shock, and pushed herself up on her hands and knees, her limbs trembling violently. Grady held out his hand and she took it as he pulled her to her feet. He motioned to the top of the cliff. "See that pointy rock up there?" Grady asked her. "It's sturdy. You can use it to help pull yourself up."

She knitted her brow and stammered, "I'm going to have to c…c….climb?"

"I'm going to give you a boost." The earth rumbled and the sound of rocks breaking rose above the churning noise of the ocean. "Like right about—*now*!"

The outcropping was rapidly disintegrating, exposing more of the horrific landing site below. Grady formed a stirrup by interlocking his hands and Allison quickly stepped into it. "Keep your hands against the side of the cliff to stay steady. Let me know when you've grabbed the rock!"

He hoisted her up another few feet and Allison lunged forward. "Got it!"

"Great! Then let's get you out of here."

He gave her a final push and she scrambled onto the path.

Grady's eyes panned the terrifying panorama of ocean, boulders and falling rocks as the outcropping shrank toward him.

Allison yelped with alarm. *"Grady!"*

Grady thrust his hands skyward, tightening his grip around the jagged rock, then he scaled the side of the cliff just as the final stretch of outcropping collapsed beneath his feet.

Chapter Twenty-Two

Grady fixed Allison a mug of coffee and carried it to her where she sat on the sofa. While the coffee was brewing, he'd started a fire and draped a throw blanket over Allison's shoulders. She was still shivering from their horrid ordeal. "Are you sure you don't need to see a doctor?" he asked worriedly.

"No, really. I'm fine. I mean, as fine as I'll ever be after *that.*" She shot him a kind smile and the small bandage he'd applied above her left eyebrow rose. Allison's hands were scratched and she'd incurred more scrapes and bruises during their roll on the outcropping, but thankfully her injuries were minor. Grady was relieved they both hadn't suffered more damage from their harrowing experience. The gash on his hand wasn't deep enough to require stitches. He'd been able to clean it and cover it with gauze and medical tape before tending to Allison's small scrapes. He'd located a first-aid kit in a kitchen closet and was grateful to find it well stocked.

Allison viewed the dressing covering his hand with concern. "How's your cut?"

"Not as bad as it looked," he answered truthfully. Grady didn't even remember it happening. It must have occurred during his rushed scramble to safety, when he'd been clinging to that jagged rock. The wound had bled a lot at the outset and he'd had to keep his fist tightly clenched to stem the bleeding during their trek to the cottage. They'd hobbled along, with Grady supporting Allison around the waist with his other arm. Her steps had been as wobbly as a new colt's, and he'd feared she might faint at any minute. Fortunately, she'd been able to walk on her own, which had been good for keeping her circulation going, and her stability had improved once they'd reached the flatter portion of the footpath leading to the cove.

"Thanks for the coffee," she said, taking a sip. "Having something hot to drink helps. The fire feels great too."

"Can I get you anything else?"

Allison slowly set her mug on the coffee table, then laced her fingers together and attempted to stretch out her arms. She grimaced and pulled them back, resting them against her chest. "My arms are a little sore."

"Allison, there's an emergency center a short drive away, or we could always go into—"

"No, seriously," she said, stopping him. "I'd like to stay here. I don't think there's anything the doctors could do other than tell me to take two aspirin and call—"

"That's a great idea," Grady put in. "But not aspirin, ibuprofen. Do you still have some in your purse?"

She nodded gratefully. "Yeah, I'm sure that would help."

"I'll go and grab you a couple of tablets."

"That would be great. The bottle's in my pocketbook by the chair."

While Grady tried to exude calm confidence on the outside, underneath he swore his pulse was beating double-time. That had been such a close call he could scarcely stand to think about it. If he hadn't been watching out the window when he had, he never would have seen Allison fall. A chill gripped him and cold fear settled in his belly. Everyone could have lost Allison forever: her family, her friends, her coworkers…and Grady. A lump welled in his throat when he realized how devastated he would have been. While he'd barely known her prior to this trip, yesterday she'd begun opening up to him. Then, this morning, they'd had that silly fight, which Grady badly regretted.

And somehow, amid their playacting in front of Allison's friends and the inherent subterfuge, Grady had found himself starting to care for her. That was the *ping* he'd felt in his heart. When he was being honest, Grady realized he'd felt a hint of that the moment he'd agreed to this caper. Was that *why* he'd agreed? Because he'd been secretly attracted to Allison?

Grady hoped that hadn't been part of his motives in coming here. He had an exclusivity agreement with Kate, and he didn't like to think of himself as a two-timing man. That simply wasn't Grady. If he was ready to move on from Kate, then he'd own up to that fact and break things off properly before beginning a relationship with anybody else. Maybe Grady should never have become involved with Kate to begin with. If his grandmother could see right through their phony arrangement, then he should have been able to see the issues with it too.

Grady had been kidding himself to think pretense was enough. Just because he and Kate behaved like a couple to the outside world, that didn't mean they operated as one in their hearts. The irony was, Grady felt like he'd had more of a real relationship with Allison in just this short while than he'd had with Kate in six months. And his and Allison's "relationship" was an out-and-out ruse.

Grady entered the bedroom and his gaze snagged on the dresser, where he'd left his cell phone charging. He hadn't answered Kate's text asking how things were going in Maine, and now he was at an even greater loss about what to tell her. One thing Grady knew for sure. He needed to have a serious talk with Kate—in person. When he and Kate had started dating, they'd both agreed the arrangement would benefit each of them. But Grady saw more clearly now that relationships couldn't be handled like business deals. Perhaps he'd gone with that approach because he'd been gun-shy.

The betrayal by Meg had not only kicked him in the gut… It had broken his heart. Grady hadn't believed that heart could be put back together, so the arrangement Kate proposed between the two of them had sounded good. Now, Grady found himself wondering if his old ticker wasn't stronger than he'd given it credit for. Since his breakup with Meg, Grady had thought of himself as the Tin Man, someone who no longer had a heart at all. Yet, Allison didn't make him feel that way. She made him feel different—and special, even when she was utterly exasperated with him and professing to hate his guts.

Grady spotted her purse by the chair and popped it open, searching for the medicine bottle. As he found it, his fingers grazed against something else: Allison's box of condoms. While he'd joked to himself about Allison being a "party girl" in the beginning, it was easy to see that wasn't who she really was. The woman was totally hands-off, and had even appeared embarrassed that she'd seen him sleeping in his boxers. Someone like her keeping birth control at the ready somehow didn't compute. What if she *had been* telling the truth, and the package was for Kate? No, that didn't make much sense either, Grady thought, shaking his head.

He quickly extracted two tablets from the ibuprofen bottle, then dropped the bottle back in Allison's purse, snapping it shut. He didn't need to be examining Allison's personal items anyway, and what she carried around was honestly none of his business.

Grady turned to grab a cup of water from the bathroom and the comfy queen-size bed came into view. In a flash, he had a vision of taking Allison in his arms and laying her down on it. Of him gently placing her head on the pillow, and her long golden hair catching the fire's glow as it had the night before. Her beautiful blue eyes staring up at him, her sensuous lips full and inviting… And Grady, wanting to give her everything.

"Grady!" Allison called from the sofa. "I think somebody's here!"

Grady snapped to attention as another car door slammed shut. It had to be one of the other couples, maybe Brevard and Queenie returning from the store.

Grady quickly filled a small paper bathroom cup with water and hustled out of the bedroom, cradling the two tablets in his good palm. *What* had he been thinking? Was Grady out of his mind? Okay, that settled it. Whether Allison ever became romantically interested in him or not, he was definitely talking with Kate when he got home. The vision of Allison had thrown him. He'd never thought of Kate in those terms, not even once.

"Hey! We're ba-ack!" It was Queenie's sunny voice. Then suddenly she gasped. "Girlfriend! What's wrong?"

Chapter Twenty-Three

A little while later, Queenie, Brevard, Grady and Allison were seated around the hearth with their lunch plates. Brevard had started a new pot of coffee and Queenie had insisted on making grilled cheese sandwiches for everyone. She served them nice and hot off the griddle, each with a big dill pickle and a side of chips. Allison sank her teeth into the crispy, buttery toast holding melted cheese and sighed. "Thanks, Queenie. This is absolutely delicious."

"Superb," Grady agreed, crunching on a potato chip.

"Pish-posh! It's the least I can do for you two! What a nightmare you went through."

They'd told her and Brevard all about it and the couple had listened with astonished faces.

"We're so glad you're all right," Bernard said, adjusting his glasses. "Are you quite sure neither of you needs to see a doctor?"

Both Grady and Allison tried to insist they were fine. Allison was at least as fine as she could be under the circumstances. She thanked her lucky stars, the heavens and Grady that she was alive. She also owed a private debt to her mother, whom she believed had been with her in spirit. Perhaps a mother's love truly was strong enough to transcend dimensions and the bonds of time.

"Well, Grady, look at you!" Queenie said, savoring her sandwich. "You're not just the perfect boyfriend, now you're a hero too."

Allison saw Grady's neck color beneath his open collar. "I think *hero* may be too strong a word," he said modestly. "Allison had a role in this as well. She was incredibly brave under the circumstances. A lot braver than I would have been in her position."

"Now you're just being magnanimous." Allison twisted her lips, then said coyly, "There's no getting out of this, Grady. You'll always be a hero to me."

A big voice boomed, *"I can be your hero, baby!"* It was Bruce. He and Carla had just walked in the door juggling shopping bags. They'd caught the tail end of the conversation, and—as if on cue—Bruce had burst into a bawdy rendition of the Enrique Iglesias song.

Carla slapped him playfully across the front of his jacket. "Ha-ha! Okay, honey. You can cut the karaoke." She gave a lighthearted giggle, then glanced around the room, her face registering worry.

"Guys," Bruce asked seriously. "What's wrong?"

Allison found herself wishing that Deb and Patrick were here as well, so they'd only have to go through the story one more time. But Queenie had told her they'd gone on a full day's bike ride and had taken a picnic lunch with them.

By the time Allison and Grady got through their second detailed telling of events, Allison felt exhausted. It was as if by sharing the story she was experiencing the entire ordeal again.

"We offered to take them to the clinic," Brevard explained.

"Yeah, but they were both too stubborn to go." Queenie stood and began clearing their plates, and Grady got up to help her. "No, you don't," she told him. "Just sit right back down, sugar." She sent her lover a pointed look and scolded, "Brevard, get your lazy bottom off of that chair and come help Laticia."

Brevard shot to his feet, appearing embarrassed, and cleared a few empty coffee cups. "Anyone want more?"

Allison and Grady both shook their heads. Allison had consumed enough caffeine and she wanted to get a good night's sleep. Her aching body had certainly earned it.

Bruce was eyeing her carefully as if he sensed her discomfort. "Well, if you won't go to the clinic," he said. "It's a good thing the clinic could come to you."

"That's right!" Carla replied, her cheeks glowing. "There's a doctor in the house!"

Everyone agreed that Bruce should look Grady and Allison over. And, a little reluctantly, Allison and Grady conceded it was a good idea. So Bruce grabbed his medical bag from his car and took them back to the master suite one at a time to give each a thorough going-over. He checked for reflexes and concussions, tested the condition of their hearts and lungs and carefully examined the minor injuries Grady had tended to, telling him he'd done a fine job. When he returned to the great room and officially proclaimed the couple safe and sound, the others cheered.

That was right when Deb and Patrick walked in the door, wearing biking outfits and holding backpacks and their bicycle helmets. They exchanged glances, then looked questioningly at their friends. "Is...something going on?" asked Deb.

While Brevard got started making the rub for the short ribs, Allison and Grady recounted their story one last time, Patrick and Deb sitting beside Allison on the edge of the sofa.

Patrick hung his head and blew out a hard breath. "Tough break. I'm so sorry that happened to you guys."

Deb looked both Grady and Allison in the eye, then patted Allison's hand. "Well, we're certainly glad that you're okay."

Allison genuinely appreciated everyone's concern, but at that moment she was dead tired. She just hoped she could last until dinner. Afterward, she might be going straight to bed. She glanced at Grady, who likewise looked beat.

"Those short ribs look fantastic," she said to Brevard as he carried a tray of them to the grill outdoors. "How long did you say they have to cook again?"

He appeared pleased she'd asked. "I brown them first, then put them in a pan with a beer mixture. Cover that up and it slow cooks for three hours."

"Yum!" Carla said, as the others also voiced their approval.

"Sounds very tasty," Grady agreed, but Allison noticed him sneakily hiding a yawn. He'd probably be just as eager to make an early night of it as she was.

Deb and Patrick left to shower upstairs and Carla went to help Queenie in the kitchen. Bruce said he was going to check on Brevard and see if he needed help with the grill, but he turned to Grady and Allison first. "Are you sure you don't need anything stronger for the pain? I can make a pharmacy run before dinner." They both declined with many thanks.

When he'd left, Allison confided to Grady, "I might take a glass of that delicious wine later. It will probably knock me right out and make me sleep like a baby."

Grady nodded and shifted on the sofa, positioning a pillow behind his back.

"You're sore too, aren't you?"

"Just a little," he said, but that sounded like a lie.

"Maybe you should have two glasses of wine."

Grady laughed. "Maybe tomorrow, I'll go out and buy us a whole new bottle."

Allison shyly licked her lips, feeling her face color. "I'd like that."

Grady settled his gaze on her and something passed between them. He was searching her eyes, looking for something. And Allison found she was searching too. Who was this man, this Grady O'Brien? And how had he suddenly made such a huge impact on her life? It wasn't just about him saving her; it was about other things too. "Grady," she said, "I never properly thanked—"

"Please don't."

"But I…you…I mean, without you..."

"No, Allison," he said hoarsely. "Without *you*. Without you nothing would have been the same."

"And how are the patients?" Queenie's voice interrupted. She glanced uncertainly at the two of them, understanding she'd intruded. "Oh! Oh, I see… Well, don't mind Queenie." She set two goblets of wine on the coffee table before them, then spoke softly, backing away. "Brevard and I opened our merlot. We thought we'd share."

Grady lifted a glass and handed it to Allison while she nervously fiddled with her hair. Had he just said what she thought he had? Was Grady actually implying…? No, she had to be imagining things. Grady wasn't interested in her as a girlfriend. Not a real girlfriend anyway. He'd simply come to care about her as a person. Besides that, Grady already had a girlfriend! "So," Allison said like it was the most natural thing in the world, "how's Kate?"

Grady stared at the lock of hair Allison had twisted around her finger. "Okay…I guess."

Allison quickly unwound her hair and placed her hand in a ladylike position on her glass. "You mean, you haven't spoken with her?"

"Spoken, no." Grady seemed to hedge. "But we've texted."

"Great!" Allison said a little too brightly. "Maybe I should text her too!"

Grady rolled back his shoulders. "Sure, if you'd like."

"Ask her how the conference is going?" Allison went on. "Or about the weather in San Francisco, or her flight there or…?" She realized she was babbling and suddenly stopped, cupping a hand to her mouth. "Grady, I'm sorry. All this Kate talk!"

He viewed her curiously. "Well, she's your roommate. Of course you're interested."

"And she's your"—Carla walked by and Allison caught herself just in time—"sister!"

"Right." Grady's eyes trailed Carla as she disappeared down the hall, giving them a little wave. Queenie was in the kitchen busily peeling potatoes and humming, Deb and Patrick were still upstairs and the other men were outside.

For a few minutes, Allison and Grady sat silently, listening to the crackling of the fire. "Maybe I should bring in some more logs?" Grady offered.

"I think you'd get in trouble," Allison warned him. "We're under strict orders to stay put."

"I feel like a kid in time-out," Grady said, and Allison giggled.

"Me too." She swirled the glass in her hand. "But kids don't get to drink wine."

Grady thoughtfully tilted his chin. "No, they don't."

Allison impulsively lifted her glass toward his. "Cheers."

He clinked her glass. "What do we drink to?"

"How about…to Kate?" The instant Allison said it, she regretted it. Why, oh, why couldn't she stop *talking* about the woman? Allison felt a rush of heat when she realized it had been her conscience speaking. When Grady had looked at her the way he had, she'd *wanted* him to be interested in her romantically. In her heart, she'd wished for it.

"To Kate?" Grady frowned and tipped up his glass. He sat still a moment, apparently contemplating something. Then he took a long swallow of wine, as if he were downing a bitter pill. "To Kate it is," he said at last.

Chapter Twenty-Four

Allison struggled into bed, her bones aching. After enjoying the delicious dinner Queenie and Brevard prepared, they'd graciously excused themselves and retreated to their master suite. Nobody questioned the issue of them being wiped out. What a day! What an experience! "Thanks for letting me take the bed tonight," she told Grady as he slid into his sleeping bag. Since it was supposed to get colder tonight, he'd worn sweatpants and a T-shirt to sleep in. Allison appreciated his being more modest. Particularly after the thoughts she'd had about him earlier, seeing his bare-chested manliness on display definitely wouldn't do. Allison needed to find a way to put her attraction to Grady out of her mind, but the more she fought it, the more she seemed to feel it.

He sighed and dropped his head back on the pillow. "I don't think anything could keep me awake tonight."

Allison could relate. They'd forgone building a fire and sipping more of Grady's marvelous Montepulciano in favor of taking mild painkillers and heading to bed. Bruce had supplied a prescription-level ibuprofen that he kept in his bag for emergencies, which he said would help them sleep better. Even Grady hadn't refused that offer. He must have taken more of a bruising than he'd been willing to admit.

Allison studied him in the lamplight, observing the rugged contours of his face covered by dark stubble. The fact that he hadn't shaved only added to his sex appeal. Not that Allison was considering Grady and *sex* in the same sentence. Absolutely not. Allison suddenly thought of the condoms in her purse and slapped her forehead. No way. But, yes, she had. She'd sent Grady into her purse after—

"What's wrong?" he queried, sitting up partway.

Allison covered her face with her hands. "The condoms!" came her muffled reply.

Grady sat up fully, drawing up his knees and resting his elbows on them. The sleeping bag scrunched around him, bunching up around his legs. "The condoms. Hmm, yes." He turned her way and Allison peeked at him from between her fingers. "I meant to ask you about those, actually."

Allison wanted to die. No, make that double-die. Not really, of course. She'd already had one chance today and *actually* almost dying was no fun. "I totally forgot they were there," she said, her face infused with heat. "When I asked you to get me my medicine."

Grady's eyes twinkled. "Funny thing. I'd kind of forgotten about them too."

Could Grady tell she liked him? That would make matters so much worse. Maybe he really did believe she'd bought them for him. What kind of person would that make her? Someone who'd intentionally planned to coerce a guy into cheating on his girlfriend?

Allison gave an embarrassed moan. "I know you don't believe me, but they really were for Kate. She asked me to buy them because I was already going to the pharmacy."

"I know. That's what you said."

Allison shot him a desperate look and put on her most innocent face. "Grady, I couldn't have...wouldn't have... I mean, that's just not the sort of thing I'd do—or prepare for. I mean, you're seeing my roommate!"

"And she's your good friend." Well, Allison didn't consider Kate a *good* friend. It wasn't like they hung out together very often. Apart from the girls' nights they undertook with mutual friends, Allison and Kate rarely did anything together at all. There was nothing the matter with Kate. She and Allison just didn't naturally gravitate toward the same interests...or values, Allison thought with a frown. Here, Grady thought Kate was so loyal. If he only knew. Once again, Allison decided it wasn't her place to tell him. There were certain things that had to be between Grady and Kate. It wasn't up to Allison to get in the middle. Besides, what if she'd somehow misinterpreted things, and Kate wasn't as bad as she thought? "More to the point," she answered. "Kate's your *girl*friend."

Grady heaved a sigh. "Yeah, well... We'll see about that when I get home."

"What's that supposed to mean?"

Grady held her gaze for an extended beat and Allison's heart hammered.

"Allison..." he asked thoughtfully. "When did you buy those condoms for Kate?"

"Oh, I..." She was thrown by the question. "What?"

"I mean, how long ago?"

"I don't remember. Sometime last week. She said she, um…" Allison felt herself flush. "Needed them for your trip."

"Our trip to Jamaica?"

"That's what I assumed."

"But that was canceled by Saturday."

"Yeah? So?"

"So, if she asked you to get them after that, then they weren't for our trip. I mean, not her trip with me."

Allison worked the puzzle in her mind. Did Grady suspect Kate was cheating on him?

Grady rubbed the side of his cheek. "If only I knew the date of that purchase."

"There might be a receipt in my purse!"

Grady locked on her gaze with a serious look. Then he lifted her purse from beside the chair and handed it to her. Allison sat up and took it, opening it up and digging around inside. "Yes! Here it is." She glanced at him and his face fell, like he already knew the answer. "Tuesday."

"Of course it was Tuesday," Grady said with a bitter edge. "I knew they couldn't have been for me."

Allison's head reeled. "What do you mean?" she asked softly.

"Kate and I don't…" He hung his head.

What? They didn't? "But your arrangement. You're exclusive."

"Kate and I cut a deal, but it doesn't include sex."

Allison feared the worst. Had Grady been injured or incapacitated somehow? Was it even possible he didn't like…?

He evenly met her gaze. "I'm not gay, if that's what you're thinking."

It didn't make sense. A big, sexy guy like him. "Then, why?"

"One word." He turned away, his expression pained. "Meg."

Chapter Twenty-Five

Allison feared she'd pried too deeply and had pushed Grady into revealing things he didn't want to. "Grady, I'm sorry. It's not any of my business. I never should have asked."

His face was dark and stormy, and he seemed miles away. "We were engaged to be married," he uttered, as if on autopilot. "I thought we were in love." Grady swallowed hard. "That…she loved me."

"I don't see how she couldn't—"

"Well, she didn't. Not really," Grady snapped. "I found the two of them together. Meg and Trevor, my *ex*–best friend." He pinched the bridge of his nose and paused. When he met her gaze, his eyes were steely. "Trevor was going to be my best man, can you believe that? I mean, *the best man and the bride*—what a stinking cliché."

Allison's heart broke for him. She couldn't imagine what it would feel like to be deceived that badly by two people you loved. She struggled to offer some words of comfort, or wisdom, but all she came up with was a heartfelt, "Oh, Grady…"

"Yeah, it was bad. But I'm a big boy, you know? I got over it."

Emotion welled within her and she longed to put her arms around him. "How?"

Grady set his chin. "By moving to Marydale," he said with determination, "that's how. It was the perfect job, and the perfect opportunity to get away from Seattle and those—"

"Memories," she whispered in sympathy.

He met her gaze with a sad smile. "I was going to say *people,* but yeah, same difference."

Allison was hesitant to ask him more, but she had the sense he wanted to talk about it. That maybe he needed to confide in someone.

"I haven't told this to anyone," he said, underscoring her thoughts. "Thank you for listening. Maybe I needed to get it out."

"And Kate?" she asked carefully. "How did she come into the picture?"

"Like a bulldozer, quite frankly."

His candor made Allison laugh, and she quickly covered her mouth with her hand.

"It's okay to agree," he said with a touch of melancholy. "Let's just say I didn't know what I was getting into. Or maybe I did. Or thought I did, anyway."

Grady inhaled deeply, then let out a breath. "Kate was the solution to a lot of my problems. When I arrived in Marydale, I wasn't in the dating mood, and yet…"

His words fell off and Allison guessed, "There were interested ladies?"

"A few," Grady acquiesced. "In any case, there was that…and then there were all those business dinners and events."

"You needed a partner."

"In certain ways, yes. But I wasn't ready for anything deeper. I explained this to Kate and she agreed. We worked out a deal to keep each other company, and appear as a couple when situations demanded it."

"But all those trips?"

"Kate arranged them, and truthfully I didn't mind. It was good to get away once in a while and take my mind off the job. Especially since it was clear there were no strings attached. Though that's not the picture Kate wanted to paint for her sister."

"What do you mean?"

"Never mind. That doesn't really matter." Grady shook his head. "What does is that I never told Kate about Meg. And I'm definitely not sleeping with her." His lips twitched and that old sparkle returned to his eyes. "Maybe *she* thinks I'm gay?"

Allison mulled this over, trying to remember if she'd ever seen Grady and Kate appear affectionate, exchange hugs or kisses. To her surprise, the answer was no. It hadn't stood out for her one way or another, as some couples were simply more private in their displays of affection. Now Allison understood that Grady and Kate hadn't been amorous in private either.

The revelation was mind-blowing. Was Grady and Kate's relationship even more of a sham than Grady and Allison's? She approached this gingerly, but her curiosity was getting the better of her. She wanted to understand how far Grady and Kate's relationship had gone. "Didn't she ever, you know, want to? I mean, did she ever...?" Allison stopped when she felt herself turning red.

"Suggest it?" Grady said. "Only once, but then she blew it off and acted like she was joking. It didn't matter to her, she said. Kate wasn't ready for a physical relationship any more than I was. Maybe she has her baggage too. I never asked. We didn't share with each other that way."

Grady's confession answered so many questions Allison had been harboring in her heart. On the surface, his relationship with Kate appeared to be no more real than his short-term arrangement with Allison. Viewing this from the outside, Allison might have judged Grady to be someone who enjoyed playing the boyfriend role. But looking at his face, she knew that was wrong. He was hurting and conflicted, probably much more than she knew. The words came out on a breath. "So the condoms weren't for you."

Grady stared at her earnestly. "No."

"That begs the question—?"

"Exactly."

Allison lay back in the bed while Grady reclined on the floor, both of them staring at the ceiling. What on earth had Grady done? He might as well have gone ahead and told Allison he had plans to take over her company too! Grady hadn't meant to get into that whole sorry story about Meg, but when Allison had looked at him with those big blue eyes, he'd found himself opening up to her. In truth, it had felt good to get that long-buried secret out in the open. Now, Allison knew the real deal about him and Kate too. What must she think of him? That he made a habit of playing the pretend boyfriend, like it was some kind of second job?

"Grady," Allison asked quietly. "Do you think Kate's really in California?"

He blinked at the thought. There was an option he hadn't considered. When he'd started putting together the idea of Kate buying birth control, he figured she'd been planning a tryst with someone in San Francisco. Maybe there wasn't any conference at all. How was Grady to know?

What a perfect way for Kate to test the waters with someone else, and what an ideal method for getting rid of Grady in the meantime: send him to Maine with Allison. That was just like Kate, to be conniving when she just as easily could have admitted their arrangement was no longer good for her by suggesting they call it quits.

"You're thinking she used us?" he asked Allison.

"I…just don't know."

Grady thought hard about this, but he didn't know either.

"I mean, it might have been convenient—if she was planning to see somebody else—to have you out of the way."

"But why go to all that trouble? Why not just dump my sorry tail?"

"Maybe Kate wanted to hedge her bets, in case the other situation didn't work out."

In a scary way, Allison had a point.

"Besides," she added a bit mischievously. "I've seen your tail, and it's *not* sorry."

Grady turned to her agape. "I don't believe it."

"What?" Allison asked with mock innocence, but she was blushing madly.

"You were flirting with me."

"Was not," but there was a little lilt in her voice that contradicted that.

"Allison Murphy," Grady said, putting on his best Irish brogue. "I'm surprised at you." He quirked a grin. "I might even tell my grandmother."

"Ha!" Allison grabbed an extra pillow from beside her and lobbed it at him. "You will not!"

Grady reached out and grabbed the pillow in midair before it could smack him in the head. He couldn't believe his luck. Allison was actually starting to like him. Grady didn't know how his spirits could feel so light when the previous conversation had been so dour, but all at once he was floating on air. He sleepily glanced around the room, spotting Allison's robe on the chair and more of her clothing strewn across the floor, but those things hardly seemed to matter anymore. Nearly losing your life really put a little bit of domestic disarray in perspective. Grady hummed softly to himself, thinking he'd take Allison's room chaos any day if that meant she was sleeping safely beside him.

He reached up and turned out the light, only to hear Allison demand, "Give me back my pillow."

Nope. He was holding it tight and keeping it with him the whole night through. More than anything because it smelled like her. "Good night, Allison!"

He thought he heard a tiny huff and then the sound of her rolling over.

She was starting to like him all right.

She was starting to like him *a lot*.

Chapter Twenty-Six

Allison woke to Carla's jubilant cries. "Woo-hoo! Pajama Day!"

She sat up quickly, the room coming into focus. Oh yeah, she was at the beach. *With Grady.* She spied him standing by the front windows and her heart melted. He might be going out with Kate at present, but from the way he'd spoken last night he was reconsidering that. Theirs didn't sound like an ideal relationship anyway.

Grady noted she'd risen and nodded out the window. "Can't get that in Jamaica," he said, grinning. Allison slipped out from under the covers and hurried over to see.

"Oh my, Grady." Magical white flakes danced through the air as snowdrifts banked against the dunes, now capped white like the faraway waves. "It's gorgeous."

He gave her a warm perusal, then spoke, his eyes never leaving hers. "I couldn't agree more."

Allison tried to think of a snappy comeback, but all her energy was focused on his mouth, and how heavenly it would feel meeting hers. Not this morning, or even today. But someday... Yeah, someday, once the thing with Kate was straightened out.

Grady's cell buzzed on the dresser and he viewed it with annoyance.

"Don't you want to check that?"

"It's probably Kate," he said. "I texted her earlier to ask about the weather."

"In San Francisco? That's clever."

He lifted his phone and scanned the message. "'High of fifty-five and sunny.'" He shrugged. "She could have gotten it off a weather app."

"That's true." Allison thought for a minute. "But either way, she's there and we're here."

"Wherever *there* may be," Grady added.

"Well, there's no way to know until we get home, is there?" Allison said lightly. "That is, unless you want to call her sooner and—"

"No," Grady said firmly. "The discussion I have with her needs to be in person."

"Then I have a suggestion," Allison said, mustering her courage. "Why not forget about Kate for today? I mean, not *forget* forget. Just not worry."

A slow grin spread across Grady's handsome face as he slid open the top dresser drawer and dropped his phone into it. "Consider it done."

Allison couldn't help but giggle. "My, you're compliant this morning." She rolled her eyes in an exaggerated fashion. "*So* much better than yesterday."

"You're being a little less bellicose yourself."

Her eyes widened. "Bellicose? Ha!"

Grady gave a low chuckle. "Doesn't matter, Allison. I like you either way. Both ways, actually."

Once more, he'd rendered her tongue-tied. Grady was so full of compliments this morning she didn't know what to think, other than that he was starting to fall for her. Could she dare to hope?

He leaned forward and asked in a husky whisper, "What's a pajama day, anyway?"

"It's a snow day for adults!" Allison grinned happily. "We stay in, make popcorn and hot chocolate, build a fire and play games!"

Grady slowly stroked his chin. "All that in one day, huh?"

"Queenie, Deb, Carla and I have been holding them since college."

"Do boys get to come?"

"If you mean the boys here, of course."

Grady mouth tipped up in half a smile. "I'm in."

They decided to freshen up and join the others in the great room. Allison made a move toward the bathroom and winced, nearly toppling over. Grady steadied her shoulders in his hands. "Hey, whoa. Are you all right?"

"Still sore, I guess. In my arms and shoulders mostly." He loosened his grip, but didn't let go. He apparently was still worried she might fall. "But my legs are achy too."

"It's no wonder you hurt all over. Your body was under a lot of stress and that roll wasn't exactly gentle." He shot her an apologetic look. "Sorry about that."

"You don't need to apologize for saving me, Grady. I'll always be grateful for that."

"I know what might help," he said with growing enthusiasm. "A nice hot bath. We've never properly put that claw-foot tub to use."

Heat flooded her face at the thought of them in it together. "What are you suggesting?"

"A bubble bath for you! I think I saw some bath salts in there. They were on the rack by the towels."

Allison had to agree that a bubble bath sounded soothing. The tub was there for the taking, but so far she and Grady had only showered in it using the updated tub-to-shower conversion.

"That's not a bad idea, actually." Allison massaged the back of her neck and Grady dropped his hold.

"Good, then it's settled," he said. "You go on and get started. I'll fetch some coffee for the two of us. After all, it's my turn."

"Grady…" she said with a flush. He couldn't possibly intend to bring it to her while she was bathing?

Grady chuckled in understanding. "No worries, Allison. Your modesty's safe with me. I'll ask Carla to take it to you. She's obviously awake."

"Yeah, but…" The idea of sipping her morning coffee in a hot bubble bath while snow swirled down outside sounded heavenly. But wouldn't Carla think it strange that Allison's own boyfriend couldn't bring it to her?

"But what?"

"That might look weird. Don't you think? Won't she wonder why you can't bring it yourself?"

"You know, I've been thinking about that. This whole pretend boyfriend thing."

"What about it?"

"Given everything we went through yesterday and my confessions to you about Meg and Kate, do you really think it's necessary we continue—?"

"Yes," she broke in adamantly. "I do."

"But your friends are such nice people, I'm sure they'd understand. I'm also starting to feel a little bad about deceiving them."

Nooo. What was happening here? Grady couldn't back out of their deal now. It was true her friends had accepted him and that was great all around. But what a desperate fool she'd look like if they discovered the truth. Allison was enjoying feeling a part of the couples group—for the first time *ever*—and she didn't want Grady to ruin that for her. Was their arrangement really so untenable to him? They only had a few more days left.

"Grady, I'm sorry about what happened with Meg, really I am. What she did was inexcusable and I can understand it taking a while to get past that."

Grady furrowed his brow.

"Okay, more than a while. A long time. She was horrible, she was, and I'm sorry about Kate too. Neither of us is sure exactly what she's up to, and I understand it doesn't look good. But I don't know how owning up to our ruse in front of my friends could make things any better. In fact, that would make things a billion times worse."

"Worse? For who?"

"For me," she admitted hoarsely.

"I see." Grady's features softened. "Look, Allison, I don't want things to be any more uncomfortable for you than they have to be. I thought that maybe by telling the truth, and getting things out in the open, the rest of the week would be less difficult."

"But admitting to my friends that I've been lying to all of them?" she asked with incredulity. "I don't see how."

"I just thought the stress of pretending might soon take its toll. I mean, look at you! You're so beat up from yesterday, you can barely walk. You need to rest and regroup. Be yourself rather than—"

"I am being myself," she told him. "In fact, I've never pretended to be anyone else. What you see is what you get, Grady. You can take it, or leave it."

Silence stretched between them as snow thudded against the windows.

Grady reached out and gently cupped her cheek in his hand. "I think you know what my answer is."

Allison held her breath and her pulse quickened.

"I'll take it, Allison. I like you just the way you are, and I wouldn't change a thing about you. I just wish…" He took a step closer and there was longing in his eyes, deep and soulful.

"Yes?"

He brought his other hand to her mouth and lightly traced her lips with his fingers. "I think you know what I wish."

Desire flooded her. Oh, how she wished for him too.

Grady lowered his face toward hers and she tilted up her chin.

"That's why I hope you'll forgive me," he said as her lips parted. "If we wait."

Allison inhaled sharply.

"Allison, darling…" Grady tenderly stroked back her hair and cradled her cheeks in his palms. "I want this to be so much more than pretend, but there are things I need to settle first." He searched her eyes. "Can you possibly understand?"

Allison nodded numbly. She felt faint from his very proximity and the heady scent of his skin. Though she suspected Kate didn't deserve it, Allison couldn't ask Grady to be anything less than he was: an honorable man. She couldn't believe how seriously she'd misjudged him, but that had been in the beginning, which now seemed a million years ago. "I know you want to do the right thing."

"I think we both do." When he said it, the words rang true. Allison didn't want to be the cause of further trouble between Kate and Grady, when their relationship was obviously troubled enough. If these feelings that were emerging between Allison and Grady were authentic, they could keep a few short days until after Grady got home and broke it off with Kate. But oh, what a torturous wait that was going to be, Allison thought, stifling a moan.

Grady softly kissed her forehead and shared a warm smile. "Now, what about that bath?"

Allison felt a cold shower might be more appropriate, but she wasn't prepared to say that. Especially not after Grady had so forcefully put on the brakes.

"Why don't you get it started," he continued, "while I grab your coffee? Cream, no sugar." Grady winked and Allison's heart fluttered.

Her head was still in a tizzy when he left the room. It seemed too good to be true, but it wasn't. Grady had alluded to starting something genuine between them: not a fake relationship, but a real one. Once they returned to Marydale, and Grady and Kate had settled things, Allison and Grady could start dating in earnest. Allison didn't know whether Kate would be upset or feel relieved. She'd clearly not been happy with Grady, as she often badmouthed him and tended to have a roving eye.

Allison had imagined before that she'd have to invent some kind of breakup-with-Grady story for her friends, but if she and Grady became a bona fide item, perhaps she wouldn't have to. There'd be that minor matter of Kate being Grady's "sister" that they'd have to address. But maybe they could find a way to explain that, when she and Grady put their heads together?

Allison smiled at the thought of her and Grady as a couple, marveling at how the fit felt so right. There were so many things she liked about him, and she was sure she'd find more. It was evident that Grady appreciated what he saw in Allison too. Plus, there was that knock-your-socks off chemical attraction, that major *zap* that Allison felt when Grady was near.

There was a rap at the door and Allison scuttled toward it in her robe. The tap was running and her bath was nearly full, big sparkly bubbles foaming in an arc and steam rising above it.

She cracked open the door and Grady's arm poked through holding a mug. "Coffee for my lady!" *His lady.* Allison's heart danced. She couldn't wait to be Grady's lady for real. Just the idea made her giddy.

"Thanks so much!" she said, taking the mug. Then she shut the door with a grin, not bothering to lock it. Grady wouldn't disturb her now; she understood that about him. He was the patient kind. Apparently, a lot more patient than Allison, who couldn't wait to get her arms around his sexy neck.

Allison set her mug on a stool by the tub, discarded her robe and sank into the water with a silent squeal. *Yes!* she thought, kicking her feet and pumping her fists until water splashed around her, making the bubbles crown higher. *Yes, yes…yes!* Ahhh, the warmth felt good… She sank down languorously in the suds, a happy glow on her cheeks. *If I'm Grady's lady, then that makes him…my man.* Oh, she liked the sound of that. She liked it so much, she feared another gleeful squeal coming on, so she quickly ducked her head under the water and let one rip.

Chapter Twenty-Seven

Grady didn't know when he'd spent a more relaxed afternoon. After a lazy breakfast at the table, the group had gathered around the fireplace to play games. True to the intent of the day, the women wore their pajamas. Grady noted the guys all appeared in sweats, likely because their "pajamas" were as presentable as his were. Meaning, they probably slept in their underwear or in nothing at all.

They'd begun with a few rounds of cards played on the coffee table, progressed to a group party game and then played charades. In between it all, the designated cooks for the day, Carla and Bruce, made turkey sandwiches and fixed popcorn and hot chocolate. Or rather, Carla fixed hot chocolate while Bruce supplied beers for the guys.

Brevard had just taken a turn pantomiming "Dancing Queen," and everyone fell back in hysterics when Allison finally guessed the song. He'd done The Robot, The Moonwalk, some wild disco moves, and had even imitated a Mamba, pointing first to himself and then to Queenie.

Queenie's eyes had widened in hilarity as she kept asking, "What? *What?*"

Unable to answer, Brevard had pressed his lips together, swept a surprised Deb off the sofa and done a ballroom dip.

Brevard took a bow and the group broke out in applause.

It was Allison's turn next, but Carla checked her watch. "Gosh! It's already five o'clock. Should we take a break before dinner?"

Everyone remarked on how the time had flown and agreed a breather was in order. Queenie was still laughing. "Who knew my man could *move!*"

Her man, hmm. Grady smiled at the sound of that, thinking he'd grin even more to hear Allison claiming him as her own.

"Well, *my man* wasn't too shabby," Allison playfully contended. She shot a glance Grady's way and continued, "I thought his *Interstellar* was out of this world!"

Grady basked in the glow of Allison's claim on him, wondering if it was just for show or if she was coyly flirting back, since he'd called her "my lady" earlier. Everyone laughed, recalling Grady's attempts at acting out the film title. He'd a hard time thinking of what to do, so he'd held his fingers up behind his head like Martian antennae and then flattened his hands together like a flying saucer. He'd alternated these moves, as people guessed everything from *The Devil Wears Prada* to *E.T.* to *Beverly Hills Chihuahua*. Carla thought his spaceship was a taco.

Brevard cast his gaze to the hearth. "Fire's burning low," he declared. "I'll go grab another stack of wood."

Patrick shot to his feet. "My legs need a stretch. I'll help you."

Carla and Bruce were already working in the kitchen concocting a wonderful-smelling oyster stew, and Deb and Allison offered to set the table. Queenie, who claimed exhaustion from laughing so hard, had gone to take a nap.

Brevard and Patrick turned to Grady, issuing him a silent command to come along. "Sure, yeah! I can help." Though he wondered why. They couldn't need to carry in that many logs at once. The men waited until they were all outside to cut to the chase.

"So," Brevard said, piling logs into Grady's outstretched arms. "Queenie wanted me to talk to you. You know, man to man." Grady recalled Brevard's wild rendition of "Dancing Queen" and subdued a chuckle. Brevard paused to adjust his glasses and stare at him. Uh-oh, this was serious.

Patrick cleared his throat.

Grady looked at him incredulously. "Deb sent you too?"

"No, I just came along as backup."

"Backup. I see," Grady said, although he didn't. "Guys, what's this about?"

Brevard lifted a heavy log from the pile and held it up high. Grady instinctively recoiled, his gaze darting from one man to the other. For the life of him, they looked like a couple of mafia guys. Secret mafia. Underground stuff. Really dark and scary.

"Calm down, man," Patrick said. "We're not going to hurt you."

"Not yet, anyway," Brevard said, and Grady's throat constricted.

"What?"

Snow swirled around them in the darkening night, and for a paralyzing moment neither man spoke. At last

Brevard said, "That thing that happened with Allison yesterday."

"Her accident?"

"Yeah, that. You didn't have anything to do with it, right?"

Brevard's log teetered threateningly overhead.

"Do with it? I…was only trying to help her!"

"That's all that we wanted to know," Brevard said stonily.

"Right," Patrick reinforced. "That you're one of the good guys."

"And that you won't break Allison's heart."

"Her heart?" Grady's voice warbled.

"Because if you do…" Brevard's log came down so fast it smacked against the stack in Grady's arms with a *crack*.

Grady jerked and something clattered beside him.

"Grady?" It was Allison's voice, kind and gentle. "Grady, are you all right?"

Grady opened his eyes in a daze to spy the hazy glow of the fireplace before him. A mug and a beer bottle were on an end table by his elbow, but the beer bottle had been knocked onto its side. Thankfully, it was empty. Grady glanced around in confusion, realizing he must have hit it in his sleep.

"I think you dozed off," Allison said sweetly.

Across the way, Patrick was reading a golfing magazine and Brevard was focused on his laptop. *It must have been a dream.*

Grady heaved a sigh, feeling like he'd dodged a bullet. Then he met Allison's eyes, and inwardly accepted that his biggest challenge lay ahead. Grady understood he was falling for Allison and he hoped she was developing feelings for him in return. Yet Grady didn't want their real relationship beginning with more cover-ups and lies. Sooner or later, he'd need to tell her about his Total Wines expansion, and how he'd planned to make an offer on Bella Fortuna Wine Designs. Grady couldn't deny that he'd still be thrilled if the acquisition worked out, but that was no longer his top priority. Since he'd come to Maine, his goals had changed. They now had way more to do with Allison than her business.

Grady was seriously struggling over how to explain that to her while sounding sincere. If he mentioned the business deal at all, would she immediately push him away, believing that was what he'd been after from the start? In the beginning, maybe it had been, but that wasn't Grady's sole ambition now. He'd shared things with Allison he'd never shared with any woman since his breakup with Meg. He'd also sent Allison some pretty clear signals indicating his interest in her. But if she knew about his earlier designs on her company, would she trust that any romantic interest was authentic, or would she accuse him of more playacting in search of personal gain?

"Sorry, yes. I must have fallen asleep."

"Don't be sorry. You've got plenty of reason to still be worn out from yesterday."

"Yeah, you too."

"We can make it another early night, if you'd like?"

Brevard and Patrick stopped what they were doing to raise their eyebrows at each other.

"Cut it out, guys!" Allison said, but she was laughing. "In any case, I'm on a mission from the kitchen. I'm supposed to tell everyone dinner is ready."

Brevard shut his laptop. "I'll get Laticia." He stood at the same time as Grady, and a menacing image of Brevard holding a huge bludgeoning instrument came to mind. Brevard met his gaze and lifted a log from the holder by the fire. Grady backed away so quickly, he nearly stumbled. Brevard shot him an odd look and tossed the log on the fire, where it immediately crackled and whined. "You all right, Grady?"

The words *won't break Allison's heart* rang out in his mind. Grady swallowed hard. "Yeah, um…fine."

Allison watched Brevard slowly climb the stairs while he kept a wary eye on Grady.

"What on earth is wrong with Brevard?" Allison whispered.

Grady cleared his throat and replied, "I have no idea."

Chapter Twenty-Eight

A few hours later, Allison and Grady told the others good night and retired to their room with a couple of fresh wineglasses. The weather was predicted to be just as bad tomorrow, so the group had voted to stay indoors and watch movies. They had enough in the way of leftovers to scrounge lunch together and jointly agreed that ordering organic pizza for dinner sounded good. Deb and Patrick had scoped out the family-owned pizza place in town and had proclaimed its wholesome ingredient list "Deb approved."

The following night was Allison and Grady's turn to cook, so they'd need to pick a menu and purchase supplies. Since Thursday was St. Patrick's Day, they all thought it would be fun to eat at the local Irish pub. Then, their final night together, they'd hold their group potluck. Allison was amazed at how the week was whizzing by, and pleased that everyone appeared to be getting along with Grady. She didn't know what weird thing had transpired between Brevard and Grady before dinner, but by the time dessert was served, everyone seemed to be over it.

"Do you want me to light the fire?" Grady asked after their door was closed and latched. Allison hadn't even noticed he'd laid a fresh one.

"When did you do that? Bring in more wood?"

"This morning while you were bathing. I wasn't sure when we'd be using it again, but with the weather today…" He motioned to the darkened windows, where tiny specks of white dotted the night. "I thought it would be good to be ready."

Allison smiled at his thoughtfulness. It confounded her that Kate had said, *Grady never thinks about anybody but himself.* That only proved how little Kate knew him. There was a whole other Grady right beyond Kate's reach that she'd never had access to. In a way, Allison felt sorry for Kate, but in another way she didn't. While Allison didn't like to think of herself as possessive, believing that Grady had selectively revealed his kinder, gentler side only to her made her feel special. "A fire would be awesome." She set the glasses down by the corked bottle of wine. "Should I pour us each a glass?"

"I'd love a nightcap, Allison. Thank you."

Grady had to be an expert fire builder, because he started a healthy blaze with just one match. "Impressive," she said, motioning toward the hearth with her glass while handing him his.

"Yeah, well, I've done a bit of camping. I've learned it pays not to waste resources. A little preparation goes a long way later."

"Like perfectly placed kindling and positioning the logs at just the right angle."

He cocked an eyebrow. "Seems like I'm not the only one who knows about fire starting."

Boy, wouldn't she like to start a fire with him. Allison recalled the warmth of his touch on her lips from this morning and her temperature spiked. "I got a badge in it."

"Merit badge?"

"Girl Scouts."

Grady laughed. "That's right. I forgot. You're a nature girl." He studied her a prolonged moment. "Hey, you wouldn't like to...? What I mean is, how long has it been since you've gone camping?"

Allison thumbed her chest and sputtered a giggle. "Me? Gosh. Has to have been ten...no, make that twelve or thirteen years."

"That's what I figured." His face fell in disappointment. "Probably not your thing anymore."

Allison couldn't imagine anything more romantic than being alone with Grady in the great outdoors. "I didn't say I wasn't interested." Her tone said she definitely was.

Grady smiled in surprise. "Great! Then maybe we'll go sometime? I mean, later. You know."

"I know exactly what you mean," she said, unable to believe they were actually discussing it. Grady hadn't out-and-out said it, but it was clear that he wanted to date her. "Although..." Her eyes traveled to the closet where they'd stashed the sleeping bag. "I don't own any camping equipment."

"No worries. I've got plenty to keep us covered."

"I was talking about a sleeping bag."

"Darling," he said, and her heart fluttered. "I've got a spare."

Allison felt herself flush, but her color deepened when he winked and added, "It's a double."

"Grady O'Brien!" she said with fake haughtiness. "I'm not that easy."

"I never imagined you were," he returned smoothly. "I was only thinking of keeping us warm."

His eyes sparkled in the firelight and Allison felt more than warm; she was sweltering. "Ha-ha! Good one!" Allison set down her wine and retreated to the bathroom, walking backward as she went. "Just going to grab some water!"

But before she filled her glass, she ran the tap icy cold and splashed some on her face.

Grady sat in the chair by the fire and took a slow sip of wine. It had been open a few days but was still holding up. A very good year. He was excited to think Allison might actually go camping with him. Kate wasn't into it, and he'd never bothered to try and convince her to accompany him on any of his treks through the Virginia mountains or along the Appalachian Trail.

It would be something altogether different—and fun—to venture into the wilderness with Allison. He'd only been razzing her about the double sleeping bag. He'd never push Allison into something she wasn't ready for. And the truth was, he wanted to feel ready himself. Somehow he imagined it would be a whole lot easier to entertain those notions about her than it had been to think about becoming intimate with Kate. But another part of him knew a deeper secret.

Allison wasn't a casual-sex kind of girl, and he wasn't that sort of guy. If they wound up together that way, it would be because they'd built something significant and expected a future together.

The bathroom door opened and Grady's hand jerked, nearly causing him to spill his wine. He hadn't even started *dating* the woman, and he was already contemplating forever?

Allison reappeared, her face scrubbed pink like she'd just washed it and her hair up in a ponytail. She held two glasses of water in her hands. "I brought one for you."

"Thanks." He stood and offered her the chair. Other than the bed, it was the only sitting space in the room. She declined, saying she was happy to sit and visit on the bed again.

Grady sat back in his chair while Allison propped herself up against some pillows. "You're just angling for squatter's rights," he teased.

"Huh?"

"You figure you get on the bed first, you get to stay there."

"That's not true." Allison picked up her wine. "I'm happy to take turns if you'd like. Tonight, I'll take the floor."

"Sorry," he said briskly. "It's mine. Already claimed it."

"Suit yourself," she said with a grin.

Allison was still recovering from her bruising and Grady knew she'd be much more comfortable in the bed. Therefore, he wanted her to have it. He was used to sleeping in a lot of hard places. And being in tough spots, he reminded himself, thinking of Kate. "I think I'd better send Kate a message."

"What will you say?" Allison asked softly.

"Just that we need to talk when we get home." He stood and walked to the dresser where he'd stashed the phone in a drawer this morning. "I feel like it's only fair to give her warning. I mean, put her on notice that a serious discussion is coming."

"Are you breaking up with her?" Allison cupped her hand to her mouth. "I'm sorry. That was too blunt. And, frankly, none of my business."

Grady put down the phone and went to her, sitting on the side of the bed. He rested his hand beside hers on the comforter, but didn't dare touch her. If he did, he might be tempted to take her in his arms. "Allison." He leaned toward her and his hand slid over. Their skin was so close he swore he felt the tingles of her touch. "It certainly is your business, because I need you to know that I am who I say that I am."

Her face was awash with guilt. "I don't want to be the cause of trouble between you and Kate, or the reason—" She dropped her chin.

"You're not. You have to believe it. Things never would have lasted between me and her. They weren't real, can't you see? Kate and I, we were never meant to be together. With her, there was always winter." He brought his hand to his heart. "In here, way down deep. But now…" He dove into her eyes, which were as blue as an April sky. "I feel springtime. Everything inside of me. The part of my soul I thought had died—frozen up—is experiencing a…" He searched for the words. "Very satisfactory deep thaw."

"That's beautiful." A single tear rolled down her cheek and Grady resisted the urge to stroke it back with his thumb.

"It's the truth. You do believe me?"

Allison nodded and he smiled gently.

"I'm glad. Now, let me text Kate."

Grady dispatched the message quickly, then returned his cell to the dresser drawer. It buzzed almost immediately, but he ignored it, retaking his seat in the chair.

"You're not going to check that?"

Grady sipped from his wine, observing the fire. "Not tonight."

Allison understood that he needed some space, but their quarters were tight. There was nowhere else for Grady to go to be alone with his thoughts. Except for out on the porch, where it was freezing.

Laughter sounded from the great room, indicating that the others were still awake, talking animatedly or playing games. "If you need a few moments, I can go back out there with the others."

"No, stay." He locked on her gaze and Allison's heart thudded. "I mean, please." He smiled softly but that smile looked a little sad. "I like having you here."

Allison spoke to herself, almost in a whisper. "Endings are hard."

"Yeah, they are."

She took a swallow of wine. "At the end of the day, I might be shopping for another roommate."

"It's probably something you should prepare yourself for. We don't know how Kate's going to take this double-whammy. Our breakup and the news that I'm falling for another girl."

Allison gripped the edge of the comforter in her hand, hoping she wasn't dreaming. Grady was falling for her, just like she was for him. That wasn't just marvelous, it was a miracle, particularly given where they'd started. And yet, it was hard to feel happy while Grady's expression exhibited pain. He shook his head and said hoarsely, "I don't deserve you, not really."

Allison fought the urge to go to him. "Of course you do. I'd like to think we're made for each other.

Isn't that how it's supposed to be? Getting hit by a Mack truck?"

Grady chuckled in surprise, his dark mood suddenly lifted. "A Mack truck?"

Allison stammered in embarrassment. "Um, yeah. You know. It just—*wham!*—smacks right into you? Bowls you over! Often when you least expect it?"

Amusement danced in his eyes. "What does?"

"Love!" Allison bit into her lip when Grady blanched. Had she actually just said that? Okay, where was the sinkhole that was going to appear beneath the bed and swallow her up?

Grady finished his wine in one long swallow, then spoke gently. "Why don't we just take things one step at a time? All right?"

"My thoughts exactly," Allison replied, her face flaming.

Chapter Twenty-Nine

Allison was glad the next day was Movie Day because the last thing she wanted to do was open her big mouth again around Grady. Shortly after she'd dropped the "L" bomb, both she and Grady had feigned sudden exhaustion and quickly prepared for bed. Allison didn't know if she was falling in love, but she sure felt like she'd been worked over by something. She was probably just sore from her harrowing ordeal near the lighthouse, and her achy body was messing with her mind. Not to mention her heart. Hey, it was anatomy, and everything was connected in one way or another.

Grady sat beside her on the sofa, clearly engaged in the film they were watching, the fourth installment of a long saga set in a fantasy realm. While Allison enjoyed the series too, she'd had a hard time focusing on the movies. She kept reliving last night's faux pas and wishing there was a way to take it back, when—of course—there wasn't. Grady had been really nice to her today and once again had brought her morning coffee, but he'd skipped the flirty bit about calling her his lady. In fact, he'd pretty much eliminated flirting altogether.

It was still cold and gray outside, but the sky had stopped dumping precipitation on them and it was supposed to clear up tomorrow. Wind whistled down the chimney, fanning the flames of the fire and causing them to leap higher. When the doorbell rang and their pizzas arrived, everybody cheered. After a short bathroom break, the group gathered around the table. Queenie, who was dressed in a sparkly top and designer jeans, popped open the lid of a pizza box and a heavenly aroma escaped. "Mmm, pepperoni." She looked cheerily at the others. "What are y'all gonna eat?"

Brevard jokingly nudged her and stole a piece. "Move over, woman. I like pepperoni."

She sharply arched her eyebrows. "Who says I'm your woman?"

Brevard stunned them all by boldly leaning toward her and planting a kiss on her lips. "I do. Any objections?"

The group hooted and hollered, while Queenie adjusted the shoulders of her top. "Not at the moment." Then, when Brevard turned to accept Bruce's high-five, she stole the pizza slice off his plate and placed it on hers. Everybody laughed, including Brevard, who helped himself to another piece, then passed around the box. Deb and Patrick declined the pepperoni and each had a slice of vegetarian instead. Allison couldn't decide, so she had one of each.

Carla made a ravenous sound and sank her teeth into a piece of the plain cheese pie. She and Bruce had skipped out on the second half of the film fest, claiming they were sleepy and needed a nap. Patrick had to keep adjusting the volume on the television to disguise the noise from squeaking bedsprings upstairs, but nobody commented on it. When the doorbell rang and the pizzas arrived, Carla and Bruce had miraculously reappeared. Allison noticed Bruce helping himself to three slices, one from each box.

Deb addressed Carla and Bruce with a purposely blank expression on her face. "Looks like you woke up hungry."

Carla ran a hand through her orange hair and shot a sideways glance at Bruce, who lifted his beer and said, "Yup."

"So!" Carla said, changing the subject. "Allison and Grady, tell us! What's on the menu for tomorrow?"

Allison and Grady exchanged looks because, honestly, they hadn't talked about it. Allison had been so intent on keeping her foot out of her mouth, their obligation had slipped her mind. "It's, uh…"

"A surprise," Grady offered. "And be prepared, everyone. It will be tasty!"

Allison's friends nodded, appearing pleased as they continued chomping on their pizza.

Carla grinned at Allison, her cheeks still flushed from…whatever. "You really picked a great guy."

"Uh-huh," Queenie agreed.

"Absolutely." Deb lifted her glass of wine. "Here's to Grady!" She studied him with sympathy. "Thanks for putting up with all of us."

"Yeah, and not running for the hills," Bruce added with a chuckle.

"He did go cliff-diving though," Brevard observed, and everybody moaned.

Queenie snapped to attention. "You shouldn't make light of that."

"It's okay," Grady said. "Because it's true."

"At least he was diving for *you*." Carla pointed at Allison. "Now, that's true love."

Allison's face steamed. Was it her imagination, or did Grady purposely avoid her gaze?

Bruce broke out in another rendition of "Hero" and Carla elbowed him.

Grady glanced around the table, smiling at everyone but Allison. "It's an honor to be here, and it's been great getting to know all of you."

"You sound like it's coming to an end." Patrick took a sip of wine. "We still have half the week here."

"And there's always Italy!" Deb said, raising her hand. "Let's not forget about next year. It's not too soon to plan for it."

Allison wasn't sure she was ready to think about next year. She was already getting nervous about next week. After Grady and Kate had their talk, she and Kate were bound to have some sort of confrontation. Since Allison wasn't the confrontational type, she hoped it would go smoothly. Without a lot of yelling and screaming. Kate could get loud that way. Luckily, Kate had never turned her bad temper on Allison. But given the circumstances, that could very well change.

If Allison could stay focused on what might happen beyond that—her and Grady being together—then maybe that would make any interim discomfort tolerable. The trouble was, Allison had a strange sensation in her gut, and it felt suspiciously like fear. She'd been so drawn to Grady and had begun to hope for a relationship, but since she'd said that "love" thing he'd been acting differently, like it was too much too soon. And it probably was. Maybe Allison was wrong anyway. She'd never really been *in love*. Had never once succumbed to that delirious emotion she'd read about in books and seen portrayed in movies. She'd actually started to wonder if the whole thing was a myth.

Still, a secret part of her heart held out hope that someday she too might find *the real deal.* Grady O'Brien was the real deal, she just knew it. Allison didn't need an app or a website algorithm to help prove that; she sensed it way down deep.

When Bruce went to retrieve more booze from the kitchen, Grady leaned toward her and lowered his voice. "You okay? You've been awfully quiet today."

"Yeah, fine," she whispered back. "Just thinking."

His blue gaze washed over her. "Me too."

Allison wondered if she should apologize for seeming to rush things, but decided that even mentioning the topic again would make it worse, so she pressed her lips together and kept mum.

Bruce returned and handed Grady a beer, then began a lively discussion about the oddest emergency room admissions he'd ever seen. Everyone else had their own stories about some bizarre injury they'd endured or knew of befalling someone else. After a while, they were on to sports, before Queenie dragged the conversation back around to the latest outlandish fashions. When Deb checked her watch and exclaimed, "Wow, it's almost midnight," everyone was stunned. Cleanup was easy and they all mutually decided to call it a night. For the past few nights Allison had looked forward to having alone time with Grady. Now she found herself dreading it.

Was Grady going to tell her he'd thought the whole thing through and that one week with Allison was enough? Maybe he needed a breather after his bust-up with Kate, rather than rushing headlong into another relationship? Allison couldn't deny that thinking was sound, even though it gave her a horrible knot in her stomach. If Grady didn't want to follow through immediately, he'd probably never follow through at all. It was just like when a guy says *I'll call you* without actually taking your number. But Grady had her number, didn't he? At least, in the figurative sense. He knew just where Allison stood because she'd worn her heart on her sleeve.

Well, if that's what Grady was going to say, then Allison would just have to suck it up and deal with it. This whole week at the beach had been a fantasy world anyhow. She had a business to run back in Marydale, and it was one that sorely needed her attention. Things hadn't been going well at Bella Fortuna Wine Designs, and she'd been researching ways to reorganize without cutting staff, since hers was a small operation with only five employees.

Every single one of them depended on their jobs to get by. She employed two designers, a bookkeeper, a marketing manager and a personal assistant. Though Allison did most of the lead artwork herself, she had the other artists tweak her ideas and, when she got stuck, present concepts of their own. If she had to make cuts somewhere, it would be most logical to consolidate those two design jobs into one. But Phillip was a single dad and Kayla had just announced she was expecting her first child. How could Allison possibly choose between them? She knew she couldn't.

Allison had to do something soon. She just didn't know what.

Chapter Thirty

"You're deep in thought," Grady said, closing the bedroom door behind him. "You've seemed that way all day."

"I was just thinking about work," she said, happy to steer the conversation away from anything personal. Like her *love* life. Yeesh.

"Your company? Bella Fortuna Wine Designs?"

"Yeah."

"You haven't talked much about it. I've been meaning to ask."

They were out of Grady's wine and too tired for more drinking anyway. Allison sat down on the bed and sighed. "I suppose I've been trying not to think about work."

Grady sank down in the chair. "Yeah, I've been kind of avoiding that too."

"I thought Total Wines was planning some big expansion?" He looked caught out before she reminded him, "You were telling the others about it, the first day."

Grady slapped his forehead. "That's right. We are."

"What does that mean, exactly? Buyouts? Acquisitions?"

"A few."

Allison's face fell in a frown. She knew all about those. Firsthand.

"If you're worried about the companies we take over, I already told you—"

"I remember your speech."

"It wasn't a speech, Allison. I didn't write it out and rehearse it."

"Touché."

"What's that supposed to mean?"

"You're very quick with a comeback, aren't you?"

"I'm not the only one."

She haughtily raised her chin. "No matter what you say, I can't believe it's always good for the little guy when big business moves in."

"Always? No, maybe not. But ninety-nine percent of the time—"

"That's an inflated statistic."

"Says who?"

Allison couldn't keep the hard edge from her voice. "Says me."

"And here I thought we'd come all this way." Grady's eyes flashed. "What makes you so bitter, Allison? What is about *big business* that you detest so much? At first I thought it was me that you disliked, that it was personal. But I'm starting to sense it's a whole lot more than that."

She stared at him flatly. "My parents, if you must know, ran a bookstore. It was put out of business by the big chains."

"I'm so sorry. When was this?"

"Nine years ago this spring."

"That must have been tough on your family."

"It was hard on all of us, but hardest on my mom." She turned away as her eyes stung. Allison willed herself not to cry. She didn't want Grady's sympathy. In fact, she was beginning to believe she wanted nothing from him at all. Why did she have to give in and let herself become attracted? It had all been just a game from the start. A hugely fabricated production, and she and Grady had been the stars. Now those stars were crashing and burning. The foreboding she felt was overwhelming. Like something really, really bad was about to happen.

"What about your mom?"

Allison steeled her emotions and met his eyes. "She died, Grady. She'd had cancer and it came back. The stress of the bookstore folding was too much. While my dad helped support the business, it was really my mother's endeavor. She put everything she had into it until…"

"Oh, Allison." Grady stood from his chair. She held out a hand to stop him as a tear rolled down her cheek.

"Please. Stay where you are."

"But this is all wrong. I want to hold you."

"No, you don't," she snapped. "Your loyalty's to Kate."

"For now, yes. But just for the next three days, until I have the chance to tell her."

Allison vehemently shook her head. "I don't want you if you're not free."

"But Allison, you're not making sense. I'm telling you I'm going to be free! As soon as possible. On Saturday."

"And then what, Grady?"

His eyes glistened. "I thought you knew."

"One step at a time, right?"

Grady blew an exasperated breath and raked his hands through his hair. "What's wrong with one step at a time?"

"You're putting on the brakes."

"For here? Well, yes, I am. I explained all that. I thought you were okay—?"

"I didn't mean 'for here'! I was talking about the future."

"What future?" His voice rose, apparently louder than intended. Then a sharp, penetrating silence followed.

There. He'd said it, and it was exactly what Allison had been fishing for. But instead of feeling gratified, her heart broke into a million tiny pieces. How foolish she'd been…hoping he might be her forever guy. Grady wasn't any sort of Mack truck. He was just a Greyhound bus on its way out of town.

Chapter Thirty-One

Grady had a hard time sleeping and it had nothing to do with being on the floor. He had so many things going through his head, it was difficult to know how to sort them. At least now he understood more about Allison's beef with big business, and his soul ached for her, losing her mother so young. Grady could only imagine the toll that had taken on her family, and on Allison, as well. Still, likening what had happened to her parents with his dealings at Total Wines was like comparing apples to oranges. Grady was intent on helping smaller companies strengthen their operations via allegiances with his. He didn't aim to shut any place down or put people out of jobs. Allison had it so wrong, but the more he tried to convince her, the less she seemed to listen.

And what was that slap in the face about the future? Could Grady be faulted for wanting to take things slowly? He'd already laid his heart on the line and explained fully about his arrangement with Kate, including his intention to break it off. Not only that, Grady had opened up about Meg. Now he found himself questioning the wisdom in that.

Maybe he'd been more swept up in the illusion of this week at the beach with Allison than he should have been. Being around her friends, who totally bought into their couple act, only made the ruse seem more real. But it wasn't real, Grady reminded himself. Everything that had gone on between him and Allison had been a big, fat lie.

Okay, not everything… Grady recalled the heat of her stare this morning. He'd brought his hand to her cheek and his heart had pounded so vigorously he'd feared it would beat through his chest. He would have given anything to hold her. The whole world to kiss her. Had he only been deluding himself when he'd thought she'd felt those things too?

In just a few short days, he and Allison had been through so much together, including their harrowing escape from serious injury—or worse. Perhaps the experience had bonded them somehow. With Grady serving as Allison's rescuer, he'd subconsciously grown protective, and had begun to think of her as his. To imagine what his life might be like with her in it. But permanently? Allison had thrown him for a loop by even hinting at it. She couldn't possibly have known he'd secretly thought of it himself. The future certainly wasn't anything couples discussed this soon in the game. He and Allison hadn't even had their first real date!

Grady grumpily fluffed his pillow and rolled onto his side. The remnants of the fire burned low, softly shedding purplish-golden light from its dying embers. First, Meg had kicked him in the gut, then nothing about his situation with Kate had seemed right. Now, Allison was asking too much. To top it all off, Allison had made her disinterest in dealing with large corporations patently clear. Grady could forget about any attempts at buying out Bella Fortuna, and would just have to come up with an alternate plan for his foreign expansion when he got home. It wasn't like he didn't have options; there were other label suppliers he could investigate. Yet none of their products would appeal to the savvy European market the way that Allison's could.

Grady shut his eyes and tried to sleep, realizing he couldn't solve any of these problems tonight. Tomorrow, he and Allison would return to their role as the happy couple before her friends, and would have to prepare lunch and dinner. They hadn't even decided what the meals would be yet. During her hasty preparations for bed, Allison had said they could discuss it in the morning. She'd seemed mad at him, and Kate was clearly ticked. He'd glanced at her slew of text messages earlier and she'd written, *What's to talk about?* Ten minutes later, she'd sent another text asking the same thing. Two minutes after that, she'd demanded, *Grady! Tell me now!* But he couldn't tell her now. Grady wanted to do that in person. One way or another, no matter what shook down between him and Allison, Grady was determined that he and Kate should call it quits.

Grandma O'Brien had nailed it. Kate wasn't the woman for him. Neither was Meg—obviously. He'd begun to hope he could develop something meaningful with Allison, but now Grady just didn't know. His head was all screwed up and his emotions were in a jumble. All he could do was hope things would look clearer in the morning.

Allison awoke wondering how she was going to get through this day. She was in a quandary over whether to say anything further to Grady or let things drop. The more they talked about what might happen after the beach, the tenser the conversation became. Perhaps she'd been wrong to so openly share her feelings with Grady, but if she couldn't be honest with him, maybe he wasn't the guy for her.

Was it her fault she'd been swept away? He might not have appreciated the Mack truck comparison, but the analogy was pretty accurate. Grady had come on full force, flattering Allison with his attentions, remembering details about her preferences. Next, he'd courted her friends with his fine wines and witty repartee. To add insult to injury—or near-injury, anyway—Grady had gone and saved her life!

How could he do all that and not expect Allison to fall for him? Especially when he'd stood so close and indicated that he wanted what she'd wished for too? She thought she'd seen it in his eyes: the very same longing she felt. Was that also part of Grady's act? Had he simply been toying with her? Playing some kind of game? But toward what end? What on earth could Grady hope to gain from her?

She'd risen early to find Grady slumbering soundly by the fireplace, and had showered and dressed quietly, before walking to the kitchen to get some coffee. The whole house was asleep, so she'd had to start the first pot. The group typically went through several during the course of the day.

Allison stared out the window as the coffee brewed, watching the sun peek over the horizon. The snow had completely stopped and last night's winds had scattered what was left of it throughout the dunes. Temperatures were expected to rise today, and the warming sun would likely chase away any last signs of the snowfall.

The ocean had calmed and waves rolled onto the beach in a steady rhythm while gulls dived for the sea. Beyond a faraway crest in the waves, she spied the humped back of a dolphin rising up out of the water, then dipping back below. Another dolphin followed a few feet behind, and then another. An entire pod was swimming together. They were headed toward the point, the bend in the shore where the lighthouse stood.

Allison's heart stilled as she recalled those terrifying moments when she'd held on for dear life, suspended by that spindly tree on the outcropping. If it hadn't been for Grady coming to her rescue, she wouldn't be here now, and for that she'd always be grateful. Allison felt a wave of shame, thinking that it was possible she'd been too hard on him. Had she been expecting too much in too short a window of time?

Just look at everything Grady had done for her, and with no thought of receiving anything for himself in return. He'd even risked his life. Allison thought back to the casual boyfriends she'd had and had a hard time imagining any of them placing themselves in similar danger on her behalf. In every way Allison could think of, Grady had proved himself to be an honorable man. He'd been completely honest with her about everything, including Meg and Kate. And he'd done her an enormous favor by coming here to begin with.

Allison knew she couldn't let the tensions between them fester. She needed to address them straightaway. Being open was a two-way street. She'd been forthright with Grady about her feelings, and he'd shot straight with her as well. And when he had, she'd blown a gasket. Could Allison really blame Grady for wanting to take his time? Especially after what he'd been through?

Of all the men Allison had been involved with, Grady O'Brien was head and shoulders above the rest. Maybe she didn't like what he did for a living, but perhaps that was because she'd never fully paid attention when he'd attempted to explain the nuances. Each time he'd tried, that ugly tangle of emotions and grief concerning her mom had risen to the surface and completely obstructed her view.

Grady couldn't possibly be the heartless businessman she'd originally conceived of. Now that Allison had gotten to know him as a person, she had to believe he was different. At the very least, she owed it to him to give him a chance. She should also probably say she was sorry for pushing too hard. If she kept pushing, she might just succeed in pushing Grady completely away, and in her heart, Allison knew that wasn't what she wanted.

Chapter Thirty-Two

Grady opened his eyes to see Allison entering their room holding two mugs of coffee. He must have finally dozed off, and slept like a rock.

She smiled tentatively. "I brought one for you: black, with sugar."

"Thanks, Allison." He sat up groggily and accepted her offering, blinking at the light streaming in through the windows. Yesterday's storm had apparently washed out to sea and today promised to be a beauty.

Grady took a sip of coffee, savoring its warmth. He hadn't known what to expect of Allison after last night. He was grateful her attitude had improved. They had the rest of the week to get through and, hopefully, more time beyond that. During those dark and dreary after-midnight hours, Grady had tried to talk himself out of becoming involved with her. But seeing Allison now, with her beautiful blond hair in its morning disarray, he knew it would be impossible to walk away.

He cared for Allison, he really did. She was talented, sweet and pretty, and her strong bond with her friends was a testament to her commitment and kindness. And when she looked at him with those heavenly eyes, Grady found himself completely captivated. He had a sense they could build something together. Something terrific, if Allison would grant him some time. Perhaps she thought he was backing out because he'd balked at the words *love* and *future*. If that was her impression, she'd misunderstood his reaction. It wasn't that Grady didn't want those things too, or that he couldn't hope for them...eventually. But he knew himself better than Allison did, and Grady was a cautious man.

"Allison, about last night—" He started to speak, but her words overlapped with his.

"Grady, I…"

"Yes?"

"You first." She set her coffee on the bedside table and sat down on the bed. Grady opened his mouth to speak, but then she stopped him. "No, wait. I'd better go." She drew in a deep breath. "Before I lose my nerve."

Just then, Grady's cell phone buzzed from the drawer in the dresser. "Go on."

It buzzed again and she glanced in that direction.

"Let's just ignore it."

"Okay, here's the deal." Allison pressed her lips together and her chin trembled. "Grady, I do—"

The blasted phone buzzed again, and then again. Then a fifth time!

Allison sighed and rubbed her neck. "Maybe you should get that?"

This was all Grady needed: more text messages from Kate. "I'll just turn off my phone," he said as it continued to buzz. What on earth was Kate doing? Sending one angry diatribe after the next?

"What if it's important?"

"I can answer later." He started to climb out of the sleeping bag, but Allison was quicker. She got to her feet and strode to the dresser, sliding open the drawer.

"I'll bring it to you."

"You don't need to—"

She smiled congenially and picked up the cell. "Already done!" Allison brought it to him and it vibrated loudly in her hand. "Someone's very persistent," she said, passing it to him. As she did, her gaze snagged on a message and her face paled.

Grady stared at the phone and his world stood still. It wasn't a text message at all, but a string of e-mails from his assistant, Diane. Each one concerned a deal-in-progress and she was sending him the paperwork to review. He'd asked her to have the contracts on his desk by Monday, but Diane was always trying to prove her efficiency by getting a jump on things. She had arranged the e-mails in alphabetical order according to the subject line.

Allison scanned Grady's first unread e-mail, the one that sat at the top of his in-box, and her jaw dropped. "'Bella Fortuna Buyout'?" She turned her stunned gaze on Grady and his heart stopped. Her expression was cloudy, her eyes misting over. "I'm afraid I don't understand."

Though it seemed impossible to admit this now, Grady had been so confident of his success, he'd gone ahead and commissioned the paperwork so he'd have it ready. He spoke past the lump in his throat. "I've been meaning to talk to you about your company…" He reached for the phone, but she snatched it back in disbelief.

"So it *is* about my Bella Fortuna? Oh, my gosh! Oh…my…gosh!" She spun on her heel, angrily turning away from him and punching the e-mail open. "The *paperwork you requested last week,* Grady?" She wheeled back on him and there were daggers in her eyes. "And why haven't you said anything about it?"

Grady swallowed hard. "I was going to, but then so much happened—"

"Yes, it did, didn't it?" Her eyes widened in incredulity. "And now I know the reason." She bit back her tears. "For everything!"

"Allison, wait." He tried to stand from his sleeping bag, but she pressed her hand into his shoulder and pushed him back down.

"For what? More lies?"

"I've never lied to you," he said, his throat raw.

"Oh, I beg to differ!" She chucked his cell onto the bed. Allison brought her hands to her head and shook it. "It all makes sense now. Your eagerness to come on this trip, the smooth way you won over my friends, the ultra-sneaky way you tried to woo me! No wonder you said we needed to take our time! The ink hadn't dried on the contract, because I hadn't signed it yet! Jeez!" She blinked at him, startled. "Did you somehow arrange the cliff thing too? Go up there and loosen some rocks?"

"Now you're talking crazy." He shoved the sleeping bag from his legs and stood, facing her in his boxers. "I would never do a thing like that. Put you in mortal danger. What kind of guy do you think I am?"

"I don't know, Grady. What kind of guy are you? It seems I don't know you at all! That whole thing with Meg? Was that a lie too? A ploy to gain my sympathy?"

"Allison, no—" He reached for her and she backed away.

"I have one question for you. Why my company? Why Bella Fortuna Wine Designs? Because you thought it could help you?"

"Not only that. It could help you too!"

She gritted her teeth, striking fear into Grady's heart. He'd never seen her so incensed. "Grrrr…Grady!"

He jumped.

"I'm so disappointed in you I can't believe it."

Grady extended his hands, palms down. "Maybe if you just took time to calm down, we could talk about—"

"What? Are you planning to lay out your proposal? Deliver a formal pitch? No, thank you, Mr. O'Brien. Whatever you're selling, I'm not buying!" Allison grabbed the jeans and sweatshirt he'd left neatly folded on top of his suitcase last night, and hurled them at him. "And, here's a news flash for you. I'm not *selling* either!"

Grady clutched his clothes to his chest, his entire universe caving in. So this was what a supernova felt like. He'd gone from brilliant to utter nothingness in seconds flat.

Allison closed her eyes and blew out a hard breath. When she looked at him again, her gaze was polar. "I think you'd better leave."

"Leave?" He nearly choked on the word. "You mean like go on a walk, or for a drive? Get out of your hair for—?"

"No, Grady," she said, her expression ominous. "I mean *go,* as in hit the road. Head back to Marydale."

"You're kidding."

She pointed to her cheek and gave a bitter, pinched-up smile. "Does this look like kidding to you?"

"But, what about the rest of the week? Your friends? And you?" He shook his head numbly. "How will you get back?"

She gave a little huff. "Don't worry about me. I'm sure I'll manage without the fabulous Grady O'Brien coming to my rescue."

The woman was impossible. She wouldn't even listen. She was throwing him out? Just like that? Grady yanked his sweatshirt over his head and tugged up his jeans. "Yeah, well, in that case," he said caustically, "you'd best steer clear of any cliffs." Then he threw the rest of his belongings into his bags and stormed through their private outside door, slamming it shut behind him.

Allison raced into the great room and opened the front door to see Grady's car peeling out of the driveway with its windows lowered and loud opera music blasting from its stereo. Queenie came thundering down the stairs wearing a leopard print bathrobe and slippers. "Sugar, what happened? I thought I heard screaming!" She stared out the open door and at the empty spot where Grady's car had been, then set her worried gaze on Allison. "Oh, no, baby. Oh, no…"

Allison collapsed into tears, falling into Queenie's outstretched arms. Then she broke down and told Queenie everything.

Chapter Thirty-Three

Grady intended to drive straight to Virginia, but he found himself taking a detour through Boston instead.

"My boy!" Grandma O'Brien pulled back the door with a pleased smile. "Why on earth didn't you say you were coming?" She wore a simple gray shift and what she called sensible shoes over thick stockings. A lilac and navy crocheted shawl draped around her shoulders, and her hair was in a silvery bun. Her slate-blue eyes were the same as Grady's and the years hadn't diminished their luster. She hugged him tightly around the shoulders, then beckoned him forward. "Come in, come in! It's blustery outdoors!"

Of all the people in the world Grady felt he could talk to, his grandmother came in at number one. While he loved his folks dearly and they loved him, his mom and dad were very reserved—both in their reactions and with their emotions. In contrast, Grandma O'Brien always said what she felt, and meant what she said. He'd loved that about her since he was a little boy. As he'd grown into a man and realized what a rare gem she was, he'd come to love her even more.

"So, lad," she said as she shuttled him indoors. "What brings you to Boston?"

"If it's all right with you, I'd like to stay with you a couple of days."

"Of course, of course! Go get your bags and I'll put the kettle on."

Grady understood that nothing could be discussed without a nice cup of tea. Before she turned toward the kitchen, she gave him a sly perusal. "I won't be wrong in thinking that this is about a girl?"

Grady heaved a sigh and shoved his hands into his jeans pockets. "You won't be wrong."

"And it's not that Katie Fagan we're talking about either," she said, with a knowing nod. What was his grandmother, clairvoyant?

"Grandma, how did you—?"

"My Grady wouldn't come to Boston unless it's serious. This one—whoever she is—is special. Now! Let me start that tea, and we can talk about it."

Two pots of tea later, Grandma O'Brien set down her delicate china cup with a thoughtful look. He'd gone ahead and told her the whole sordid story. He didn't see the point in sugarcoating things around his grandmother. Not when she could see straight through him anyway.

"Well, Grady, I must say, that's a fine kettle of fish you've gotten yourself into. More like a stew actually."

"I know it sounds bad."

"No, not bad. Just a wee bit complicated." She adjusted the shawl around her shoulders. "So, tell me. Is this company, Bella Fortuna Wine Designs, really worth it?"

Grady frowned. "I don't know. I mean, it seemed like the right fit in the beginning. But now, I guess if it doesn't happen, I can live without it."

"And the girl?"

Grady thought back to that heart-pounding moment on the cliff, when Allison had begged him not to drop her and he'd said he'd never let her go. The situation had been so intense, with both their senses heightened. It was life or death, and when he took Allison's hand, it was almost like she'd saved him and not vice versa. Since his breakup with Meg, he'd been going through the motions, but not really living the way a man should live. Allison made him want to be that kind of person again. Someone who could trust a woman with his heart.

"Can you live without her?"

Grady shifted in his chair. "I can live without a lot of things if I put my mind to it." And he could too. Hadn't he proven that with his move to Virginia? He didn't need Seattle with its host of unhappy memories. Just like he didn't need Kate, or Allison Murphy for that matter. Grady was good at business, but he was an expert at moving on.

She leaned forward and studied him a long moment.

"Ah, but you don't want to. Do ya, now?"

"I never said—" Grady tried to look away, but Grandma O'Brien grabbed his chin, turning him to face her.

"Ya didn't have to say a thing. It's written in your eyes."

Again with the eyes? She'd said something similar about Kate when she'd met her, but that assessment had not been complimentary. Grady should have guessed it was a mistake introducing a casual girlfriend to his grandma. She'd known something was wrong with their relationship right away, though she'd blamed it on

Kate. Grady understood that was easier for her than faulting her own grandson.

"It doesn't matter what I want," he told her. "Allison kicked me out, remember?"

She released his chin and gave his cheek a pat.

"Out of the beach house, yes. But not necessarily her life."

"That's what I've been trying to tell you. There's no hope here."

"Grady O'Brien, bite your tongue! There's always hope. That's precisely why you came to see me. You knew that in your heart, but you needed to hear the words out loud. The way you describe her, Allison sounds lovely. She may even have a touch of that Irish temper."

"I never said she was Irish."

Grandma O'Brien arched an eyebrow. "You can have the temper without the nationality, lad. In any case, a woman who asserts herself is a strong woman in my mind."

Great. She hadn't even met Allison, and already his grandmother was taking her side.

"But the O'Brien men are made of strong stuff. They've always been tough enough to take it. Just look at your late grandfather."

"Grandpa? What does he have to…?" Grady viewed her with surprise. "You don't have a temper. I've never known you to get angry with anyone."

"That's because you never asked your grandfather. He was the salt of the earth, solid. But not so good at showing his emotions, even though he felt them deeply. A bit like your father, I suppose." She shot Grady a wink. "I was a frightful newlywed, I was. Always yelling and screaming." She gestured dramatically toward the ceiling. "Bringing the whole house down."

"Seriously?"

"Mark my words, I was a terror." She chuckled. "But that was only because I didn't understand how greatly your grandpa loved me. Once I learned that, it was fairly smooth sailing." She appeared wistful a moment, her gaze on the china tea service. It was then that Grady recalled it had been one of her and her late husband's wedding gifts. She lifted the pot, offering to refill his cup, and Grady accepted. She handed it back to him with a melancholy smile. "I loved your grandpa a lot in return. He was a very good man. And so are you, Grady. That's why I know you'll make a fine husband one day."

"Thanks, Grandma." It was hard to get to *husband* from where he was now. His "ex" Meg had betrayed him, he was about to dump Kate and Allison had just sent him packing. No matter what his grandmother thought, the sting of Allison's rejection had felt final. What was worse, Grady couldn't fathom a way to fix things. He actually *had* planned to buy her company in a calculating, premeditated manner. Now that Allison knew the truth, he couldn't very well retract it.

His grandma eyed him astutely. "When I said you were in a stew, you may have mistaken my meaning. A stew can make a marvelous meal. Sometimes you just have to let it simmer. You give Allison a little space to think about what she's missing. Meanwhile, you can think about it too." Grandma O'Brien's blue eyes twinkled. "Mark my words, the two of you will be coming back together."

His grandmother was being so kind. He only wished he shared her confidence. The doubt must have shown on his face, because she took his hand and squeezed it. "Don't worry, lad. If Allison has half the smarts you say she does, she's not going to let a man like you slip away. You're a wonderful catch, Grady, and I'm not just saying so as a relation. I'm speaking as a woman."

Chapter Thirty-Four

Allison morosely sipped her drink, tuning out the revelers around her. But she was only wallowing on the inside. Outwardly, she was doing her best to appear perky. Allison was tired of being the downer in the group, and weary of ruining everybody's vacation. Her friends had taken the news about Grady pretty hard, meaning they were all furious at him. At least, they were trying to act furious, but the women were doing a better job of it. Bruce had slipped up, saying that Grady wasn't actually a bad guy, before Carla had elbowed him. And Queenie had to squelch Brevard's comment about Grady's daring rescue. Patrick was the only man who hadn't rushed to Grady's defense, mainly because Deb had sternly crossed her arms and shot him a don't-you-dare look.

"Here, Allison." Carla enthusiastically reached across the table and tilted the miniature food coloring bottle over her mug. "Yours isn't green enough."

Allison couldn't believe she was drinking green beer. Then again, it was St. Patrick's Day. "I'm good, thanks!" she spouted as cheerfully as possible.

Carla was their party planner. Apart from packing green food coloring in her purse, she'd bought them all festive headbands. They held glittery shamrocks bouncing high on tiny springs like alien antennae, and made them all look like lucky Martians. Never mind that no one in Ireland wore anything like this. Ever. Not even in mythology.

Brevard's headband was apparently bothering him, because he kept trying to prevent it from knocking against the earpieces on his eyeglasses. Every time he repositioned it, his glasses popped forward off his nose and then he had to fix them. When he slid them back on, the headband rose off his head. Poor Brevard; it was a losing battle. Though he seemed to be keeping a sense of humor about it. He took a big swig of beer and Allison watched his lips turn green. She glanced around at their group, noting they all looked like they'd been sucking on lime-green popsicles.

They were seated around a large table that was actually two tables pushed together in the smallish pub. Despite the meager offerings on the menu—bangers and mash, lamb stew, burgers and sandwiches—the place was packed. Perhaps because it was one of two restaurants in town. The other was the organic pizza place, a carry-out and delivery operation that didn't sell beer. As such, Ye Olde Irish Pub was the natural happening spot for tonight.

After spilling her guts to her girlfriends yesterday, Allison was relieved to be somewhere that served as a distraction. She didn't really want to talk about Grady anymore, because that only dragged thoughts of him to the surface, when she was working her hardest to push them under—and keep them there. The other women had been very kind and reassuring, but also a little upset that Allison had felt the need to deceive them. Okay, Carla had been upset, in her sweet Carla way. Queenie had gone ballistic, ranting on about how Allison should have trusted them enough to tell them the truth, but then she'd stopped and apologized when she'd realized she was only making Allison sob harder. Deb, in her typically neutral manner, had reserved judgment. In the end, they'd all said they were sorry for making Allison feel so much pressure. That it wasn't what any of them had intended.

They'd concluded with a tearful group hug, then Deb had offered a practical solution to their sudden dinner problem: the four women could make it a girls' night and fix something together. The Mexican meal theme, complete with tacos and margaritas, was Carla's brainstorm. That third margarita had seemed like a great idea to Allison at the time... It looked a lot less appealing in retrospect this morning. Allison had woken up with a horrible headache and a big case of Grady hangover. She still couldn't believe how far he'd been willing to go to seal his deal. No wonder he'd jumped at the chance to play her boyfriend. Allison's heart ached at the notion that he'd been so calculating. He'd underhandedly tricked her into believing he was something he wasn't: a guy who was starting to fall for her.

"Allison?" Queenie, who was sitting to her right, nudged her. Allison looked up to find a waiter with a notepad waiting to take her order. She hadn't even noticed him appearing at their table, but apparently everyone had given their orders but her. "What would you like, sugar?" Queenie asked her. "A burger maybe?"

"Perhaps she'd like something Irish?" their waiter asked, putting on a brogue. Allison couldn't help but think of Grady and her heart sank. She wanted something Irish all right. But what she wanted was in an alternate universe with no connection to reality. If only Grady had been the sort of hero Bruce sang about, rather than a manipulating jerk, he might be sitting here with her now. Kate's bitter words haunted her and they held a searing truth. Grady made a pretty good package—on the outside. But for Allison, it was what was on the inside that mattered most. She'd gotten a glimpse of Grady's soul and it was a dark, dismal and profit-driven place. "I'll just take the burger, thanks," she answered, forcing herself to smile again. "With fries."

She took another sip of beer, determined to go easier on the alcohol tonight. St. Patrick's Day or not, one was her limit. Deb was seated on her left and had volunteered as their designated driver, so she wasn't drinking. She waited until the conversation picked back up among them, then patted Allison's arm in solidarity. "You made the right choice," she said sotto voce, pretending to be talking about the menu. But Allison was smart enough to know that she wasn't.

Chapter Thirty-Five

Grady returned to Marydale a day ahead of schedule. Since he had extra time on his hands and an abundance of pent-up energy, he decided to dedicate them to his house. He was refitting the windows with contemporary replacements that had no framing on the bottom half and let more light in. He'd already replaced the ones at the front of the house and was working his way around to the kitchen. Unfortunately, when he lifted the smaller window that went over the kitchen sink, he noticed its frame had separated in one corner. He thought he could fix it with some wood clamps and a special carpenter's glue he kept on hand, but when he checked the bottle, he found it was nearly empty.

Grady tugged on his jacket, intending to make a quick trip to the hardware store to pick up what he needed. It was tough letting things "simmer." The more he thought about his disastrous ending with Allison, the more driven he was to fix it. But he had to fix things with Kate first. After his serious conversation with his grandmother, neither of them had mentioned his love life again. Instead, Grady had taken his grandmother out to lunch, then had set about making handyman repairs to her place. Every time he visited, it seemed more work needed to be done. But Grady didn't mind the physical labor. It felt good to keep busy and helped him keep his mind off his worries.

He'd been struggling over what to say to Kate, and ultimately decided the truth was best. The arrangement they'd made had been fine in the beginning, but it now seemed a detriment to both of them. Grady's heart wasn't in it, and he could never give Kate more than he already had. *Besides, she's already giving what she's got to somebody else,* Grady thought bitterly, recalling the condoms. Grady parked in front of the hardware store and climbed from his car, eying the restaurant next door, where he and Kate had gone for their first date. They'd had lunch in a cozy booth in the front window, but had never appeared as head-over-heels in love as the couple sitting there now. Grady blinked hard, then had to look again. *Wait a minute! Is that Kate?*

The slight woman with short brown hair had her arms wrapped around some guy's neck and was devouring his mouth in a massive make-out session. She broke away and threw her head back in laughter before glancing out the window. Kate's eyes locked on Grady's and her jaw dropped. The man with her turned and followed her gaze. All at once they were both looking at him like he'd just arrived from outer space. Grady's head reeled. Kate was here in Marydale? What about the conference in San Francisco? Had Allison been right? Did Kate even go at all?

Grady stood on the sidewalk, transfixed, while passersby bustled around him on their way to run lunchtime errands. Kate quickly said something to her lunch partner and scooted out of the booth. The next thing Grady knew, she came flying out the restaurant door and landed at his feet. "Grady!" she said in shock. "What are you doing back so early?"

He viewed her in disbelief. "Weren't expecting me, I see."

Kate huffed. "Of course I wasn't expecting you." She set her hands on her hips. "What does it look like?"

"Uh, cheating."

"Cheating? You can't be serious. Beau's just an old friend."

"A very close friend, it seems." Something about the name rang a bell. Grady examined the guy, who lifted a menu in an attempt to shield his face. "Wait a minute. Wasn't that the name of the guy you dated in college?"

"You never answered my question," she demanded, like Grady was the one in the wrong. "What on earth are you doing back in town?"

"What about San Francisco?" he countered.

Kate twisted her lips in thought. "The conference was canceled."

"Canceled. How convenient."

"Where's Allison? Did you drop her at home?"

"No, she's still at the beach."

"I knew it," Kate spat viciously. "You screwed that up too."

He peered into her eyes, wondering how he could ever have found them pretty. At the moment they just looked cold and judgmental—as if Kate should be the one judging. "It seems the only screwing that's been going on has been here in Marydale."

Kate smirked and lowered her eyebrows.

"Let's just say…what you won't supply, Beau's happy to provide."

That was hitting below the belt and Kate knew it. "If you were so unhappy with me, why didn't you call things off? I would have been glad to oblige."

She flinched just a little and set her lips in a thin line. "You think you're so special. Like every woman should wait for you. Well, here's the deal. I'm tired of waiting."

"Waiting? But I thought we agreed—"

"Agreements change, Grady."

Grady cocked his chin toward the restaurant. "Obviously."

"Look, I was going to tell you." Her features softened, but not a lot. "After you got back tomorrow."

"Tomorrow? Why not before?"

Grady shook his head, the truth dawning. Allison had been right to suspect it. Kate had wanted Grady out of the way so she could test the waters with someone else: her old boyfriend Beau. If that didn't work out, she'd still have reliable old Grady around to take her on expensive trips and show off to her sister, while she secretly back-stabbed and dissed him. He narrowed his eyes at her. "I get it now. I was your backup plan."

"Backup plan? What are you talking about? Don't be ridiculous."

"Tell me something, Kate. Have you already texted Marie photos of the new guy? Because if you haven't, you'd better get busy."

She stared at him, befuddled.

"You might also want to change your cell wallpaper."

Grady angled toward the hardware store, amazed at how easy this was. Walking away from Kate. He hadn't a shred of remorse or any qualms about the decision. He only wished he'd made it sooner, before Kate had made such a fool of him. He sauntered down the sidewalk feeling about a hundred pounds lighter than he had just a few minutes before.

"Grady O'Brien!" Kate shrieked. "Don't you walk away from me!"

Without turning around, he raised his hand and waved good-bye. Then he casually pulled back the hardware store door and stepped inside, its chime tinkling.

Chapter Thirty-Six

Allison opened her apartment door and called out, "Hello! Anybody here? Kate, I'm—" She stopped dead in her tracks when a guy wearing a towel emerged from the bathroom, and he sure wasn't Grady. He had short blond hair and medium-brown eyes, and was about six feet tall. He didn't seem the least bit embarrassed to be standing there half naked. His eyes crinkled in a smile. "Hi there," he said, his British accent evident. "You must be Allison."

Allison set down her travel bags with a *thunk.*
She'd ridden with Deb and Patrick to
Washington and they'd put her on a train to Marydale.
Allison felt like she'd been thrown for a loop. If she'd expected to see any man in her apartment, it wasn't this one.
"Where's Grady?"

"Long gone, I'm afraid. *Finito.*"

Kate appeared from her bedroom. "I've just finished clearing out Grady's opera CDs, what should I—?" She halted suddenly and stared at Allison, then at Beau, then back at Allison again. "You're home."

"Of course, it's Saturday." Allison was still staring at the guy, who viewed her curiously. Even if Grady had broken up with Kate the minute he got back, Kate was moving pretty quickly to already have dropped another man in his place. Hang on. What was Kate even doing here? Wasn't she supposed to be in San Francisco until tomorrow? "I thought you weren't due back until Sunday?"

"Long story," Kate said dismissively.

"Oh, yeah?"

The guy watched them, apparently interested in what Kate had to say. She swatted his arm with a CD and gave a flirtatious laugh. "Go on and put some clothes on, Beau. Certain things here are meant for my eyes only."

Beau? Wasn't that Kate's old flame from college? The guy Kate mentioned as being "the one that got away"? Of course, this was normally after a couple of beers, and she generally said it to her other girlfriends and not directly to Allison. Beau cinched the towel around his waist and ambled to the bedroom, glancing over his shoulder before he shut the door.

"So," Kate said, eying Allison oddly. "I hear the beach was a bust."

Allison removed her vest and scarf and hung them in the coat closet. "Went as well as expected, I guess." For some reason, she had the instinct she shouldn't tell Kate everything. Why was Kate's old boyfriend in their apartment? Could it be that Allison's hunch was right and that Kate had been two-timing Grady while he was away? "How was the weather in California?"

"Funny thing about that." Kate flipped through the stack of CDs like she was shuffling cards and staged a frown. "The darn thing was canceled. And after everybody went to so much trouble."

Right. Allison would buy that about as readily as swampland in Florida. Allison met her roommate's eyes, then asked unabashedly, "And Beau? How does he fit into this pretty picture?"

Kate waved her hand. "Beau and I go way back. It was such a coincidence that I happened to run into him at the college during the week. He was here for an interview. Math department," she said, smiling. "Word is, he got the job."

Allison threw a glance at Kate's closed bedroom door. "Looks like he got more than the job."

"Don't get your panties in a bunch. I already broke up with Grady."

"*You* broke it off?"

"Yeah, and he took it kind of hard too. But what do you expect? It's not like the man has options."

"I thought he was such a great package?"

"On the *outside,* Allison. No woman in her right mind would date him seriously. Grady's got issues. God knows what they are, but he's got them."

Allison's blood started to boil. Okay, so Grady might be sneaky in business, but he was a person after all. A genuine flesh-and-blood person, with a heart and real feelings. While he'd explained the nature of his relationship with Kate, he'd never said an unkind word about her. "Maybe you don't know Grady as well as you think you do."

"My, my. Defending him. That's a new twist."

Just then, the doorbell rang and Allison answered it. A flower delivery man held the most stunning bouquet of a dozen long-stemmed roses arranged with sprigs of baby's breath. They stood elegantly in a tall glass vase tied with a pretty red ribbon. Allison thanked the man and accepted the flowers, but as soon as he'd gone, Kate stepped forward and snatched away the card wedged in its slim card holder. "Obviously for me."

She pulled it from its envelope and rolled her eyes. "Poor Grady. How pathetic. Who knew he was the begging type?"

She shot Allison a superior look, then scanned the card, her face scrunching up. "*One cup of coffee? Cream, no sugar. My treat*? What's this supposed to be? Written in code? And why did Grady leave his cell number at the bottom. I *know* it, for crying out loud. I've got it on speed dial."

In spite of herself, Allison's spirits soared. She'd tried to forget him, push him out of her mind. But she hadn't been able to do it completely. It wasn't like she wanted to see him, or even talk to him in person, but the fact that he'd made this gesture touched her heart. Unless he was merely trying to get her to sign a contract again. Allison heaved a heavy sigh. "Sorry, Kate!" she said, plucking the note card and its envelope out of Kate's hand. "But I think these are for me."

"You?" Kate asked mockingly. "You must be joking."

Allison flipped over the envelope and held the front of the card toward her. *Allison Murphy* was typed in big, block letters above their apartment's address.

Kate gasped in understanding. "Something happened at the beach, didn't it?" she asked, her eyes flashing. "You didn't actually…? You promised me, Allison! Not in the same bed!"

If anyone was guilty of two-timing, it was Kate. Grady might have his faults, but he definitely wasn't a cheat. Given her behavior, did Kate really deserve to know that? Allison approached her and saucily raised an eyebrow. "Who said anything about a bed?" she asked lightly. "Maybe we did it on the floor." Then she carried her bouquet to her bedroom, leaving Kate standing there with her mouth agape.

Chapter Thirty-Seven

Allison walked out of her regular Monday morning meeting with her design team more determined than ever to save her company. She didn't have the heart to fire either of them, but if something didn't change soon, she'd have to cut back their hours. She'd come into the office on Sunday and had spent all day poring over her books. In the past six months, things had gone from bad to worse. Allison needed to face facts. Her business was failing. The clients that had been her bread and butter were turning away in favor of cheaper alternatives.

While Allison's labels weren't extremely expensive, they were more costly than those offered by the majority of her competitors. That's because they were better. Each of her personalized designs was handcrafted with the particular client's needs in mind. Allison was also committed to using only natural or recycled materials and that commitment had cost her. She'd lost a handful of clients this year, and her in-box revealed that a few more were considering bailing if Bella Fortuna Wine Designs couldn't offer more competitive terms.

Allison had already trimmed expenses everywhere she could and had even taken a cut in her own salary. There was nowhere else to go. You couldn't squeeze blood from a stone. She'd spent all last night thinking about it and had barely slept a wink. The knocking noises coming from Kate's room hadn't helped a lot either. Beau was still there and wasn't leaving until Wednesday. She was definitely getting a new roommate soon, or maybe she'd go live on her own. Yeah, right. Like she could afford that, when she couldn't even properly compensate her employees.

By the time the sun rose, Allison had decided on a plan. While she was proud, she certainly wasn't stupid. She'd never let pride stand in the way of protecting the staff that had been so loyal to her. Allison had hired them at the outset, and they'd stuck with her through lean times. All of them were great people who shared her artistic vision. Plus, they were individuals with their own financial demands and families. She couldn't let them down.

The sweet aroma of Grady's roses had filled the room throughout the wee hours of the morning, reminding her of his proposition. He'd said that Total Wines helped the companies it took over by offering greater security and benefits. Could Allison really believe him? It was difficult to know without thoroughly examining his offer. Yet, rather than consider it, she'd rejected it out of hand. Perhaps that's because his approach had left something to be desired.

If Grady had asked her about a deal straight out, rather than undertaking such convoluted shenanigans, she might have been more inclined to trust him. Instead, he'd jumped on the pretend-boyfriend-for-the-week bandwagon, which had muddied the lines between them. Allison frowned to herself, realizing it took two to tango. She couldn't lay the blame for what happened in Maine on Grady. She'd played an equal part in their deception.

The saddest thing about their time together was the dismal way it ended. Grady's flowers had been a form of apology. Maybe she needed to say she was sorry too. And not just because she was hoping to save her company. Because her heart broke a little more each time she recalled the devastation in Grady's eyes. He'd been shocked beyond words when she'd told him to leave, then he'd launched his parting missive about Allison staying away from cliffs. She'd said she didn't need him to rescue her, but it hadn't felt that way when Grady had nearly taken her in his arms. In that pulse-pounding moment, her heart had surrendered to his.

As much as she'd tried to deny it, Allison had fallen for Grady while they were together at the beach. He'd won over her friends and charmed her heart in a way she didn't think possible. Grady was smart, gregarious and fun, and honorable in his personal life, even though Allison had questioned his integrity on the job. Now she wished she hadn't done that. She wouldn't have been drawn to him if he was anything but a good man. A good, brave man, who had literally risked his life for her. And when his blue-gray gaze washed over her and that dimple settled in his cheek, Allison felt like she'd been struck by lightning. Or, more accurately, hit by a Mack truck. And Mack trucks like Grady O'Brien didn't rumble through Marydale every day.

Grady didn't expect to hear from Allison right away. He reasoned that she needed time to think about it. She'd been so livid with him at the beach, he'd been convinced she never wanted to see him again. Perhaps she still didn't, but it was worth a try. Man, this simmering was hard business. When she didn't call on Saturday, he'd thought, okay, so she'd just returned from her trip and was unpacking. On Sunday, he'd stayed busy sanding the hardwood floors he was refinishing, but he'd kept his cell nearby and had periodically checked it. Now, it was Monday and he was back at his desk, sorting through the messages that had come in while he was away. His e-mail in-box was flooded, and his stack of phone messages towered high. Yet the one text or call he'd hoped might come in on his phone eluded him.

Diane's paperwork was in order, and the agreements were ready to sign. It would be a simple matter of overnighting the bulk of them to the businesses he'd negotiated with, then the acquisitions team he'd put in place would get rolling to ensure smooth transitions. He flipped through the stack, extracting the contract with Bella Fortuna Wine Designs, and began to stuff it in his shredder. But something stopped him at the last minute. The terms were incredibly generous, and really beneficial to Bella Fortuna. What if Allison changed her mind?

Yeah, right. That would be precisely after she accepted his offer of coffee, which was looking like never. Grady switched on the shredder beside his desk and fed the document into it, thinking he could always print out another contract copy, should the need arise. Though he'd forgo that deal in a heartbeat if it meant Allison would give him another chance.

The shredder was humming so loudly, he almost didn't hear Diane rap at his door. He always left it ajar, so she stood on the threshold, gripping a white cardboard box with an ornate gold seal. "Sorry to disturb you," she said, "but this just came in from the bakery."

Diane was fresh out of college with a bachelor's degree in business administration. She always dressed in a suit and kept her jet-black hair back in a bun. She never wore makeup as far as Grady could tell, her sole fashion accessory being a really cool pair of bright red cat-eye glasses that sat against her alabaster skin. She was the epitome of the polished professional, and Grady had no doubt she'd go far. In fact, he planned to promote her at the end of the year.

"The bakery?" Grady switched off the shredder to make sure he'd heard her correctly. Oh, no. He hoped it hadn't begun already. Women bombarding him with cookies at work. Could the word that he was newly "single" really have gotten out so quickly? He supposed it was possible Kate had changed her Facebook status. Heck, she'd probably even done it while he was in Maine.

"Yes," she said promptly. "Marydale Confections, the bakery on the corner."

He'd walked by the window several times, but had never been inside. "Was there a note?"

"Just this yellow sticky one." She held it up with her right hand. "It came attached to the box."

"Don't keep me in suspense."

She steadied her glasses and read, "*I thought these might go with our coffee.* Kind of odd." Diane looked up. "There's no signature or anything. Just a phone number."

A grin tugged at the corners of Grady's mouth. "What kind of cookies are they?" he asked, as if he didn't know.

Diane shrugged and popped the box open with her fingernail. She peered down inside and lifted a business card from some crinkly tissue resting on top. "The card says Irish Soda Bread Cookies." She flipped it over. "The bakery's contact information is on the back. Do you want me to call and see who sent—?"

Grady grinned so broadly his cheeks ached. "No thanks, Diane. I think I've got it."

She set the box on his desk and when her back was turned, Grady silently pumped the air with his fist. But on the inside he was shouting, *Ye-es!*

Chapter Thirty-Eight

Grady arrived at the appointed place holding the box of Allison's cookies. She was already seated on a bench by the park's central fountain. Kids played on the big grassy slope beyond it, some of them flying colorful kites while parents hovered and instructed from nearby. It was a beautiful springtime day, but the sun paled in comparison to Allison's brilliant smile. She wore her ski vest over a sweater and a pretty white scarf, and held two carry-out cups of coffee.

"I was supposed to get the coffee, you know," Grady said, settling in beside her. Her light perfume wafted toward him and he resisted the urge to move closer. Grady would need to play it cool if things were to go off right.

"Yeah, but I figured I owed you one." She handed him a cup. "For doing me a favor in Maine. Two favors actually." She thoughtfully set her chin against her cup lid. "Hmm. Maybe there were more than two. I'll need to think on that."

"I took the floor," Grady offered helpfully.

"That's three."

"What were one and two?"

"Going to Maine to begin with, and saving my life."

"Those were good ones," he agreed.

"I just thought of a four! My Montepulciano!"

"Yes, there was that." Grady repressed a grin. "You know, not so long ago, you were enumerating the ways you despised me."

"I'm sorry, Grady." She appeared sincere. "I was upset, and speaking in anger."

A lump formed in his throat. "I never meant to hurt you. It kills me that you believe I'm—"

She lightly touched his arm. "I don't believe that anymore. I've had time to think about it, and I was wrong." Sunlight glimmered in her hair and she looked like an angel straight out of heaven.

"I was wrong too. I was hurt when you pushed me away. Angry. More angry than I should have been. It took me a while to figure out why." Grady gathered his nerve. "You may have thought it was all pretend. But it wasn't, really. Not on my end anyway. I was honestly starting to care." He stopped himself. "I mean, I do care. Still."

He gazed into her eyes and his heart pounded.

Allison shyly ducked her head. "The roses were lovely."

"I'm glad that you liked them," he said, swallowing hard.

She peered up at him through long, dark lashes. "You want to know something funny?"

Grady waited.

"Kate thought they were for her."

"Nooo…"

"It's true! I practically had to wrestle them away from her."

Grady chuckled. "I'll bet that was a sight to see."

"Believe me, Beau would have watched if he could..." She quit talking, turning crimson. "I'm sorry. I didn't mean to mention—"

"It's all right," he told her calmly. "I know all about the ex-boyfriend popping back into the picture— during the precise week I happened to be away."

"What a coincidence," she said wryly.

"My thoughts exactly."

"It's a shame to learn we were right about Kate."

"Doesn't bother me," Grady said honestly. "I just hope Beau knows what he's getting into."

Allison laughed. "Well, presumably...since he's dated her before."

"Burn me once..." Grady said.

"Yeah, but he's a grown man."

"Too true. You never know. It could work out between the two of them."

They sat a moment in silence, enjoying their coffees and the light breeze. At length, Allison said, "This may come as a bit of surprise, but I wanted to ask you about Total Wines' proposal for Bella Fortuna."

Grady choked on his coffee. "Excuse me?" he said after catching his breath.

"I'm serious, and I'm not asking in a bad way. This isn't a trick or anything, if that's what you're thinking."

All at once, he understood. Of course it was about the proposal. Here he'd been hoping Allison wanted to see him for personal reasons. Boy, what an idiot Grady was. He tried to remain professional, fighting the burn in his chest. "What do you want to know?"

"Well, for one thing, I'd like to read your offer."

"After everything you said—and think—about *big business*? Why?"

"Maybe I've reconsidered."

"I see." He briefly turned away, watching the gurgling waters of the fountain.

"I'll shoot straight with you," she said, recapturing his attention. "Bella Fortuna is in trouble."

His brow creased with worry. "How deep?"

"You might be surprised when you see the numbers."

"Will you show them to me?"

"Yes. That's what I've been trying to tell you; I'm willing to consider your deal. I mean, if it can really help the way…" Her lips trembled and she seemed on the verge of tears.

Grady steadied her chin in his hand. "Allison, I'm very good at making magic happen. Pulling proverbial rabbits out of hats. I've saved more than one firm that was going under. I may be a mess when it comes to being a boyfriend, but in business I know what I'm doing."

"This is my company, my baby. And my people—"

"I'll fix it for you, I promise. If you don't like Total Wines' terms, you can walk away."

She nodded and he slowly released her.

"It must have taken a lot of courage for you to tell me that. To ask me to help Bella Fortuna. I'll do everything in my power to make it work for everyone concerned. Don't worry, I'll look out for your employees."

"Thank you, Grady. I really appreciate that." Her eyes were teary, but beautiful just the same. "And you're not, you know."

"Not what?"

Her voice quaked, but she smiled as she wept. "A mess when it comes to being a boyfriend. Actually, you were a pretty great one."

He reached up and gently stroked back her tears. "Why don't we see if we can try that for real?"

She looked lovingly into his eyes. "One step at a time?"

"I was thinking the first step should be a date."

"What do you call this?"

He considered it a moment, then said, "A pre-date."

Allison giggled and dabbed her cheeks with a napkin. "Fine, then for our *first date,* do you mind if I make a suggestion?"

He viewed her happily. "No, not at all."

"I was thinking of the opera."

"The opera?" Grady laughed so hard, he nearly lost his grip on his coffee.

"Puccini, specifically."

"But why?"

"Because I've never been to one." She grinned sweetly. "Who better to take me?"

"Who better, indeed?" He took their coffees and set them aside. "I've got to warn you though, it's an *opera.*"

"What does that mean?"

"There will likely be hand-holding, and physical displays of affection..." he said, pulling her close. Color rose in her cheeks.

"Grady..."

"Maybe even kissing, and a hint at *amore...*"

Allison's eyes sparkled when she asked, "Are we talking about what happens during the show or afterward?"

Her mouth tilted up toward his and something ignited inside him: a deep, powerful yearning. No woman had ever moved him the way that Allison did, and he wanted her in his life now more than ever. "Oh, darling," he said, brushing his lips over hers, "I hope both."

Allison whimpered into his kiss and tugged him up against her, clearly desiring him just as much as he needed her. He kissed her softly at first, then intensified his ardor, following her cues. When she lightly nipped his bottom lip, Grady groaned, feeling pure pleasure pulse through him. *One step at a time* wasn't going to be easy with Allison, when everything in his soul wanted to race straight ahead. Yet, he was determined to do right by her and be the kind of boyfriend she deserved.

Grady cradled her in his arms and they were lost to each other for a long, luxurious time. Then, after an extended bout of PDA on the park bench, they both admitted they'd worked up an appetite—and decided to open the cookies.

Chapter Thirty-Nine

Six weeks later, Grady took Allison to meet his grandmother in Boston. His parents lived in Seattle and they were planning to see them at Christmas, after Grady met Allison's family in Charleston over Thanksgiving. Grady wanted Allison to meet Grandma O'Brien first, as he'd explained the special bond they shared.

The minute the kindly older lady opened the door, her face brightened. "Why, Grady and Allison! Aren't you two a pair?" She wrapped them both in a warm hug, saying how happy she was to see them, and invited them inside. The house smelled of fresh-baked cookies and a pretty tea service sat on the coffee table by the couch in the living room.

"It's such an honor to meet you, Mrs. O'Brien."

"Please, call me Abigail." She smiled sweetly. "All my friends do."

Grady handed her a wine bottle. "Meet our first creation in the Bella Fortuna line. It's a prototype. We roll out the full venture next spring."

Abigail slowly turned the bottle over in her hands, carefully studying its label. "Lovely, isn't it?" Her chest puffed out with pride. "Imagine what you two can do when you make babies!"

"Grandma!"

"Well, don't be wasting any time in getting to it. I won't be here forever, ya know."

Allison glanced at Grady and his color deepened. "She gets a little overzealous at times," he whispered as Abigail scuttled toward the kitchen.

"Make yourselves at home! Just going to put the kettle on."

One step at a time, Allison thought to herself. Not that the idea of making babies with Grady didn't sound terrific. Only, given the fact that they weren't even engaged, it would likely be a while. That was okay with Allison. She'd learned to savor every moment as it came.

This past month and a half had been a whirlwind, starting with a fantastic night at the opera and ending with Total Wines' smooth acquisition of her company. Bella Fortuna Wine Designs had become a Total Wines subsidiary, remaining wholly intact. Better than that, Allison had been able to hire more staff and provide better perks for her existing employees. She didn't know how he'd done it, but Grady had pulled more than a few rabbits out of several hats, and her once-faltering operation had become the poster child for Total Wines' expansion success.

If she had ever questioned his motivations in business, she had no qualms about his moral integrity now. Grady was every bit as honorable in his professional realm as he was in his personal life with her. And oh, how he'd swept her away. He'd taken her to dinner, the movies, museums…even canoeing, hiking and camping! A little to Allison's dismay, Grady had brought her a separate sleeping bag, rather than the double one. But she understood he was being cautious.

It wasn't like Grady didn't want her. She could feel it in every ounce of her being. It was more like he was waiting for something.

"Any minute now!" Grandma O'Brien called cheerfully. While Allison and Grady had gotten settled on the sofa, she'd carried the tea service to the kitchen, refusing their offers of help as she did. "Oh, Grady!" she hollered a few seconds later. "Come here, lad. I do believe I'll need a hand with this after all!" After saying that, for some reason, she chuckled.

"Do you need my help?" Allison queried.

"No, lass! You just stay put!"

What seemed an eternity later, the two of them returned from the kitchen. Grady balanced a tray holding the teapot, three cups, milk, sugar and a plate of cookies as his grandma paraded beside him, a pleased look on her face.

"Well!" Allison said. "This looks delicious."

Grady sat next to Allison on the sofa and Abigail took the Queen Anne chair catty-corner from her. "Would you like to pour, dear?"

"Pour? Oh, ah…" Allison was frightfully embarrassed. She'd never actually served tea before, and wasn't clear on the protocol. "I'm not sure I know how to do it."

"Go on now, pick up the pot. It's not that hard. I'll help you."

She instructed Allison on how full to fill each cup and waited until Allison put the pot down. "Good," she said encouragingly. "Now you ask us if we want cream or sugar."

Allison had a hunch Grady took his tea the same way he took his coffee. "I've got this," she said confidently, recalling every episode of BBC television she'd ever seen. She turned to Abigail first. "One lump or two?"

"No sugar for me, dear. I take mine black."

Allison guessed how Grady wanted his, but why was his mouth twitching? "Grady?" she asked him. "Is something wrong?"

"No, darling." He smiled pleasantly. "All's right in my world. How about you?"

Allison studied him quizzically, thinking he was acting awfully weird. "Good, great. I'm fine."

Grady nodded and extended his cup, apparently waiting for his sugar. Allison straightened her spine and leaned forward, lifting the sugar bowl lid. She could do this, of course she could.

"You're doing fine, dear," Abigail said warmly.

Then something glinted in the light. No way! But it was! A gorgeous solitaire offset by rubies sat in the empty sugar bowl. Allison's heart raced, and her cheeks flushed hot. What on earth did this mean?

"Heavens!" Abigail said, peeking over her shoulder. "Will you look at that! It's my old engagement ring."

"Imagine that," Grady said, without a hint of surprise.

Allison stared at them both, unable to believe…unwilling to hope…

"Funny thing about that ring," Abigail said to Allison. "It brings very good luck. The luck of the Irish, we like to call it. Grady's grandfather had it made for me many years ago. I never believed I could part with it until now."

Allison's eyes felt warm because she thought she knew where this was going.

"I'm very particular," Abigail said with a wink. "Only the best for my Grady."

Next, Grady stunned her by sliding off the sofa and dropping down on one knee. He pried the ring from the sugar bowl, then took Allison's hand. "My sweet," he said, and she laughed through her tears. "Grandma O'Brien has never offered her ring to anyone, but she did to you—sight unseen—and you want to know why?"

"I saw it in his eyes," Abigail cut in.

Grady sent her a petitioning look, but it was lined with kindness.

"Well, what do ya know?" his grandma said suddenly. "Seems I forgot to turn the kettle off." Then she disappeared from the room as Allison's world went fuzzy. Could this really be happening? Could Grady actually be…?

"Allison," he said, taking her hand. "I know things began in the wrong way, but I want to spend the rest of my life making them right." He shot her a grin and his dimple deepened. "I mean, if you'll let me."

He kissed the back of her hand and her heart fluttered.

"You make me the happiest man on earth, happier than I ever thought I'd be. It seems a lifetime ago now, but I meant what I said on that cliff. I never want to let you go." He slid the gorgeous two-carat ring on her finger, positioning it just above her top knuckle. "You think I rescued you that day? No way. You're the one who saved me. Who made me able to feel again and love deeply. And I promise you this." He gazed at her earnestly. "I've never loved anyone more deeply than you. You're my moon and my stars and my sun, and I never want to watch another sunset without you. Say you'll be with me for the rest of my life." His Adam's apple rose and fell. "Say that you'll marry me, Allison Murphy."

Tears blistered down her cheeks and her hand trembled. "Oh, Grady. I will."

Allison couldn't have imagined feeling this happy, but things were about to get even better. He slid the ring fully on her finger and took her in his arms. Her heart beat double-time when he gave a husky growl and whispered, "I've been saving it up for you, darling... Get ready." Then he kissed her so passionately she heard wedding bells ring.

Epilogue

Queenie strode onto the patio and swept her arms across the broad landscape. Purple hills rolled in the distance, where cypress trees towered high. Wild sunflowers in the foreground turned their faces to the sun as a herd of sheep ambled by. The sky was bright blue and brisk winds riffled her colorful kaftan. "I'll never get used to this view. It's gorgeous!"

Brevard wrapped an arm around her waist. "Maybe we should come here on our honeymoon."

"Honeymoon? What honeymoon?" Her eyebrows arched. "Please, Brevard. One honeymoon at a time."

They all sipped their bubbly and everyone, including Brevard, laughed. They'd done it! They'd made it to Tuscany in March. Allison never could have imagined a year ago that she'd be coming here married. Shortly after Kate learned about Allison's budding relationship with Grady, she'd moved out of their apartment to move in with Beau, who was relocating to Marydale. With her company more secure and profitable, Allison was able to handle the apartment rent by herself for the remainder of the lease, and now she'd be moving in with Grady. They occasionally saw Kate and Beau around town, and both couples were cordial to each other. Though Allison could never imagine the four of them becoming good friends. Allison's lifelong best buddies were right here.

Grady pulled her into a hug and whispered, "Having a good time?" She was having the time of her life, thanks to him, and she said so. After their early March wedding, they'd vacationed in Maine at the very same beach house the group had rented the year before. Only, Allison and Grady had gone there alone. They'd safely made it to the lighthouse more than once, and had fun "breaking in" every room in the place, as Grady called it.

Allison flushed, recalling Grady's vigor. He was still showing evidence of it in Italy, which was why Carla had pulled her aside and asked with a knowing smile why Allison was walking like a cowgirl. Allison didn't mind the good-natured teasing from her friends. She could see how happy they were for her. Allison was happy for them too.

Brevard had finally finished his book, and to his— and Queenie's—delight it had become a *New York Times* best seller. Brevard kept hinting at marriage, and, though Queenie had not yet said yes, she seemed to be growing less resistant to the idea.

Bruce had completed his residency and opened a practice with a small group of doctors he'd met in medical school. He and Carla were expecting their first baby, so she was the only one not drinking real champagne. From the glow on her cheeks, it hardly seemed to matter. She was a brunette this year, and Allison thought it suited her. It might even have been her natural color, but Allison wasn't sure.

Patrick and Deb were as companionable as ever. No one could guess if they'd eventually tie the knot, and not a one among them would dare to ask the question. They seemed happy the way they were. Allison knew that *she* was happy. She couldn't imagine a more perfect life than the one she had. She stretched out her hand and examined her diamond as it glittered in the natural light, perfectly complementing the gold wedding band beside it. "You like it a lot, don't you?" Grady asked, nuzzling the side of her neck.

Allison sighed, thinking if he didn't stop, he'd have to carry her back to the bedroom, and she was having enough trouble walking as it was. "I love it," she said. "I really do. But not nearly as much as I love you."

He pulled her up against him and shared a sexy grin. "Luck of the Irish to ya."

She breathed against his lips. "Luck of the Irish, Grady."

His mouth moved in for a kiss.

"Hey!" Queenie shouted. "Get a room!"

Grady laughed heartily and scooped Allison up in his arms. "We might just do that."

Then he carried her into the villa and took her breath away.

The End

A Note from the Author

Thanks for reading *The Borrowed Boyfriend*. I hope you enjoyed it. If you did, please help other people find this book.

1. This book is lendable, so send it to a friend you think might like it so that she (or he) can discover my work too.

2. Help other people find this book: Write a review.

3. Sign up for my newsletter so you can learn about the next book as soon as it's available. Write to GinnyBairdRomance@gmail.com with "newsletter" in the subject heading.

4. Come like my Facebook page: https://www.facebook.com/GinnyBairdRomance.

5. Connect with me on Twitter: https://twitter.com/GinnyBaird.

6. Visit my website at http://www.ginnybairdromance.com for details on other books now available at multiple outlets.

If you enjoy sweet romantic comedies, you might like my novel *My Best Friend's Bride*. Keep reading for an excerpt here.

MY BEST FRIEND'S BRIDE
A confirmed bachelor gets asked to marry his best friend's girl.

From *New York Times* Bestselling Author GINNY BAIRD, a new laugh-out-loud romantic comedy...

My Best Friend's Bride
Relationship expert Jillian Jamison is in a bind. While her first book was a successful bestseller, her second tome tanked. Now, her publisher wants a spin on the third book, Married Love: Keeping Those Home Fires Burning, that's up close and personal. With financial pressures mounting and sole responsibility for her aging grandfather, Jill feels forced into wedlock in order to appease her publisher and keep her job. But it's only for a year, and she's devised a plan with her long-term friend. When Brad backs out due to problems with his real girlfriend Susan, Jill fears she'll be left standing alone at the altar. Then Brad offers a solution: Jill can marry the one man on earth she despises...his handsome best friend.

Hunter Delaney is a confirmed bachelor and that's how he likes it. When his best friend, Brad, approaches him with an unusual contract, he's determined to run for the hills, especially since the name on the paperwork is international celebrity Jillian Jamison, the woman who spurned him in high school. Hunter would rather do anything than spend twelve months of his life saddled with her. But he has a soft spot for Brad, who's in a predicament, so Hunter agrees to consider Brad's proposal. When Hunter learns he's getting passed over for a promotion because the family-oriented client only wants to work with someone who's married, this clinches the deal.

Hunter is "in" for as long as he can stand it. Jill is not thrilled with the arrangement either. But really, what choice does she have? Even if it has to look authentic on the outside, between her and Hunter it's just pretend. Besides, she reasons rationally, she's already got the dress...

Chapter One

Jillian Jamison strode off the tennis court feeling disconcerted. She'd bested Brad at singles, and normally would have relished her victory. The trouble was that Brad hadn't made it much of a match. Generally, his returns were hard and his serves were fierce. Today, he'd scarcely made an effort. Jill eyed him sideways, wondering what was up.

Brad dabbed his brow with the towel draped around his neck. "Nice job!"

"Hmm, yes." She bent to tuck her racket into its bag. "Almost amazing."

Brad shrugged, sweat glistening inside his open collar. He had a nice physique and a muscled chest. Too bad Jill wasn't drawn to it. That would make things *so much easier.* He grinned and dimples settled on either side of his mouth beneath a mop of sandy-colored hair. "What can I say? You're a natural."

Jill smirked. "And you're a natural-born liar. Okay, Brad. I'll bite. What are you hiding?"

His face fell in a wounded fashion, but Jill silently called his bluff. She'd known Brad Tate since the second grade, when his family had moved in across the street from hers. They'd gone to grade school together, and had taken swimming and tennis lessons together—right here at this very club. Later, he'd been shipped off to prep school but they'd kept in touch. And now, as fate would have it, they were getting married. *Well, no, not really. Fate's got nothing to do with it.*

"You're always so suspicious," he said. "You know I enjoy winning just as much as you do."

"Uh-huh."

"You've just really got your game on today."

"Right."

"I've never seen you in finer form."

Jill adjusted the headband that swept back her dark bangs and narrowed her eyes.

A grin tickled the edges of his mouth. "Come on, Jilly. Take a compliment."

"All right. If that's how you want to play it."

She was irritated with Brad for about a billion reasons, not the least of which was his throwing this game. Lately, he'd been acting funny. Reticent, almost. Like he was having doubts about going through with it. She started to walk away from him, but he stopped her, laying a hand on her arm. "Okay, all right. You've got me," he admitted. "You and I do need to talk, but not here."

She studied his eyes, questioning. They stared back at her with compassion and concern. "Let me buy you a drink at the grill."

Jill checked her watch. "It's ten in the morning."

"Bloody Mary?" he said, knowing she'd be tempted.

Jill twisted her lips, thinking this must be bad. Worse than bad.

When she didn't answer, Brad pressed, "Champagne mimosa?"

Jill heaved a sigh, deciding she needed to keep her wits about her. "I'll take coffee. Sounds like I might need a double shot."

Jill set her cup down so fast it clattered against the saucer. "You want me to *what*?"

Brad leaned forward to hush her. "Jilly, folks are gawking."

She blinked, spying heads swiveled in her direction. Everyone was dressed in tennis or golf attire. Some *were* already drinking Bloody Marys and mimosas. Now she wished she'd ordered one as well. Maybe one of each!

"I didn't say that you had to," he went on. "I'm just asking you to think about it."

She was certain she'd misheard him. "About marrying your best friend?"

To her astonishment, Brad nodded.

"But I thought—" Her voice cracked, rising a decibel. She caught herself and continued in a whisper. "I was marrying *you.*"

"Of course, you're marrying me," he hissed back. "That's what we agreed."

Oh no, now she felt the *but* coming.

"But…"

Zing! There it was! Jill bit into her bottom lip.

"Yes, Brad?"

"Here's the thing." He grimaced, apology in his eyes. "It's Susan."

"What about her?"

"She's getting cold feet."

"She's not the one getting married."

"I guess that's kind of the point." He took her hand on the small tabletop. "Hey, you know that I love you."

Yeah, she loved him too. Just not *like that*. He knew it. She knew it, and both totally agreed. They were practically family, for goodness' sake. This was all about their deal. "Brad, what are you saying? That you're not going through with it?" She gasped, grasping the calamity of the situation. "The wedding's only six weeks away."

"That's the great part," he said. "The invitations haven't gone out yet."

"Deposits have been paid."

"For the caterer and reception, yes. But the date can be changed without losing that money."

Jill folded her face in her hands. They were in too deep to pull out now. She looked up, meeting Brad's eyes. "Did you explain it to her? About the circumstances, and how we'll have separate rooms?"

"Of course. But Jilly, it wasn't enough." He dropped his voice back into a whisper. "She freaked when she saw the dress."

"What dress?"

"*The* dress, and you in it. Made the society page of the paper."

Jill's mind flashed back over the arrangements they'd made with the wedding planner. She'd been so caught up with other preparations, she'd failed to check last Sunday's edition for the engagement announcement. As far as Jill knew, Brad had briefed his girlfriend, Susan, on their entire agreement. Up until now, she'd been fine with it. It was only for a year, after all, and there was so much at stake. Jill stared at Brad, agape.

"I can't believe you're backing out now, and letting me down this way."

"Don't you see? I'm trying to fix it!"

"By having me marry *Hunter Delaney*?" She said the name like it was some sort of disease.

"By offering a solution."

"The answer is a definite no."

"You haven't seen him in a long time."

"Thank goodness I haven't had to."

"Hunter's changed, Jilly."

"Sure he has. Next you'll be telling me leopards wear stripes."

"He's not the guy you remember."

"Mostly I recall he had a car. With a big backseat." She gritted her teeth, speaking through them. "He wanted me to get in it."

"We were seniors in high school!"

"Thanks a whole heck of a lot for the prom date."

"You were going to go solo."

"Maybe I should have."

"He never touched you, you said so."

She straightened and wrapped her fingers around her coffee cup. "Doesn't mean he didn't want to."

"Lots of boys wanted to," he told her honestly. "You were one of the hot girls, Jilly. The hot, brainy babes. No one could get next to you. You can't blame a teenage boy for trying."

She huffed. "And this is the man you think can live twelve months under the same roof with a formerly *hot and brainy babe*—in separate rooms?"

"I wouldn't say formerly."

"Flattery will get you nowhere. At this point, I'm ready to lift this tennis racket off the floor and clobber you." She grasped the neck of the bag with her right hand. "I trusted you, Brad!"

He flinched and sat back in his chair. "You know I'd do anything for you, Jilly." He lowered his voice.

"Anything but sacrifice my own happiness. When Susan was cool with everything, I thought, okay... But now?" he said, looking downcast. It was clear that Brad didn't want to disappoint her. Just as it was evident that he couldn't risk losing Susan. Brad was in a tough spot.

Jill suddenly felt like a heel. But this wasn't all about her. There was something in it for Brad too. "What about the money?" she asked him. "Your share?"

He slowly shook his head. "It's not going to mean anything to me without Susan. It was supposed to be for *us*—me and her. A way for us to get started on that dream we've always chased."

Jill sighed, then recited, "Starting a B and B in the San Juan Islands."

"Yeah, that. Only we can't on our teacher salaries, and it would take years to save up." Jill knew Brad came from money, but that he'd never ask his family for help. He still had access to this club only because it was one of his parents' membership perks. His parents had tried to discourage Brad from going into high-school teaching, hoping his expensive education would pay off in a more lucrative job. They'd never really approved of his decisions, including his romantic interest in Susan Miller, a fellow math teacher at Brad's school. The only time they'd gotten the tiniest bit excited about his choices was when he'd announced he was marrying bestselling writer and international personality Jillian Jamison. Their pride and admiration lasted as long as it took to explain the marriage was a sham. At that point they reverted to being *extremely disappointed in him.*

Maybe if she closed her eyes and counted to ten this would all go away. Just last week, things had been on track. "I don't get it," she said. "Susan no longer wants the money?"

"She says she no longer wants the *stupid San Juan Islands*—her words, not mine; between you and me, I still think they're great. It's just they're suddenly not so important anymore. Neither is that wad of cash, which Susan now calls tainted…foul. Ill-gotten gains. She's scared that if I go through with this, it will curse our relationship forever. No matter how far away we move, we'll never outrun its stench. Plus, she *was* visibly upset about seeing you in the dress. It made it all so real."

Ill-gotten gains? That sounded more like Susan's mother talking than Susan. Susan's mom was a retired English teacher. "Susan talked to her mom, didn't she?"

"Yeah, but that's the only person, I swear!"

This web of deceit was growing larger by the minute. Jill absolutely had to keep this under wraps or the whole thing would fall apart. Brad's parents knew the truth; so did Susan and her mom. Who would be next?

"Don't look now," Brad cautioned. "Here comes trouble."

Jill glanced at the door to see Cassandra Evans approaching, her short golf skirt swishing from side to side. "Well, well," she purred. "Look what the cat dragged in. Two little lovebirds."

Brad smiled tightly above the rim of his cup. "Morning, Cassandra."

She barely acknowledged him, turning her attention on Jill. "Saw the engagement announcement in the paper, so I guess it's official." She fanned manicured fingernails across the air in front of her with a dramatic sweep. "'The Lady Matchmaker Takes a

Groom.' *And,*" she added bitingly, "*for more than six weeks!*"

"It never said—" Brad started before Jill cut him off.

"I'm sorry that it pains you." Jill frowned sympathetically at Cassandra. "That I'm marrying first."

Cassandra straightened on long, tanned legs. "That part doesn't worry me in the least," she lied. She folded her arms in front of her and cocked her blond head, her bob bouncing. "I'm much more interested in your next book." She homed in on Jill's eyes. "What's it about?"

Jill's words were clipped. "Probably not you, Cassandra."

"Oooh, being evasive, are we?" She scrutinized Brad up and down, and he squirmed in his chair, uncomfortable with her perusal. Jill waited expectantly for her next barb, trying to think up something witty to say. Anything to drive this woman away. Cassandra Evans, her nemesis. The one who'd picked on her since the ninth grade. And who'd lost to Jill as senior class president. And who'd come in a close second to Jill's valedictorian. Cassandra, who'd aspired to write great literature but now worked for a gossip magazine, the sort that spied on celebrities with long-lens cameras.

"Don't you have someone to interview, Cassandra?" Brad to the rescue!

She narrowed her eyes at Jill. "I'm much more interested in the discussion right here, and this sudden cacophony of wedding bells. How *sweet* that you've known each other forever—
almost like a brother and sister—and now you're getting hitched. Have you carried a torch all that time?"

"Brad and I were just leaving." Jill pushed back her chair, but Cassandra reached out and grabbed it, settling her claws on its high back.

"Don't think I don't know something's up with this little wedding deal." She cut a glance at Brad. "And, I'm going to find out *what.*"

Jill watched Cassandra stride away, her heart pounding.

"Don't let her get to you," Brad said. "She doesn't know anything."

"Yeah? And what will she think if I switch grooms?"

"That you've done better? Traded up?"

"Brad, *puh-leeze*… Don't let me down." She reached out and gripped both his hands in hers. "Pretty please, with jalapeños on top!"

"Stop trying to play to my weakness."

Jill fought back the heat in her eyes, thinking of her grandfather. "What about mine?"

He squeezed her hands in his. "I'm suggesting a solution, Jill. One that can work for all of us."

"Oh, great. And your *solution* has me play-marrying a guy I can't stand?"

"Play is the operative word there, as in pretend. Besides, how do know you still won't like him? You haven't seen Hunter in nearly twelve years."

Jill felt trapped, as if Brad had painted her into a corner. There was no way out that wouldn't leave messy tracks everywhere. If she didn't marry soon, she'd lose her book advance money. Without that, she couldn't help her grandpa. But this wasn't just anybody they were talking about as a replacement for Brad! Famed womanizer Hunter Delaney had recently moved to neighboring Parkland. He'd graduated from prep school with Brad, then had gone to an Ivy League college prior to accepting a job on Wall Street. Now, he was in business marketing of some sort and had taken a position at a prestigious advertising firm in the city abutting Sugar Hollow. It didn't matter if he'd improved himself professionally. Personally, Hunter was still a lout. Word was, he'd left a trail of broken hearts from Boston to Brooklyn. Who knew how many other women he'd crushed on his way here? No way was Jill sidling up next to him at the altar. Pretend or not. Not for any amount of money.

"Absolutely not," she stated firmly. "No way, no how."

Brad released her hands, then dropped his bombshell. "That's too bad. Hunter will be bummed."

Jill's jaw dropped so fast it nearly smacked the table. "You mean you've talked to him?"

Brad reached into his gym bag on the floor and pulled something from it. He nodded and extended an envelope in her direction. "Signed, sealed, delivered... He's yours."

Chapter Two

One week earlier, Hunter Delaney had set down the paperwork and looked up at his best friend. "No way, no how, buddy. No can do."

"I've already explained, it's for a good cause."

Hunter shrugged his broad shoulders. "Not my fault the girl's got career problems."

"You do recall who we're talking about, right? Jill Jamison? *The* Jillian Jamison."

"Hard to miss. She's in the media all the time." Hunter absently stared at the door through which two attractive women had just entered. They were obviously alone, and definitely prowling. Their eyes panned the sports bar in a predatory fashion, until the redhead found Hunter. He gave her a slow, sexy smile, then quipped sotto voce, "I'll take the redhead, you can have Goldilocks."

"I'm taken."

"Yeah, twice." He turned back to Brad and lightly shoved his shoulder. "Maybe you should ease up on that. Having a fiancée and a mistress doesn't look good. Not when one of them's a…" He spoke in a conspiratorial whisper. "…*relationship expert.*"

"I'm sorry," a woman's voice said. "Do I know you?"

Hunter turned to see the gorgeous redhead standing by their table. "I couldn't help but notice you," she continued. Pretty dark eyes sparkled, indicating interest. "You look *so* familiar."

Brad abruptly scraped back his chair and stood.

"That's because he's about to become a family man."

"Huh?"

Brad tugged at Hunter's arm, but Hunter pulled back. "Hey!"

Brad leveled a look at the redhead and spoke with conviction. "You know how some guys are. Just can't get enough."

She went pale.

Brad tried again, locking his grip on Hunter's bicep. "Come on, lover boy. A wedding rehearsal awaits!"

"Wedding?" Her voice was shrill. "Well, I never meant to…" She took a few hurried steps backward. "What I mean is… Gosh! Engaged? Are you, really?"

Hunter stood and straightened his trousers. "I…? No!"

The blonde, who'd been watching from nearby, rushed to her friend's defense. "Come on, Glenda," she said, hooking her by the elbow. "He's one of *those*."

Hunter exhaled audibly as the women walked away, occasionally turning to shoot disgusted looks at him over their shoulders. "Thanks, Brad. Thanks a lot."

"You'll be thanking me a heck of a lot more, once all of this is over."

"Oh?" He was totally unconvinced.

Brad scooped the paperwork off the table and shoved it at his chest.

"Just read the fine print."

It was Sunday, one of the days Jill customarily paid a visit to her grandfather. She also came on Wednesdays for lunch. When he'd been feeling better, she'd taken him out on little getaways from the retirement home in her car. Sometimes they ate at restaurants. Frequently, they picked up carry-out and went to the park. Gordon Jamison loved being outdoors. Now that his health had declined even further, their excursions had been reduced to visiting the interior courtyard of his building. She parked his wheelchair beside the butterfly garden, where a half dozen monarchs fluttered. "Beautiful, aren't they?"

He took her hand between his wrinkled palms and patted it. "Just about as pretty as you are."

"Thanks, Grandpa." She smiled softly. "You always did have kind words for the ladies."

"Yes," he replied wistfully. "Especially your grandmother." He glanced around expectantly past the shrubs and budding azaleas. "Where is she? Coming soon?"

Jill's heart ached as she fibbed. "Any minute."

She sat on a cool stone bench to watch a cardinal couple taking turns at a birdfeeder. She couldn't imagine how tough getting by without his wife must be for her grandfather. The two had stayed committed to each other through a long, loving marriage, and the delivery of one precious child: Jill's late mom. She hung her head, grateful for her memories, even the ones that pained her. At the age of twenty-seven, she'd lost both her parents within a year, her dad from heart failure and her mom from an incurable infection following a routine surgery. Neither death was anticipated and both had hit her hard. She was alone in the world now, except for her grandfather. Perhaps it was a blessing that, in his mind, he still had all of them.

"How are your parents doing?" he asked her. "They never come to see me anymore."

"They want to, and they will," she lied sweetly. "Just as soon as they get back from their trip."

"That's right," he said, but his expression was muddied. "I remember now. Alaska, was it?"

"Nebraska," she answered, referring to the last couples trip her parents had taken together. They were always doing things like that. Setting off on unusual adventures.

"Forget Paris, France!" her mom had chirped. *"We're hitting Rhome, Texas!"*

Jill's dad had chuckled his reply. *"Yee-haw, cowgirl!"*

Her parents' unabashed affection for one another had embarrassed her then. In retrospect, Jill was glad she had that type of exchange to remember them by. Though the time they'd shared together was cut short, they'd made the most of what they'd had. Besides that, they'd been mighty good parents. The only thing they hadn't prepared for was dying early and leaving their finances in a wreck. Her dad had planned to work for several more years, and enjoyed a lifestyle he figured his future earnings would support. When Jill's parents had passed, they'd been in debt up to their eyeballs. It had taken settling their entire estate to pay off the creditors, and there wasn't enough left over to provide for her grandfather for more than a few years. Jill had taken that upon herself, but gladly and with a whole heart. She loved her grandpa dearly.

"You're looking a little down today," he said keenly. "Is something wrong?"

"Just work worries," Jill replied, lifting a shoulder. "Those come and go."

"Well, you best tell your agent to make them scat! Have her tell that cranky publisher of yours that you're a world-famous author, ya hear? I've seen you on the television. All of us have." He was referring to himself and his fellow residents at the home. They had a large common area where they watched the evening news and the contemporary entertainment shows that followed. Jill's expertise as a relationship guru had been touted numerous times, thanks to the success of her bestselling first book, *Love Like You Mean It.* Her second book hadn't done as well. Now, if she didn't score big with this third one, she'd be out of a contract, and out of money—with no way to help her grandfather.

If she went back to her former job as a couples counselor, she'd only earn a fraction of what she did now in royalties, advances, and speaking engagement fees. Not nearly enough to pay the bills for this place. She glanced around at the gurgling fountains and pretty palmettos hedging the walkways. It was lovely and serene. Most important, her grandfather was settled here and had come to think of it as his home. "Don't you worry about it, Grandpa," she told him kindly. "Everything will work out fine. It always does."

They talked awhile longer about the weather, other residents who were his friends, how the food here was improving thanks to the new chef, and Jill's most recent book tour. Soon, the afternoon sun began to fade and Jill realized she should be pushing on. Though he always enjoyed their visits, and looked forward to them, it was clear that even her company became taxing after a point. As if on cue, a nurse arrived to tend to his personal care and wheel him to supper. "Will you be joining us in the dining room?" she inquired of Jill.

Sometimes Jill stayed, but tonight she had too much on her mind. She declined politely, saying she'd love to next time.

Jill stood and hugged her grandpa's shoulders, planting a kiss on his head. "You're such a good girl. So sweet to visit." He lightly patted her back. "Who did you say you are again? Friend of the family?"

She kept her voice steady and forced a smile. "A very close friend."

"Will you come back, then?"

"I'll be here on Wednesday."

His whole face brightened. "That's terrific! I'll introduce you to Rose," he said, naming his late wife. "I know she'd love to meet you."

Jill pursed her lips and gave a slight nod. When she spoke, the words scraped from her throat. "I'd like that." After bidding him so long, she turned and headed for the exit. As she did, the fat tears she'd been holding in broke free. Jill didn't dare lift a hand to dry them. She could feel her grandpa's eyes on her…watching her walk away. Sometimes life was harsh. Or as Morgan was fond of saying, *brutal*, Jill thought, recalling her last conversation with her agent.

Morgan Swift leaned across the small café table and frowned. She had light brown hair with frosted tips, and highlighted her petite figure with a jacket and matching slacks. She was approaching forty but looked ten years younger, except for when those worry lines surrounding her eyes deepened. Like they were doing now. "You're not going to like this, Jill, but I'm going to be brutal."

Jill slowly lowered her glass of Chablis. When Morgan had asked her to lunch, she should have expected an ambush. Instead, she'd hoped they'd be celebrating Jill's third book deal getting finalized.

"I hate to break the news," Morgan continued, "but your numbers on *Long-Term Love: Making It Last* weren't...encouraging. In fact, they kind of stunk."

Jill knew it hadn't performed as well as the first book, because it hadn't hit any major lists. Still, she'd thought it had done reasonably well. She'd been on talk shows, done interviews... "But I thought the presales were—"

"Mediocre at best." Morgan dropped her voice an octave. "That write-up in *Tempo Beat* sure didn't help."

Jill let the word slip out on an exasperated breath. "Cassandra."

"You can't entirely shoot the messenger," Morgan said. "A 'relationship expert' who can't keep a boyfriend of her own for more than six weeks *is* kind of news."

"That's not news! It's gossip!"

"Is what the article alleges true? Do you really start analyzing them by week five?"

Jill set her wine on the table and clasped her hands together in her lap. George Wesley; of course it had to have been him. Maybe Paul Thurston too. Who knew how many of her traitorous exes had spilled to Cassandra on the condition of anonymity? Could have been dozens! She cocked her chin to the side and asked evenly, "Are you with me or against me, Morgan?"

Morgan flinched, apparently affronted. "With you! Of course! It's just that..." She took a hurried sip of wine, then dabbed her lips with a napkin. "I need to know what we're dealing with here."

"I don't get what you're saying."

"I'm asking you if you can do it, Jill. Tackle a relationship for the long haul."

"You're asking me?" Jill staged a laugh. "I wrote the book on relationships, if you'll recall. A number one bestseller!"

"Hmm, yes. One on getting them started."

"What's that supposed to mean?"

"It was the second step, the part about keeping them going, that fizzled out." She shook her head sadly. "I'm going to be honest about this even if it pains you. Because your pain is my pain. We own it together."

Jill understood this was true. As her book agent, Morgan got fifteen percent. But fifteen percent of nothing was zero. Jill's stomach clenched, anticipating the next sock in the gut.

Morgan exhaled sharply. "It wasn't easy to pull this off, because Browning's none too happy," she said referring to Jill's publisher. "In fact, they didn't even *want* a third book, but I insisted. After all, we had a three-book deal.

"The thing is," she continued, "without their full backing, book three doesn't stand a chance. We need marketing support, a dynamite cover, advanced advertising, book tours!" Morgan's eyes shone with passion, and Jill recalled why she'd hired her. Morgan was not only good, she was driven. She was also as smart as a whip.

"So…?" Jill pressed. Morgan had obviously hatched a plan to make this work.

"So..." Her enthusiasm was growing so fast it was almost contagious. "I proposed we take this to the next level. Go all out!"

"Great!" Jill replied, not fully understanding what that meant. "Then they accepted my proposal?"

"Ye-es..." She drew out the word. "But not exactly as it stands."

"What do you mean, not exactly as it stands?"

"There were a few modifications." Morgan stared at her salad plate and started slowly spinning her wineglass by its stem. The goblet completed two revolutions before Morgan raised her eyes and spoke with a pasted-on grin. "Jill!" she said brightly. "You're getting married!"

Jill, who'd begun to take a sip of water, choked. She quickly lowered her glass and covered her mouth with one hand. "What did you say?"

"Married," Morgan stated matter-of-factly. "You really can't get much more long-term than that!"

Jill blinked; her whole world had gone fuzzy. Maybe she was dreaming and none of it was real? She pinched her leg through her skirt just to be sure. *Ow! That smarted!*

"Well, don't just sit there," Morgan complained. "Say something."

Jill set both elbows on the table and stared in disbelief. "That's the most ridiculous thing I've ever heard."

"It's a strategy for saving your career. Don't think I haven't studied this. Considered it from every angle. Jill, this *is* the only way. You've got to rebuild your trust with the public. Book buyers must *believe* you know whereof you speak."

"Yes, but…married?" Jill was still trying to wrap her head around it. "To whom? Did the publisher pick the groom?"

"Of course not. That's your job."

"Awesome."

"The title's been all worked out," Morgan informed her. "*Married Love: Keeping Those Home Fires Burning.* We're betting it will sell like hotcakes." She polished off her wine. "Provided you're actually married, that is."

"But I don't have to be married to write that kind of book. I've had plenty of experience, my background in counseling…case studies."

"No dice. This has to be the real deal. You with a ring on your finger. You've already duped the public once with *Long-Term Love: Making It Last.* They want to hear from *you.* You've got to make this book less clinical, more personal. Jillian Jamison practicing what she preaches!"

Jill's head throbbed. She needed this third book, she really did. She desperately needed the money. That's when a solution hit her. Nobody said she had to stay married forever—just long enough to pull off this project. All she had to do was find a guy to go along with it. That might prove a little tricky, but it certainly wasn't impossible. She already had a candidate in mind.

"How long does it have to last?" she asked. "The marriage?"

Morgan shrugged. "How long do most marriages last these days?"

"Some less than a year."

"That may be pushing it."

Pushing it a little, maybe, but the idea was starting to grow on her. Especially if she could contain it, control it, and make it her own. Jill's mental wheels turned quickly as the strategizing began in her brain. "Think about it, Morgan. I do the wedding, the big buildup…all that. It's agreed. Who can blame me if things go sour some time after? It wouldn't be my fault, or his either, as long as we tried. Just one of those things. Think of the public sympathy we could build. It might even lead to a fourth book, *Love after Love: Amor from the Ashes.*"

"Ew! Are you planning on cremating someone, or getting divorced?"

"Okay, maybe the title needs work."

"I don't know, Jill. That sounds risky. What about book sales?"

"The big push will be prerelease and during release week. I'll do the talk shows, tours—whatever it takes— to build up big numbers by then. By the time my marriage…unfortunately tanks, my book sales will be rocketing! Straight up to the stars." She sure hoped so, anyway. The book would have to earn back the advance and then some for her to cover her own obligations, as well as offer a financial enticement to a fake fiancé.

"And then?"

"With two bestsellers under my belt, I'll be a hot property, won't I? If Browning no longer wants me, I'll go to another publisher. I've got lots of great ideas. The proceeds from this book could tide me over in the meantime, if I'm prepared to give it my all."

Morgan surveyed her cautiously. Why was she acting skeptical? She was the one who'd devised this whole sordid plan. Jill was merely taking the lemons Morgan had thrust at her and making lemonade, using psychology and working things to her advantage. Jill felt her confidence surge. She was fully game-on. She could commit to marriage for a year, of course she could. It was just like accepting any job. All she had to do was hire an assistant…um, partner…in name only! That was clearly better than the alternative, rejecting this arrangement and seeing her grandfather moved to a lesser facility. She knew how her publisher worked. Browning didn't keep deals on the table indefinitely. If she was going to accept, she'd have to move quickly before someone in editorial changed their mind.

"Look, Morgan, I know how to do this. I've learned from the first book—and the second—what does and doesn't work."

"Precisely what the publisher is counting on." Morgan withdrew a contract from her purse and handed it over. "The advance I negotiated is hefty," she said. "You can't mess this up."

"I don't intend to." She unfolded the pages and flipped through them. "Wow, very cool. A much higher percentage on residuals."

Morgan preened like a peacock. "*And* merchandising. We really believe this can go big, Jill. Viral, even. Forget interviews, this could spawn an entire reality TV series!"

"*I'm* not going on television. Not in that way."

"Nobody said you had to. If a series comes out based on your book, it will profile other couples. Maybe couples having relationship troubles. Your words of wisdom will help them bring it all back together. They'll put the advice in your book to use, and the audience can watch as they heal and move forward."

Jill felt as if she'd been steamrollered. Like this idea had taken on a life of its own. Each time she thought she was totally on top of things, Morgan flattened her with something else. "I see."

"You won't have to do a thing about it, other than collect your share of the profits. That's what I'm trying to tell you. This deal is huge. All kinds of potential."

This snowballing arrangement was sounding more doable by the minute. *Potential* was code for big money. And if the sum were large enough, it could easily be shared. Okay, not half-and-half, but she could offer the groom a percentage. Jill knew just the guy in need of cash. He got bonus points for being someone she trusted.

"All I have to do is get married?"

"Yes, and you'd better make it snappy. Browning wants an engagement on the table when you receive your advance money."

"But it's okay if it's"—she hesitated on the word— "fake?"

Morgan lunged forward to grab her wrists. "Shut your mouth and seal those lips! That's the last time I ever want to hear you say that." She spoke in an urgent whisper. "For the rest of the world, it has to look real, all right? For the publisher too. Publicly? In the papers and on camera, you're a pair, all lovey-dovey. Whatever you and your new hubby-to-be do—or don't do—in the privacy of your own home is totally up to you."

Chapter Three

Hunter folded the contract and stuffed it back in its envelope, handing it to Brad. "There's nothing you can say to convince me." Brad sat back in his bucket seat behind the steering wheel. They'd left the bar and were supposedly on their way home. The only thing was that Brad had failed to start his car. "So—what? You're going to hold me hostage until I agree?"

"No. I'm just asking you to think about it," Brad said. "Like a rational person."

Hunter sputtered a laugh. "Nothing about this is rational!"

"Consider it a lease, a living arrangement."

"You're forgetting two very important points: A, I already own my condo and B, I like where I live."

Brad jangled his keys and cranked the ignition. "You think you know a man," he said, shaking his head.

"This is ludicrous, Brad. I can't believe you agreed to it in the first place."

"I already told you, she was desperate."

"Um-hum." Hunter pulled out his shoulder harness and clicked the seatbelt in place.

Brad sprang at him and latched onto his lapels. "Now *I'm* desperate. Can't you see?"

Yep, he could pretty much read that in Brad's eyes. He looked like a cross between a frightened rabbit and a chicken about to get its head lopped off. "I'm sorry, man. I feel for you, I really do. And Susan, but—"

Brad tightened his death grip on Hunter's jacket. If he didn't let go soon, he'd crease it and Hunter would have to get it dry cleaned. "You don't know what it's like. Loving someone like I do her."

"Jill?" Hunter couldn't help but say. He pressed his lips together to keep from smirking.

"No, jerk! Susan!" He released Hunter's suit coat and pushed away.

It was almost scary seeing Brad this way. He appeared borderline crazed, like he might do something unpredictable. It occurred to Hunter that perhaps he should be the one driving.

"I apologize," he said in a placating tone. "I didn't mean to make light of it."

"Yeah. Well, fine! You shouldn't have!" Sweat beaded Brad's forehead and he lifted the oil-checking rag on the console between them to dab it, leaving a black smear on his face. Maybe if Brad didn't drive such an old clunker he wouldn't have to check the oil twice a week. The sad truth was that Brad could use Jill's money far more than Hunter needed it. Financially, Hunter was doing fine.

In a last-ditch effort, Brad shot him a pleading look. "I told you about her grandfather?"

"Heartbreaking," Hunter deadpanned. "Though not my problem either."

"She's really under pressure, Hunter." Brad paused and pursed his lips in thought. "But you can't let on that you know that."

"Why not?"

"It's personal, might embarrass her."

"More personal than getting married?"

"You're not seeing the bigger picture!"

"Yes, I am, and it's a nightmare."

"Yeah, well, I'm living it."

"Maybe you should have thought that out before."

Brad glared at him angrily. "Jeez, guy, do you even have a soul?"

Hunter was fairly tough. Practically made of steel. But ouch, yeah, that pinched a little. Hunter stared at his best friend since the eighth grade. The guy whose skin he'd saved by not ratting Brad out to the headmaster after the two of them had shaving-creamed the chemistry lab. Brad was always coming up with mischievous plans and getting them into trouble. Correct that: Only Hunter got into trouble, because the administration routinely suspected him, the boisterous athlete. Timid Brad, with his keen focus on academics, had been beyond reproach. Hunter had not once squealed on Brad, and had always taken the heat. Even though every single lamebrain scheme had originally been Brad's idea.

In return, Brad had stood by Hunter, year after year, through one woman-disaster after the next. While Brad still didn't believe it, none of those breakups had been Hunter's fault. He hadn't left any of those women; they'd left *him*. The fact of the matter was that he did have a soul, and way down deep it was probably unlovable. It sure didn't know how to love back. Not that his parents had set much of an example in that department. They'd shipped him off to boarding school at fourteen and had never come to visit. Not even on family day. While he was gregarious and confident on the outside, emotionally, Hunter had donned a suit of armor that was impossible for anyone to penetrate. How many upset females had accused him of that before slamming their way out the door? Far more than Hunter cared to count or remember. "I'm not marriage material," he replied dryly. So many women had told Hunter that, and after a while he'd begun to believe it.

"That's what makes this ideal," Brad said. "You and Jill go in with your eyes open. Zero expectations." He shook the envelope in the air between them. "Other than what's written in here."

Hunter gave a weighty sigh and snatched back the envelope. He hated Brad for putting him in this position nearly as much as he disliked seeing Brad on the verge of a breakdown. Brad was the closest thing he had to a brother. A baby brother. The sort who repeatedly got himself into trouble, then required Hunter's help getting out of it. Jill Jamison, of all people. Of course it had to be her. "Okay, I'll think about it," he finally said. "But only for you."

A few days later, Hunter adjusted his red-and-yellow-striped tie in the washroom mirror. It made him look authoritative, not stuffy. In any case, that's what he hoped. He angled his head from side to side and set his jaw in a confident manner. "You've got this," he told his rugged reflection. A flicker of doubt flashed in his dark brown eyes. He cleared his throat and tried again, speaking more surely. His voice resonated in a deep baritone as he gave himself a steady thumbs-up. "You've got this."

A commode flushed and his coworker Fred Forester popped out of the bathroom stall behind him. "Got what? Catch something touching the toilet?"

Hunter startled, leaning forward to grip the edges of the basin. "Fred! Didn't know anyone was in here."

"Obviously." Fred stood at the sink beside him, washing his hands. He addressed Hunter's reflection in his mirror. "You're up for the big promotion, I hear."

"Word gets around."

"Sure does," Fred said smugly. Did Hunter imagine it, or was Fred appearing full of himself, like he knew something Hunter didn't? Then again, that was just Fred. Always one-upping everyone in the office. He was a few years younger than Hunter, but others viewed him as twice as ambitious. That's because Fred was very *obvious* in his aspirations, whereas Hunter tended to purposely underplay his.

"I wouldn't worry about it too much," Hunter told him. "I'm sure your turn's coming soon."

Fred dried his hands with a paper towel, then tossed it into the wastebasket, straightening on his reed-thin frame. "No doubt," he said flippantly. Then he turned and walked away, leaving Hunter with a sinking feeling. If Hunter was about to get good news, why did he sense the other shoe was about to drop?

Hunter's boss, Maxwell Abrams, crossed his ankle over one knee and started making small circular motions in the air with his expensive Italian loafer. Rather than remaining behind his desk, he'd joined Hunter in his office's sitting area. They now sat catty-corner in sleek leather chairs facing a low Lucite table. It held sketches of all kinds and mock-ups for new campaigns. Old man Abrams never stopped working, which was why he was rumored to need help. Word was that he sought an entrepreneurial partner to take under his wing and groom for taking over the business one day. Hunter hoped that man would be him. He'd worked hard and had landed some major accounts for the firm. Dollar for dollar, his efforts had certainly generated more revenue than Fred had brought in.

"You know I respect you as a worker," Abrams said, his silvery hair catching glimmers of sunlight through the window.

"Yes, sir. I appreciate that."

"You've got a keen eye where marketing is concerned, and that financial background of yours has only been a boon to the company."

"Thank you. It's a pleasure working here."

Abrams met his eyes. "I believe you'll go far someday."

Hunter's stomach clenched. *Someday? What about now?*

"But I'm sure you're aware," Abrams went on, "that a very big deal is at stake."

"Kaleidoscope Kids, yes, sir. I'm aware of it. Actually, I've been studying their prospectus, devising a plan—"

Abrams held up his hands. "I've got to explain this is a major account. Huge, Hunter. Landing it could completely change the financial face of this company, give us a whole new direction."

Hunter angled toward him and set his elbows on his knees. "That's why I'm determined to do everything I can to land it, sir. Just give me the word, and I'll bring that puppy home."

Abrams smiled wryly and shook his head. "That *puppy,* as you call it, is only interested in working with one kind of master."

"I'm sorry, sir?"

Abrams pressed his broad palms together. "Kaleidoscope is about kids, Hunter. *Family.* They want someone who understands that, inside out, to design the campaign. Now, I know Fred Forester is a little younger than you…"

Fred Forester? No way! He didn't have half the experience Hunter did. Plus, he was more than a little bit of a jerk. "Fred, sir?" Hunter was embarrassed to hear his voice squeak.

Abrams looked him straight in the eye. "Fred's married, and they like that. They want someone on their team who understands commitment…someone with the right frame of mind.

"Fred and Penny have been married five years. And now…" The loafer bobbed up and down. Yeah, here came the other shoe. "They're expecting a baby."

Hunter drew a breath. He had no idea Fred was about to become a dad. Hunter couldn't help but feel sympathy for the child. More than that, he felt sorry for himself. Fred Forester being positioned as his boss? That wouldn't just be uncomfortable for Hunter, it could prove disastrous for the whole office. While pretty much everyone got along with Hunter, nobody could stand Fred. What kind of supervisor would he make? Hunter couldn't believe there wasn't a way to turn this thing around. "Mr. Abrams, if you'll just give me a chance. Maybe let me talk to the Kaleidoscope people myself—"

"I'm sorry, Hunter." His look was sincere. "It's already been decided. I talked to Fred this morning and he accepted."

Of course he did, the snake! Hunter spoke frankly, because he didn't see any reason not to. "I'm really sorry to hear that, sir, because I honestly feel I'm the best man for the job. The best ad man for Kaleidoscope and the best manager for this company. I've got great leadership skills. You've seen them in action."

"Yes, and I admire that about you. Which is why I'm bringing you on board as Fred's right-hand man. He'll need someone with your talents to assist him."

The situation was going from bad to unbearable. Work directly under Fred? Hunter would have to leave the company first. The thing was, Hunter *liked* Abrams Advertising, and he'd given it his all. In the past year, he'd built relationships here, with his clients and with the staff. He couldn't just throw all that away. Nor could he stand the thought of Fred being in charge. He made one last desperate plea. "Is there nothing I can say to change your mind?"

Abrams gave a noncommittal laugh. "Only that you're getting married." He uncrossed his legs and stood. "But with a lone wolf like you, we both know that's not going to happen any time soon."

Hunter leapt to his feet, unable to stop the words that flew from his mouth. "Mr. Abrams!"

Max slowly turned his way.

"It already is!"

Abrams stared at Hunter agape. "Excuse me?"

Perspiration built at Hunter's hairline and slicked the back of his neck.

"I'm getting married," he reported evenly.

Max's brow shot up. "That so? When?"

"Soon, sir. Very soon."

Abrams sat back in his chair, apparently stunned by this turn of events. "And…who's the lucky girl?"

Hunter sucked in a breath, then spilled it. "Jillian Jamison."

"The relationship expert?" For some reason Abrams appeared amused. "But I thought she was marrying someone else. My wife, Diane, was just saying last Sunday she'd seen it in the—"

"*Was*, sir. As in, past tense. Let's just say it didn't work out."

Abrams was unable to mask the skepticism in his voice. "And Ms. Jamison decided to pencil you in? As a…replacement?"

"It's a tad more involved than that. Jill and I have known each other since high school," Hunter said. "This, um…attraction has been brewing under the surface for years."

Abrams studied him curiously. "I see. And you love this girl?"

"Almost as much as I love myself." Hunter called himself up short, realizing how awful that had sounded. "What I mean is—"

"I must say this comes as a surprise." Abrams brought a hand to his chin and sat still for a moment. When he met Hunter's eyes, he asked, "So you and your long-lost flame, Jillian Jamison, are determined to make this work? A full-fledged marriage?"

Hunter nodded numbly, not admitting he intended to make it work for just a year. Hey, many marriages only lasted that long. Why should his and Jill's be any different? By the time their agreement concluded, Hunter would be well on his way to proving himself a valuable asset at Abrams, and Fred would be caught up with baby duty.

"Well, in that case... It appears there's only one thing left for me to say." Abrams shot to his feet and held out his hand. "Welcome to my personal team, Hunter. I can't wait to see your ideas for Kaleidoscope Kids. If they're half as good as I've got a hunch they'll be, we'll lock down that account in no time. By this time next year, I might even be calling you *partner.*"

Hunter pumped Max's hand with a firm handshake. "Thank you, sir. You won't regret giving me this opportunity."

"I'm happy for the company, I really am. But mostly..." Abrams released his hand and slapped him on the shoulder. "I'm happy for you. Such wonderful news! Congratulations to you and Jill!"

Five minutes later, Hunter was back in the washroom and on his cell, furiously typing a text. He had to meet with Brad and get this deal sealed before something went wrong. He hit *send* just as someone walked into the room.

"Writing to Mommy with the bad news?"

Hunter looked up from where he leaned against the wall to see Fred standing before him. "In here again, Fred? Got some kind of condition?"

"Beats what you've got." Fred smirked. "Sore loser syndrome."

"Oh, I wouldn't be so quick to call a victory yet."

Fred paused midway into a stall, holding the door slightly ajar between them. "What's that supposed to mean?"

Hunter shrugged and shoved his cell into his pocket without giving Fred the satisfaction of a reply. It was up to Abrams to break the news, after all. All Hunter had to do now was confirm that Jill Jamison was fully on board. Of course, Brad had already assured him she would be.

Chapter Four

"You have got to be kidding me," Jill exclaimed, meeting Brad's eyes. They were still at the grill in their tennis clothes and Brad had just finished telling her how he'd explained her situation to Hunter roughly a week ago. Hunter had been so taken with Brad's story—and concerned by Jill's predicament with her publisher—that he'd naturally agreed to step right in. Hunter really had changed a lot, Brad assured her. No matter what she believed of him in the past, he was a true gentleman now. Jill stared down at the contract on the table, noting that Hunter had made several corrections with a bright red pen. If she didn't know better, she'd swear she was looking at some hapless high-school English student's first-term paper. Some of these changes were untenable. Hunter wanted *how much bigger* of a cut? "What's Hunter thinking?"

"That everything in life is negotiable?"

Jill answered combatively. "The things in my life aren't."

"Hey, don't shoot the messenger."

"Why does everybody keep saying that?" she asked, reliving her earlier conversation with Morgan, the one that had landed her in this crazy position. *Am I actually perusing a contract between me and Hunter Delaney? A marriage contract?*

"Look, Jill. It's all going to work out. Hunter really wants it to. So he made a few minor tweaks to the—?"

Jill's brow rose with suspicion. "What do you mean, 'He really wants it to'? What's in it for him?" She didn't know why, but something in her gut said things weren't exactly adding up, including Brad's assertion that Hunter had suddenly morphed into a gentleman.

Brad fidgeted with his coffee cup.

"Brad…?" she pressed.

"You can see for yourself! You're the one who added the clauses! Ten percent of residuals, and…" Brad blinked twice, like he always did when he was lying. "Fifty percent of the advance money."

"The deal was twenty, Brad. Twenty percent. How did that more than double?"

Brad sank back in his chair. "I'm afraid you'll have to take that up with him."

"You can just bet I will. This is ridiculous."

She started to stand, but Brad stopped her. "Just one more thing."

Jill took a breath, prepared for anything.

Brad spit it out quickly like he was afraid to say it. "He wants you to move into his place, not the other way around."

That was really crossing the line. From what she'd heard, Hunter owned a cramped condo in the city. Jill had a spacious country cottage with room for her pets to roam. For all she knew, Hunter's condo didn't even allow pets! Jill had so much on her mind already, she couldn't tolerate one more complication. Her grandpa's retirement home had called this morning. Their rates were going up and they wanted to make sure Jill was renewing the assisted living agreement. There were several people on the waiting list, all of whom were prepared to make early deposits, if Jill found herself unable to. As her last bill was several weeks past due, the director found it necessary to press the point. Either she paid her balance soon—*and* a large deposit toward her grandpa's next year—or her grandfather was out. Jill didn't even know where she could move him at this stage. Most nice retirement places required residents to enter when they were still eligible for independent living.

"He says he'll keep covering utilities," Brad continued. Jill's blood pumped harder and her head ached. *There are more conditions? Seriously?* "But he wants you to pay your own parking."

This sent Jill straight over the edge. Here Hunter was offered a fair—no, make that *generous*—deal, and he'd thrown the whole thing back in her face. That was just like Hunter. Arrogant, self-serving, unbearable! A real gentleman now? Ha! Had she lost her mind even *toying with* the idea that this was doable? She'd sell off every last bit of her property first, starting with this stupid tennis racket. She reached for it again and her fingers tightened around its neck. That would save her from using it as a murder weapon. First against Hunter, then against Brad. Double homicide! No, wait. Since Brad was the one here, she'd probably have to kill him first.

Jill leapt to her feet and her racket slammed to the floor. Brad watched wide-eyed as she started shredding the contract, dropping it piece by piece on the table. One of the strips curled in Brad's coffee cup, absorbing the dregs of his latte.

"Wait!" he cried in panic before lowering his voice to a whisper. "What are you doing?"

"Showing you—and *him*—what I think of this little counteroffer."

"Jilly, you're not being rational."

"Read my lips." She set her hands on the table. "I…don't…care." And she didn't! Forget Brad, and especially forget Hunter. Surely there was another way to make things work. She didn't need Brad, nor did she require the help of his conniving best friend!

"Trouble in paradise?"

Jill spun on her heels to see Cassandra had reappeared like a lurking phantom. She was toting a carry-out bag from the grill. "Are you stalking us, Cassandra?" Jill asked, reaching a hand behind her to the table. Keeping her eyes fixed on Cassandra's, she grappled for the errant pieces of paper, balling them up in her fist. Brad helped by prying her fingers apart and shoving in a few extra strips.

"Hardly." Cassandra's eyes were cold blue crystals. Cassandra tried to peer around Jill to see behind her, but Jill shifted, blocking her view, and rammed the fistful of paper strips into her purse. "I just came back to pick up my lunch order. Headed back to the office." She flipped her hair in an indignant manner. "Some of us work, you know. Even on Saturdays."

"Yes, well…" Jill pressed her lips into a tight smile. "Don't let us keep you from it!"

Cassandra obviously wasn't ready to leave them in peace. "I could have sworn I heard you two arguing… Was that Hunter's name I heard mentioned? *The infamous Hunter Delaney?*" She cocked her head at Brad. "Don't tell me your sweet fiancée has a roving eye?"

Brad answered her stoically. "This is probably one of those times when it would be good for you to mind your own business, Cassandra."

"Oh, but this *is* my business. It could be very big business indeed. Salacious details about breakups and infidelities sells copy."

Instead of offering up a biting comeback, Jill held her tongue.

Cassandra gave Jill a slow once-over, then shrugged at Brad. "Fine. You two keep your little secret. But mark my words, I'll get to the bottom of it. Where there's smoke there's fire, as they say, and there are big puffy clouds going up everywhere." Her lips twisted in an evil grin. "My spidey senses are tingling."

Jill turned to Brad as Cassandra sashayed away, her short skirt swishing. "Spidey senses?"

"I know. The woman's touched."

"Worse than that, she's wicked," Jill said. "She'll do anything in her power to destroy me."

"Maybe you shouldn't have won that tenth-grade spelling bee," Brad teased.

She wanted to stay mad at Brad, she really did. But when he gave her those darned puppy dog eyes, he made it impossible. Susan was putting the screws to him, and he'd tried to find a solution. So what if it was an abysmal one? She should at least give Brad points for trying. "Shut up. That was years ago."

Brad reached toward the floor, then handed Jill her racket. "Don't want to forget this."

"You're being very trusting," she told him, taking the racket. "I was thinking about using it to kill you only minutes ago."

Jill stepped into the sunshine, recalling for the first time in an hour what a gorgeous June day it was. She'd been so caught up in those storm clouds of thinking about Hunter, she'd nearly forgotten. She addressed Brad, who walked beside her, hanging his head. None of this mess was his fault and she knew it. It would be good of her to let him off the hook, so he and Susan could move forward in repairing their relationship. "Don't worry about it, okay?" she told him. "I'll think of something else. I have to."

Brad raised his eyes to look at her. "Maybe if you just talk to Hunter?"

"Don't think so."

"It's still possible you could reach a compromise."

Across the parking lot Jill spied Cassandra setting her lunch bag on the backseat of her shiny sports car. Was it Jill's imagination or was Cassandra taking her sweet time getting away, just hoping to catch one more glimpse of them? "Truthfully, Brad? At this point in time, I'd rather die than see Hunter Delaney in person."

"Don't look now, then," Brad said under his breath. "Because here he comes."

Jill whipped her head around to spy a handsome, dark-haired man striding toward them and sporting a broad grin. He wore a blue polo shirt and khaki slacks, and was taller then she remembered, at least a good six inches taller than her. A heck of a lot buffer too. Muscles rippled beneath his shirt as he opened his arms wide. "Jill Jamison!" Hunter proclaimed effusively. "The woman of my dreams!"

Before Jill knew what was happening, he reached for her and clamped her against his chest in a big bear hug. His frame was rock solid and he smelled of musky cologne. Hunter's arms wound around her, securing her at the waist. "Sorry, bud," he whispered to Brad, "the press is watching."

Jill stared up at him, her mind whirling. "Hunter! Just what are you doing?" She didn't know why, but her knees felt weak and her mouth went dry. She was probably in a state of shock. It wasn't like she recalled that old longing she'd had when she'd hoped to be in Hunter's arms so many years ago. Then, she'd imagined him to be a different kind of guy...the sort who could really care for a girl, and sweep her off her feet with one kiss. Not that she'd let him try, especially after learning what sort of guy he *really* was. The type who was only in it for the moment, and wouldn't have given her a second thought once she'd completely given him her heart. His dark eyes caught the sunlight as he dipped his chin toward hers.

"Making us public," he said with a grin. At once, Jill felt transported in time and she was all of seventeen again, helplessly under Hunter's spell. The next thing she knew, his mouth was on hers, all hot and heavy, his tongue sweeping in to taste hers. Jill sagged in his arms and he tightened his embrace. This was wrong. *This is insane...* But Jill found herself kissing him back, just a little at first—and then a lot. He felt so good and smelled so fine, she nearly forgot they were standing at the edge of a parking lot. Jill's temperature spiked as her tennis racket crashed to the ground. Oh man, he was good. Better than good. Hunter's skill was top-notch. Excellent. Why oh why had she waited so long? Or perhaps it was good she'd waited, until the fruit of her desire had ripened to perfection. Was it Jill's imagination, or was Hunter just as ravenous for her? Somehow her arms were around him, her wrists overlapping at the back of his neck. It was almost like she was enjoying this, wanting more of him... *What? Hunter?* Jill called herself up short and broke away, stepping back with a gasp. At least she hoped she was gasping and not panting. *Whoa.*

Hunter saucily cocked an eyebrow and spoke with a husky rasp.

"Can I take that to mean you missed me too?"

Jill cupped a hand to her mouth, her cheeks flaming. And it wasn't just her face; her whole body felt on fire, particularly the parts of her that had touched him—flesh pressing flesh. For a moment she felt faint. Brad handed Jill her racket and she used it like a cane to steady herself against the ground. "That was a little over the top for *hi, how've you been.*"

Hunter screwed up his face with mock confusion. "I thought we were engaged?" His eyes darted to a parking spot not fifty feet away, and Jill glanced in that direction to find Cassandra watching them, her jaw unhinged. She stood by her open driver's door, not bothering to hide her rapt interest. In fact, she appeared to be hastily packing away a camera. Brad had obviously spotted Cassandra too, because he leapt right in with a shrill cry. *"Engaged?"*

"Sorry, Brad," Hunter said loudly. "But all's fair in love and—"

Brad spewed his retort, immediately picking up on Hunter's cue. "You think you know a man." He motioned between Hunter and Jill. "All this time…? My girl and my very best friend? You and she…?" It was like he couldn't force himself to say it. "Unbelievable!" he finally yelped with a moan.

Jill stared at Brad in a panic before catching a glimpse of Cassandra rapidly fastening her seatbelt and zooming away. She'd gotten a scoop all right: a big one. Who knew how soon this story would be rushed to print? Yet none of the details had been ironed out. Jill didn't even know whether she and Hunter could make this charade work! And there he'd gone and spilled the whole can of beans to the entire world. Things couldn't go any more global than *Tempo Beat*. Surely, Hunter knew that. "Well, I hope you're proud of yourself," she said in a scolding tone.

Rather than appearing admonished, Hunter smiled, one side of his mouth rising higher than the other. "I thought we put on a pretty good show."

Brad nodded in agreement and shook his fingers as if fighting off flames. "Hot, hot."

Jill flushed in spite of herself.

"You did all right too," Hunter said, giving Brad's shoulder a nudge. "Really convincing."

Jill's mind was still spinning from the rapid turn of events. "When you two boys are done congratulating yourselves," she hissed at them, "maybe you can explain how bringing Cassandra in on this makes things any better?"

"Far better that she works for us, than against us," Brad explained.

"My thinking exactly," Hunter said. "You know, Jill," he told her, apparently seriously, "you've held up pretty well over the years. I don't think I'll have any trouble at all fitting the bill." He stepped toward her, playacting like he wanted to scoop her back into his arms.

"Oh, no you don't, big boy." She reached out a hand to stop him, placing her palm to his chest. His heart thumped beneath it. "You and I have some talking to do." Before this fake fiancé number could proceed any further, Jill needed a couple of answers. Like about why Hunter had agreed to it in the first place? Brad's story about Hunter suddenly morphing into a gentleman seemed to be holding less and less water. Particularly in light of that flaming hot kiss. The current rumors about Hunter were obviously true. No man could kiss like that who hadn't been around the block a time or two. Jill was just mortified that she'd given in to it. She clung to the hope that Hunter hadn't noticed and had taken her response in the vein it was supposedly given, as an outward sign to Cassandra of her new involvement with Hunter.

Brad gave a slight bow. "This is where the jilted ex excuses himself."

Jill grabbed for his arm as he turned back toward the clubhouse. "Brad! Don't go!"

"Three's a crowd, haven't you heard?" After walking a few paces, he peered over his shoulder to give Jill and Hunter an evaluating look. "You two really do make a great couple, by the way. Utterly charming." Jill seethed as he added, "Don't neglect to send me an invite!"

Jill massaged her forehead for a beat, then caught Hunter watching her. "You want to talk?" he said. "I'll talk. Shall we find a spot in the shade?"

That's when Jill looked past him to spy Cassandra's car slowly trolling back through the parking lot, her driver's side window lowered and a smart phone angled outside it.

"Film at eleven," Hunter quipped.

~ End of Excerpt *~*
My Best Friend's Bride
Available at multiple outlets now!